My Highland Wedding

Middlemarch Gathering 5

Shelley Munro

Munro Press

My Highland Wedding

Copyright © 2024 by Shelley Munro

Print ISBN: 978-1-99-106346-5
Digital ISBN: 978-1-99-106339-7
Digital ISBN: 978-1-99-106340-3

Editor: Evil Eye Editing

Cover: Kim Killion, The Killion Group, Inc.

Munro Press, New Zealand.

First Munro Press electronic publication January 2024

First Munro Press print publication January 2024

For Paul, my partner in life and adventure.

Introduction

Edwina dreams of a musical career rather than the life her grandmother is pushing her toward—that of marriage, children, and tradition. Boredom on a grand scale! Attendance at the Highland gathering is a compromise, and all is going swimmingly with not a mate in sight until *he* prowls into the ballroom. An older man—striking and confident, and everything her teenage self wished for in a partner before music and songwriting became her focus.

Shapeshifter Mikhail has come to claim his bride, and he's not leaving without her. A wife will ensure his life and household run smoothly, and he can focus on his business. Edwina isn't the willing bride he expects, but with a bit of blackmail, the wedding moves forward. His feline adores her sass, and their instant connection surprises him.

Powerless to halt this abduction, Edwina puts on a brave face and publicly accepts the hand life has dealt her, but she refuses to let this charismatic tiger shifter walk all over her, even if he makes her purr...

1

THE FORMAL HIGHLAND GATHERING ball was off to a rip-roaring start, with a top cover band belting out a song that made Edwina McClintock's right foot tap and her hips rock. The lead guitarist was perfection, and the vocalist's smoky voice had more than one shifter female and a few males studying him with interest.

Edwina grinned at her best friend, but Suzie had eyes only for the drummer.

Edwina focused on Scott, another of the Middlemarch contingent attending the gathering. "Are you asking anyone to dance?"

"Some of these shifters scare me," he muttered.

"Yeah," Liam said, the other male in their dwindling group. "It's not their teeth or their claws. It's the desperation glowing in their eyes."

Suzie joined their conversation. "Is it me, or do these shifters look reckless?"

"Got it in one," Scott said. "That's why they terrify me."

Liam grimaced. "Some of them don't have understanding folks at home. Most don't have a Saber Mitchell or a London Drummond on their team."

"True." Edwina agreed. Desperation was the right word. A vibe of hopelessness and frustration permeated the air and rang out in loud, sometimes sharp laughter. The participants danced with a fervor that matched the *bang, bang, bang* of the drums. She scanned faces, some familiar after days of shared activities and experiences. A few had left with newfound mates, like their friend Anita. Edwina made a note to text Anita since she should almost be home by now. Ramsay, the last member of their group, had disappeared, but he'd found his mate. She wasn't sure what was happening with him. Maybe Anita had heard.

A wistful sigh escaped her before she got her head back in the "gathering" game. She needed to find a dance partner, or rather partners, because she didn't want to send any male the wrong message. "We should mingle."

Scott and Liam scowled, and she rolled her eyes even though she sympathized with their procrastination.

"If I can socialize, so can you. I'll go first and show you how." She studied the nearest shifter males for a likely candidate. A flutter of murmurs to her right snagged her attention, and she angled her body. Her breath caught, and her eyes widened. "Whoa."

The shifter causing the commotion was tall and built, with an arresting presence. Every female stood straighter, and whispers raced from one shifter to the next. He strode into the room like a man with a goal. The guy was older than her by at least ten years, and his self-assurance came from his wealthy background since his suit molded his muscular body and screamed designer.

He paced a circuit of the crowded ballroom as if searching for someone.

Edwina's insides squeezed tight as his path brought him closer to her. Most Middlemarch men were black leopards with black hair and green eyes. This man's hair was dark brown and bore tawny streaks. It was slightly too long, and the urge to test those locks for softness had her fingers curling inward to dig into her palms. As if he sensed her fascination, his head cocked in her direction. His nostrils flared as he scented the air.

Edwina released a soft laugh. He probably regretted the deep inhalation because the perfume and aftershave in the ballroom made her eyes water. En mass, it was an overpowering cloud of stinky chemicals and natural scents.

When the shifter's gaze settled on those around her, she got her first full glimpse. His wasn't a pretty face since age and determination had left their stamp on him, but it was arresting and worth a second glance. She mentally added more years to his age. He was fit, his body moving fluidly beneath that designer suit. Edwina wondered which animal he transformed into and speculated it might be a feline because of the way he prowled.

There was no other word to describe his swinging yet controlled gait.

Edwina continued to monitor the intriguing male. She gasped, suddenly requiring a hit of air to clear her head.

She didn't even care if she started sneezing from the excess perfume, not when her lungs screamed for oxygen.

"Who is he?" Suzie whispered.

"I-I don't know." But something about his presence drew her and had her heart fluttering. She took half a step before she jerked to an appalled halt. Despite attending the gathering, she had no intention of hooking up with a male. When she and Suzie arrived back in New Zealand, they were packing to leave for Wellington and a university life full of music.

She was too busy for any man, even an intriguing one.

His gaze passed over her and Suzie and continued.

Edwina's breath hissed out in disappointment before she chuckled, mocking herself. A man would mess with her plans.

"Wow," Suzie murmured. "I wonder who he's searching for? I kind of wished it was me for a moment there."

Edwina laughed louder, catching the man's attention.

Blue eyes. He had striking blue eyes the color of Lake Tekapo in McKenzie country. Beautiful and stunning—a crystal blue. Those blue eyes of his widened slightly, and he halted, his gaze wandering across her face and down her red dress. Not a garment her grandmother would approve of, but it made her feel like an old-fashioned film star, and it was essential to don clothes that gave one confidence.

He straightened a fraction and changed direction, his prowl taking him to a spot directly in front of her.

Over to her right, a beautiful blonde wolf sighed.

A leggy brunette standing slightly to her left stepped forward. "Can I interest you in a dance?" she asked, not put off by his silence or his leashed power.

"No," he said without taking his gaze off Edwina.

A pain in Edwina's chest reminded her to breathe. This time, the cloud of perfume didn't assault her. Instead, she smelled him—a hint of pine and fresh mountain air.

Yes, a feline.

"I've been looking for you," he said, impatience stamped into his handsome features.

"Me?" Edwina touched her right hand to her chest, her body suddenly clammy. He was a stranger—a sexy one—and he'd mistaken her for someone else.

"Yes, hurry. We must leave, or we'll miss our plane."

"What?" Suzie demanded.

Edwina was glad Suzie asked because words failed her. She swallowed to moisten her dry mouth. The man's presence was overpowering, and her feline had gone strangely silent.

The stranger ignored Suzie, his focus entirely on Edwina. "Come," he said and extended his hand. "The minister has a deadline."

Edwina blinked, trying to make sense of his words. The man grasped her hand and lifted her right off her feet. She flew with ease, her stomach settling on his hard shoulder. Her lungs emptied with a whoosh.

"I'm here to claim my bride, and the minister awaits in the castle chapel."

Huh? He had the wrong shifter. Before she could inform him, he glided from the ballroom with long strides. A buzz of chatter followed them.

The shifter headed for the main entrance and took a

right toward the castle chapel. She bounced lightly on his shoulder, all the blood sinking to her head. His muscles flexed beneath her belly, and his breathing hadn't changed from carrying her extra weight. Belatedly, she realized he was kidnapping her. Not a single shifter had followed them—not even her friends.

What the hell? Maybe this was a prank, and she was the butt of the joke.

"Let me down!" She wriggled, but he held her with ease. She was under his complete control and confused. "Please. You have the wrong person."

2

THE WOMAN WAS UNEXPECTED, better than he'd envisaged, and a potential problem. He desired a wife who'd blend into his life and remain in the background. He'd have to bed her once or twice to mingle their scents because his family would comment if they didn't. Mikhail needed this marriage to seem real, so his grandfather stood down and accepted that he was his own man.

"Look, whoever you are, if you don't let me down in two seconds flat, I'll scream."

Mikhail withheld the grin that threatened to bloom. This urge to smile was new and entirely her fault. His cheerful expression would stun his friends since responsibility typically made him grave.

One second passed. Two. Mikhail wondered if she truly would scream. Perhaps she'd burst into noisy tears. *Too bad.* His humor faded. This marriage was necessary, and their grandmothers had come to an acceptable agreement.

This woman was his intended bride.

A piercing scream had him freezing, before flashing another of those rare grins. She possessed powerful lungs. He repositioned her body and let her slide over his shoulder and come to her feet, ruffled and full of temper. She shook herself like a disgruntled house cat and straightened her tight red dress while glaring at him the entire time.

"You have the wrong woman." She snapped her fingers in front of his nose, so close she almost did him an injury with her scarlet fingernails.

Mikhail was confident his grandmother had told him Edwina had agreed to his proposition. He tried to read her with his feline senses, but nothing. That was unusual, too. His talent for interpreting emotions was useful as an entrepreneur.

"Are you listening?" She poked his chest with her forefinger. "You. Have. The. Wrong. Woman."

He took half a step back. "Is your name Edwina McClintock?"

She blinked, her mouth falling open before she snapped her teeth together.

"I'm Mikhail Lermontov." He placed one hand on her shoulder and let his other slip around her waist. He drew her nearer and stared into her face. She wasn't a pretty woman in the way of his mistress, but she was vibrant and confident, her makeup bold to go with her red statement dress. Her green gaze settled on him, revealing a feline glint before it dissipated.

"So?" she prompted, trying to escape his touch.

She didn't move far because he stopped her. Something had broken down in communications, but that wasn't his fault. He'd signed a contract, as had she. This marriage was going ahead, which reminded him. The minister was waiting. He'd been unhappy getting rousted from his bed, so they should hustle in case the man left.

Mikhail grasped Edwina's hand and tugged her inside the chapel. "Hurry, the minister is waiting."

"What minister? You're crazy. Wait, this is a prank, right?" She whirled, only stopping when his grip on her hand halted her. "Suzie and the guys arranged this, didn't they?"

"No," Mikhail snapped, impatient with her dawdling when he needed to return home before everything went to hell. "We're honoring the agreement our grandmothers signed six months ago."

She froze and blinked twice. "What agreement?"

He cursed in his native tongue, the words gutter-level and unsuitable for a woman's ears. Mikhail sucked in a steadying breath. "The one where we get married." He tugged her hand, dragging her a few steps before she dug in her heels.

"No. Hell, no. I don't want to marry anyone."

"Then why are you at the gathering?"

"Humoring my grandmother to receive something I desire—not marriage to you."

Mikhail subdued his panic. He sent calming vibes to his tiger before focusing on his goal. *This marriage.*

Everything hinged on his marriage.

Everything.

"What do you want?" he demanded, exercising patience when every part of him desired action.

"My dream is to study music. My grandmother promised that when I returned to New Zealand, I could attend Wellington University without her opposition," Edwina said.

"She told you she would honor her promise when you *returned* to New Zealand?"

"Yes, that's what I said. *What she said.*"

"When you re-entered New Zealand," he said, understanding the trickery behind her grandmother's words.

"Yes, she—" Edwina broke off, every muscle in her shapely body tensing. "You said she signed an agreement with your grandmother."

"Yes, they are childhood friends."

"She informed you I'd be at the gathering."

"Yes, and she sent a current photo so I'd recognize you."

"She said nothing to me."

Mikhail watched the emotions racing across her face. The betrayal. The disappointment. The fury. "My understanding was you knew about this agreement and were okay with it."

"I'm not."

"I require a wife, and you are my last hope."

"Why? What's wrong with you?"

"Nothing. I need a wife to fit my lifestyle and not bother me with romantic expectations," he said. "The minister is waiting and is vocal about the delay."

"Not my problem. No matter what my grandmother

agreed to, you can't make me marry you."

"Your grandmother can return the money I sent her via my grandmother?"

"What money?"

"I believe she and her husband went on a trip and repaired the family home." Mikhail spotted the exact moment she understood that he spoke the truth. "If your grandmother can repay those funds immediately, that would fix part of the problem."

"I doubt she can," Edwina whispered. "My parents' home needed extensive repairs after a recent storm, and my grandmother gave them a loan to help them out." She studied him, deadly pale. "She got that money from you. Truly?"

"Truly," Mikhail said.

"She had no right to sign me over like a parcel." She looked as if she might cry.

Her hunched shoulders screamed of mental pain, and Mikhail wanted to hold her and offer comfort, the thought so foreign, he hesitated.

His tiger made a chuffing sound—a prompt, and Mikhail shook himself. He narrowed the space between them and embraced her. She didn't fight but quivered, and once again, the need to commiserate caused him consternation. Aware of the ticking clock—the waiting minister and plane—he reached a decision.

"Edwina, I urgently need a wife. I am within my rights to force you to marry me. You understand this. No one in the shifter world would gainsay or blame me for my actions. But what if I offered you one million dollars to marry me now and remain married for a minimum of a year? You'd lose your university place, but with the money I give you in exchange for marriage, arrange for private tutors and upskill that way. Reapply for your university place later. Would you agree to that?"

She lifted her head to catch his gaze. "How much did my grandmother sell me for?"

Mikhail hesitated. "I'd rather not say."

He'd gone into the agreement with his eyes wide open. He'd allowed his grandmother to negotiate on his behalf, but Edwina hadn't had that luxury. Her grandmother had secretly maneuvered her, so he understood Edwina's anger.

"Please tell me."

"Two million cash."

Edwina winced. "She loaned money to my parents and insisted on repayment and interest. My parents work hard, and she has the cash to help them. Unbelievable. If she thinks I'll keep quiet about her manipulation and lies to my parents, she should reconsider." She lifted her gaze to meet his, and he saw pain amongst the fiery anger. "I agree. I'll marry you and stay married for one year. You've already paid for me, so you don't have to give me a million dollars, but I would like to continue with my music. It... Music makes me happy, and this is hard enough as it is. It means putting my dreams on hold. My grandmother has fought and continually told my parents I should stay in Middlemarch. I was too wild and not trustworthy. I should've been suspicious since she didn't argue when I agreed to attend the gathering."

Guilt flooded Mikhail at his part in this deception. He'd gone to his grandmother and told her he needed a biddable wife. He'd explained his reasons. She'd agreed to help him and keep everything confidential until he introduced his new wife to the family. Edwina hadn't had the same luxury. "Are you certain?"

"Yes."

Mikhail loosened his grip and offered her his arm. "We'd better hustle before the minister loses patience."

"What about the relevant licenses and legal stuff?"

Mikhail patted his jacket pocket. "I have the necessary documents."

"Of course you do," she said. "How can you trust me to keep my end of the bargain?"

"Because if you go back on your word, I will destroy your grandmother, and unfortunately, other family members will get caught in the crossfire."

3

Edwina surreptitiously eyed the man standing beside her in the stone chapel while she tried to fashion a last-ditch rescue for herself. Nothing came to mind.

Snared like an eel in a net.

Her grandmother had sprung the trap, and she'd innocently walked into it, not guessing the lengths her grandparent would go to get her way. Her parents were happy, weren't they? Yet they'd likely faced the same hurdles presented to her now. Heat flashed to her cheeks as she berated herself. She was trying to become a better person, yet she'd been arrogant with her parents. Angry at the restrictions placed on her and putting her needs first. She shook away her self-loathing and promised herself she'd do better. An apology for a start when she next spoke to them.

Soft lights glowed around them, and two stern men with military-short hair stood as witnesses to their nuptials. The minister's robes rustled, his mouth pinching tight in abject disapproval, even though Edwina had assured him she was a willing participant.

She hadn't had an option with her abductor gripping her forearm in silent warning.

Mikhail Lermontov had planned everything. While he was a stranger, she understood his type. Bossy. Determined. Despite his arrogance, she trusted him when he said he was amiable to her pursuing her musical career during their marriage. She'd glimpsed what she'd thought was honesty in his direct gaze. Time would tell if her instincts were off.

Her mind wandered to her grandmother, the manipulative...bitch. Gods, her grandmother was lucky she wasn't standing nearby because Edwina doubted she'd bite her tongue and afford her grandparent the respect she always demanded. This was a massive betrayal. Heck, her grandmother had moved her around like a game piece, all for money. She'd sold Edwina for creature comforts. Edwina wondered if her grandfather had been complicit. She blew out a breath, frustration stalking her as she replayed her dilemma. Yeah. Probably.

"Everything okay?" Mikhail's deep, accented voice distracted her from her traitorous grandmother.

"Yes." A lie. Everything was a horrid mess.

Bare bones: her grandmother had sold her like a modern-day slave—someone with no rights. No voice. Arranged marriage was out of fashion, something done in centuries past, yet her grandmother hadn't hesitated. Edwina's suspicions should've pinged when her grandmother had put up a half-hearted fight about the gathering. Usually, she disapproved of Edwina leaving Middlemarch and was vocal about her misgivings and the dangers lurking in cities for unwary shifter women. Edwina had mistakenly thought she had given up arguing.

Edwina gritted her teeth again, fury whipping through her veins. Although Mikhail had clarified the consequences of not marrying him, he'd offered concessions for her music.

She'd have to trust him, even if that was difficult. Right now, she was clinging to her instincts and praying she'd read him correctly. Without warning, fear sliced through her, along with a shiver. Mikhail reached for her hand, and she started at the physical contact.

The minister's mouth thinned again, his eyes narrow slits. His skin flushed, and his mouth worked as if he were debating with himself. He cleared his throat, his robes swishing, and a faint hint of lavender laundry powder drifted to her. Finally, he angled his body away from them but continued to stare, to measure and come to conclusions.

Seeing this, Edwina smiled, wielding every scrap of charm she possessed while inwardly shrieking her dismay. "Should we begin now? It's getting late."

"Dearly beloved," the minister said, his tone snide. "We gather here in the sight of God..."

Edwina listened, the minister's words weighty on her soul. Marriage vows. She'd always thought she'd wed one day but hadn't imagined a clandestine ceremony with strangers as witnesses. If she thought of any man, an image of someone like the Mitchell brothers came to mind. Not them exactly, but a man of their ilk who cared and offered protection yet allowed their mate to stretch and pursue their interests. Those were the qualities she desired in a mate. Strength and consideration. Loyalty. Kindness with an edge of sexy charm.

Instead, she was marrying a shifter from Russia, a stranger, and he was a mystery, apart from his apparent wealth.

Edwina repeated her vows in a clear voice with nary a stumble. Beside her, Mikhail did the same. He pulled a golden band from a pocket and placed it on the bible the minister extended. Mikhail slid the ring on her finger, their gazes meeting, although she had no clue about his thoughts.

"I now pronounce you man and wife. You may kiss your bride."

The minister's tone had lost its sarcasm, calmer now as if reassured they'd wanted this marriage. Edwina wondered how Mikhail had convinced the man to conduct the ceremony, then decided she didn't need the answer.

Mikhail drew her closer, a glint in his blue eyes while she gaped at him wide-eyed, her heart pumping faster than usual. His lips brushed hers, tentatively then with more assertion, and she gasped at the sensations ripping through her unprepared body.

She'd kissed men before—humans and shifters—but had felt nothing. Certainly nothing electric and jarring like this. She gripped his shoulders and tugged him closer. He bit her lower lip, not hard enough to hurt but enough to focus her attention. That tiny throb had her gasping again, and this time, he took advantage, stroking his tongue against hers. Once and fleeting before he withdrew and stepped back. Her hands fell to her sides, and wordlessly, she observed him, her pulse racing, while he murmured to the minister and handed over an envelope.

Mikhail held out his hand. "Come, we must leave. The plane is waiting."

"But my friends. My possessions."

Suzie and the boys hadn't come to her rescue. She bit her lip, the truth striking her almost as soon as the indignant thought had formed. She understood why. Her abduction had likely seemed a joke, and she hadn't made a huge scene. Men had carried other women from the ballroom during the week, their initial protests much like hers. It was part of the gathering hijinks.

"Contact your friends later and ask them to forward your bags."

And with that decree, he ushered her outside.

She was married.

Edwina ran her thumb over the golden band weighing down her ring finger. Married to a shifter and stepping from one jail to another. Worse, she hadn't fought. She told herself it was because she'd needed to save her parents from her grandmother's machinations. But a tiny part of her admitted Mikhail had persuaded her to proceed with this ridiculous farce.

He was compelling and charismatic and dangerous to her peace of mind. She prayed she hadn't made the biggest mistake of her life.

Mikhail led her toward the gravel parking area in front of the castle. The two men who'd witnessed their ceremony trailed silently behind. Mikhail ushered her into the rear of a luxurious vehicle. He gestured for her to slide along the seat and joined her inside. With a glance at her, he leaned forward and pressed a button.

"Seat belt," Mikhail said.

Edwina fumbled for the belt and buckled it with a loud click. Before she had finished, the vehicle fired to life with a muted roar. Seconds later, they glided away from the castle. Edwina swallowed as fears rose to taunt her. She'd generally consider a situation before she acted, or at least she did these days. Saber and London had helped her and Suzie see they were hurting themselves by acting out.

She was a married woman.

The thought echoed through her mind, soft thumps of truth. *Ting. Ting. Ting.* The beat of reality reminded her of a percussion instrument, which led her to music.

Suzie would lecture her something fierce after their hard work to earn extra money for accommodation and expenses. But she'd gone through with this marriage to help her parents.

Now the repercussions...

Gods, she hadn't even asked if he expected her to sleep with him. As much as she found him attractive, he was still a stranger.

She turned to find him studying her. Heat rose to her cheeks, accompanied by a tingling unease and a pinch of oh-shit-this-was-a-mistake. *Huge blunder.* He remained silent and didn't shift his gaze from her. Instantly, she wanted to squirm, but she forced herself to do nothing more than recross her legs and settle against the seat. She struggled to keep her composure and thought she did well until he spoke.

"You wanted to ask me something?"

"No. Yes." Edwina swallowed and broke their visual connection while cursing her cowardice. She had so many questions.

"Go ahead," he said, that accent of his cruising across her nerve endings just so.

Her stomach swooped, and she bit her bottom lip to stop the purr building deep in her throat. Her feline's attraction to the shifter man was problematic.

"What are you?" she blurted. That heat swallowed her face again, her cheeks burning.

"Tiger."

Oh. That fit with his size and his prowling gait. His stillness. "How old are you?"

"Relatively young." His eyes gleamed with challenge.

"What does that mean?"

"You recently turned twenty-one."

"Yes." Either her grandmother had filled him in on her minor details, or he had efficient spies.

"I am forty-one."

She did a double take, blinking at his grin. "You don't look that old."

"Tiger shifters age slowly, but then so do leopards once they reach maturity." Sharp canines glinted before his lips concealed them again.

"Yes." Another thought occurred—an important one.

"Why haven't you married before?" He was older than most seeking a wife.

"None of your business," he said with a silky softness that had the hairs on the back of her neck lifting.

"You don't think that's relevant?" Edwina snapped. As soon as the words fell between them, she winced.

"We need to concentrate on making this marriage appear real, especially to my grandfather."

"Does that mean I have to sleep with you?"

Their gazes collided, and she caught the flare of heat in his blue eyes, the faint shift before he regained control. Every muscle in her body tensed while her feline purred in delight. An audible one that Mikhail heard.

"That is what married people do." His beautifully shaped lips twitched a fraction, discernable in the dim light of the car interior.

"This isn't a typical marriage," she said, tension leaking through in her words, her strident tone.

"Many people have arranged marriages."

But this wasn't what she'd envisioned. She'd wanted her music first, and the idea of a relationship had come a distant second.

Wait. What was he telling her?

Her breath hissed out. He'd thrown her when he'd informed her what her grandmother had done. It was too late now, but perhaps she should've argued, negotiated, and called his bluff instead of letting her stunned heart and feline guide her direction.

"We will share a bed. No one will believe this marriage is genuine unless our scents mingle."

Oh. Edwina stared at her laced fingers. He was an attractive specimen and appeared in excellent health. Of course, a suit could hide many sins and excessive business lunches, but given his shifter status, she imagined muscles.

"Your grandmother led me to believe you are a virgin."

Her head jerked up, and a chill ran through her veins.

"Is that not correct?"

Edwina closed her eyes, heat suffusing her cheeks again. This was so embarrassing. While it was true, her virginity wasn't because of anything her grandmother had done or said or ordered. She'd experimented, as had Suzie, but an inner instinct had stopped Edwina from going the whole way. She'd kissed and cuddled and enjoyed heavy petting, but nothing more.

"That's correct," she whispered, mortified. "What would've happened if I wasn't a virgin?"

"I would've been extremely disappointed," he said after a long pause.

Not reassuring. The strange note in his voice had her digging her fingers into her thighs. This was not the way for him to reassure her.

"W-where are we going?"

"To the airport. We'll fly to my home city."

"I see." Not true. She didn't understand this at all. "Your business is important to you?"

"Yes."

His steeliness conveyed that he wouldn't elaborate any further.

"What type of business is it?"

"Construction."

Edwina risked another glance in his direction and caught his resolute expression. Was that code for the mafia or whatever they called them in Russia? She'd heard whispers, read stories. She opened her mouth to ask, then closed it again. Perhaps it was best she didn't know if her husband was part of the mafia. Head of the mafia, given the respect the two accompanying men had shown.

"Is the city where you live—will I be able to access a music teacher?"

His lips curled, a sexy twist that had her blushing. "I'm permitting you to continue with what you consider important. I doubt hosting the odd dinner party or spending time with my family will be taxing. You will need to fill your days."

Would he be at work? "Do you work long hours?"

"It depends on our contracts."

That didn't reassure her. "Tell me about your family. Whom will I meet?"

"On my paternal side, my grandfather is the head of the family and has been since he was in his early twenties. He is a human and unaware of shifters. My grandmother, his wife, died two years ago of a virus. She had never been strong." He hesitated as if intending to add more but decided better.

"Wait, I thought you told me my grandmother is friends with your grandmother?"

"My grandmother on my mother's side. My mother and grandparents live nearby. They run a clothing store. My father died in an accident when I was a youngster, and my mother, brother, sister, and I moved in with them. I get my shifter blood from my mother's side."

Oh, dear. Keeping up the pretense would be challenging if they shared a home. "Do you still live with them?"

"No, I have a home on the city outskirts. It's close, but not too close."

"But your family sees you regularly?"

"Yes, the reason we must present a genuine marriage." His blue eyes gleamed as if he were imagining them touching each other.

Edwina inwardly railed at her predicament. She stole a glance at her watch to check the time in New Zealand. Early, but not too early, to blast her grandmother with stinging words. It wouldn't aid her situation but might make her feel better. A prickling scrutiny had her focusing on Mikhail. Her new husband studied her with interest, although reading his thoughts was impossible.

"Do I scare you?" His silky voice broke into her musings.

"It will depend on what I learn and how you treat me in the coming days." Bitterness crept into her voice. "I'm in a strange place with no support, my choices stripped from me."

A beat of silence ensued before he spoke. "I won't mistreat you, Edwina. Unless…"

"Unless what?"

"It's imperative for my grandfather to believe our marriage is real. I will lose everything if he even suspects a ruse. Normally, I wouldn't explain this to you, but I don't want you to misunderstand and cost me everything I've worked for."

He was leaving vast gaps in his telling. Why was this so

critical? Couldn't he have gone into business on his own account? "What sort of business is so important?"

"Enough questions. You will follow my instructions, and we'll get on fine."

Edwina pressed her lips together, temper fizzing. Blast her grandmother. She should've refused, but her parents didn't deserve punishment for her grandmother's schemes. Edwina relaxed her fingers and inhaled. No options left now. She'd play the long game. Renewed anger pumped through her. This was the last time she'd be her grandmother's pawn, forced to follow her instructions. *The final.*

"When can I contact my friends?"

"Later. Once you're settled in my home, and everything is moving forward as it should."

Tears burned her eyes—frustration. A lump formed in her throat. A tiny sound of vexation and anger, and fear escaped her—the groan reminding her of a trapped animal. She glanced down at her hands again, numb and despondent.

He'd taken her by surprise, however. Suzie would expect Edwina to contact her, and her friend would stress about their plans.

Gods, what a mess. A tear ran down her cheek and splashed onto her hand.

"Don't worry," he said and squeezed her arm. "Everything will work out fine. Your grandmother told me you're a sensible girl, and a year will soon pass."

A sensible girl.

Fantastic. Exactly what every woman wanted as a

descriptor.

Her hand tingled at the point of contact, the heavy heat from his skin driving away a portion of the chill in her heart. Because there was one other immediate problem she'd initially rejected. One that she believed might be her reality because of the electric awareness—something she hadn't experienced before. She suspected this tiger was her mate, and if that were the case, she'd end up stuck for longer than a year.

He'd trap her for life.

4

MIKHAIL WAITED FOR HIS friends to exit at the airport before opening the vehicle for Edwina to alight.

His wife.

The situation seemed surreal. He glanced at his wristwatch and scowled. Finding Edwina and tying the knot had taken longer than he'd allowed, but they should make up time during the flight.

A stiff breeze ruffled his hair, and Edwina shivered in her red evening gown. He propelled her toward the building that housed officials and served as the terminal. He'd secured a passport for her, which would pass inspection.

"This won't take long," he promised. "We can get you warmer clothes on the plane."

Edwina nodded but remained silent.

For the best. He didn't want her asking incessant questions in front of border officials.

Ten minutes later, they were boarding the plane, his

friends trailing them up the stairs. The cabin steward met them at the plane entrance.

"Mr. Lermontov, welcome back." The tall blonde with showgirl's legs and a lithe figure showcased by her uniform ignored his new wife.

"This is my wife, Edwina," Mikhail said, keeping his tone even despite the flash of accompanying anger. It would take time. He understood this, but Edwina would settle faster without outside distractions. And he needed to act fairly with Risha, the cabin steward. He'd taken advantage of her non-too-subtle offers before, but now he had to behave more circumspectly. "Please find Edwina something warmer to wear. We want to take off immediately, so a blanket will suffice for now."

Risha's welcome faded, but she strove for professionalism and acknowledged Edwina with a brief nod. "Take your seats, and I'll return momentarily."

Edwina frowned after the blonde before allowing him to guide her to the airplane cabin.

"Take the window seat," he said. "Buckle up because we'll take off as soon as we receive clearance." He hoped to return to Russia before his grandfather learned of his Scottish trip. He'd have questions, and it would be best if Mikhail distracted him with Edwina. One bright thing on the horizon—his mother would approve. Edwina bore an air of innocence, a freshness that most of his female companions had lacked.

"Here is your blanket, Mrs. Lermontov." Risha frowned when Edwina didn't react, focusing on whatever she saw outside.

"Thank you," he said, accepting it from Risha.

"Ready to take off now," the pilot's voice filtered through the communication system.

Risha checked everyone had fastened their seat belts before saying, "I'll be back with drinks and snacks once we reach our flying altitude."

She sashayed toward the front of the plane and disappeared. The cabin lights dimmed.

Edwina yawned and belatedly covered her mouth with her hand.

"Are you tired?"

"Yes," she said.

Mikhail forced himself not to touch her silky cheek as every instinct prodded him to do. "You can sleep soon. There's a bedroom at the rear of the cabin."

"Thank you." It was her polite voice, but anger pulsed beneath her skin. Not that he blamed her. He'd stolen her dreams. Her grandmother had implied this marriage would be welcome, and she was an amiable girl. Young, inexperienced, and perfect for the role of wife. Mikhail realized he should've approached her differently because she had spirit and was no pushover. He should've done more research, but he'd been busy. He cursed under his breath. No excuse for getting wrong-footed.

Edwina might be younger, but she had opinions and goals. She wouldn't accept orders gracefully, and he needed her obedience. His grandfather would suggest punishment, but that wasn't him, wasn't his way, and he suspected Edwina wouldn't react well to physical chastisement. His wife required wooing and respect. He'd need to treat her like a young horse and ease her into the role.

His lips curled, amusement a flash of reality. Hell, he was treading the same arrogant path as his grandfather. The last thing he wanted was to become a carbon copy of that man.

The plane taxied onto the runway and hurtled into the air. Edwina focused on the view out the window, and he wished he could read her mind. Attraction sizzled between them in the furtive glances they exchanged. An excellent start and something to work with, and that made him a bastard.

Clarice, his mistress, accused him of selfishness and only pleasing himself, and while it was true, she tolerated his ways. She'd see the girl as a rival and would eat Edwina alive, beaming while devouring her in a social situation. And worse, his grandfather would hear about any confrontation or missteps because their friends would gossip.

Hell, it was easy to imagine the rumors about his clandestine marriage.

Challenges. Usually, he relished them, but this one could destroy him if he didn't keep ahead of the sharks.

Perhaps he should've finished with Clarice. He considered and discarded this idea. He needed Clarice since the info she pulled for him was useful. She had friends and contacts, which were helpful to his business plans. The beautiful Clarice considered him hers.

Not true.

Edwina was more important to his plans.

The seat belt sign dinged, and Mikhail unfastened his and stood. "Come," he said, holding out his hand to his new wife. "I'll show you the bedroom, and you can change into something more comfortable. We'll have a light meal, and you can sleep if you wish."

Edwina brushed against him as she stepped in the direction he'd indicated. He caught a delicate floral scent and a hint of green and wildness. She'd enhanced her natural scent rather than drowning it with chemical fragrances. He liked this. He also enjoyed the delicate shiver that rippled through her body.

Mikhail's lips twitched, but he quickly composed himself.

"Can I help with anything?" Rissa asked, appearing from the front of the plane carrying a tray and his regular whisky.

"Would you like something to drink?" he asked Edwina.

"A glass of dry white wine," she said. "Thank you."

His gaze swept to Rissa, and she inclined her chin in response.

Mikhail took Edwina's arm and ignored the jolt that blazed through him. He'd encountered this earlier when he'd clasped her hand. It was unusual and something he'd never experienced before. He wasn't sure if Edwina felt this spark and hesitated to ask.

"This is the bedroom. Ah, Rissa has found you warmer clothes. Help yourself to whatever you require. The bathroom is through that door. You are welcome to use the toiletries. I'll be with my men."

"Thank you." Edwina turned away with polite

dismissal, but not before she surveyed the space, taking in the thick midnight blue curtains over the porthole windows, the massive bed with cream covers, and the throw pillows in varying shades of blue. The decor had Clarice's seal of approval. Edwina's gaze struck the bed and flicked to him. Her cheeks turned a delightful shade of pink.

Mikhail didn't hide his grin. She tempted him to stay, but he needed to speak with his men. He closed the bedroom door and strode into the cabin. Not only were they his security team, but they were his most trusted friends.

Ivan grinned. "Not what you were expecting," he said in their native tongue.

"No," Mikhail agreed, replying in the same language. "She's not a meek miss."

Gregory picked up his glass and swirled the amber liquid. "A good thing. She will need her steel to deal with your grandfather, Clarice, and other friends."

"Yes," Mikhail agreed. "I need to research music teachers."

Ivan's thick black brows arched. "What sort of teachers? Singing?"

Mikhail scowled because he hadn't asked. "I'll check with Edwina. Are either of you acquainted with music teachers? I'll need to take care with my choice."

"You mean you don't want a sexy young man to run off with your new wife," Ivan teased.

His tiger released a possessive growl that surprised him as much as his friends.

Gregory's mouth opened, amusement sliding across his features.

"I don't want to hear whatever smart quip you intend to push past your lips," Mikhail said.

Instead of cowering, his friends cackled.

"Respect," Mikhail snapped.

They laughed even louder.

He rolled his eyes, not replying since Rissa arrived with Edwina's glass of wine and a plate of canapes.

"Are you sitting here?" Rissa asked, sounding surprised.

"No," Mikhail said. "Please set the wine with my glass of whisky."

Rissa brushed past, close enough for him to receive a blast of spicy Oriental perfume. He stepped back, and she made a moue of disappointment. But she was smart enough to understand and not push him a third time.

"I'm sorry," she said. "I won't do that again. Your wife is a lucky woman."

Interesting. She'd assumed his marriage changed nothing, and his rejection had shown otherwise.

"Any word from home?" Mikhail asked before he retreated with Edwina's glass of wine.

"No," Ivan said.

Excellent. It would be best if his grandfather didn't gather a hint of his plans. Ideally, he'd settle Edwina in his home before his mother demanded a meeting.

Edwina opened the bedroom door and appeared wearing a set of navy sweats. They swallowed her, but at least they'd be warmer and more comfortable. She backed up to allow him entrance to the bedroom.

"Here's your glass of white wine," he said, switching to English and gesturing with his hand. He placed the plate of canapes on a side table. "Are you tired?"

"A little."

"You can sleep soon."

"How long is the flight? Can I contact my friends to tell them my location? I should've done that before, but I was..." She hesitated before finishing, "Off-balance."

"You're not a prisoner," he said.

Not quite the truth because her life wasn't hers to do as she pleased until he had what he needed. Once the year was up, he wasn't sure how his grandfather might act, so he'd need to consider strategies. A sliver of guilt flickered through him because, if necessary, he'd make her stay in the marriage longer. His conscience had no place in his decisions.

Her brows rose. "Aren't I? Weren't you protecting your interests by forcing me to marry you?"

"You went through with the marriage without coercion."

Her brows rose higher still, but she didn't argue. Instead, she sipped her wine. Mikhail pressed his lips together, nonplussed by her mature response. By saying nothing, she'd told him quite a lot.

Edwina lowered her voice. "Why is your business so important?"

Anger stole his breath, but not at her. She was asking astute questions. "I disliked how the business was heading before I took over control. My cousin presumes he'd do a better job. He has my grandfather's ear and isn't above pushing against my decisions."

"That must make life difficult."

"Also, my cousin is part of the Russian mafia," he said. "I refuse to let my family get dragged into that life." *Plunged back into that madness.*

"I see. Is that the reason you have bodyguards?"

"My cousin has tried to kill me," Mikhail said.

She blinked. "Am I in danger?"

Mikhail hesitated, debating if honesty was the best policy. He preferred not to lie. So much easier to keep his stories straight since he was juggling enough with his grandfather. "Possibly. Not at first, but maybe once my cousin understands the consequences of our marriage." *Children.*

Her eyes narrowed. "What happens when the year ends? Your problems will still be present."

"No," Mikhail said, even though she was right. His difficulties would return to bite him on the butt. He intended to use this time to his advantage and line up his geese. No, it was ducks, and he wanted them in neat, tidy rows. "I will handle my cousin." And he would, even if he had to kill the conniving bastard and stomp on his grave.

Edwina sipped steadily at her wine.

"Don't you want to learn about the family heirloom jewelry you'll wear to the ballet and opera?" he asked, tired of juggling the truth. She was nothing like Clarice. Nothing. "About your clothing allowance? How much money you'll have at your disposal?"

Edwina snorted. "I don't need jewelry and expensive clothes. They're not important to me."

Mikhail's mind screamed liar, but she met his gaze without flinching.

"I've done without luxuries for years to focus on my music. Why would that change?"

"What sort of music do you study? Do you play an instrument? Sing? Something else?" He surprised himself with his curiosity.

"I sing and play several instruments, but my passion is writing music. My friend Suzie also loves music, but her strength is writing lyrics. We're a fantastic team." Her enthusiasm shone through her words, and guilt surfaced in him. He quashed it, telling himself his need was more significant.

"Collaborate via the internet," he said. "What type of teacher do you require?"

"I want to improve my singing and keyboard skills and perhaps learn another instrument. Suzie will help me on the songwriting side, and I can go through the university course with her, even if I'm not there in person. A remote course is a possibility."

"You have my approval to do all of that. Find a suitable option and let me know how much you require to pay for it."

"Thank you," she said, placing her glass on the small tray.

She had eaten none of the food.

"Are you not hungry?" he asked.

"I'm more tired. It has been a long day." She hitched up the loose sweats. Although she wasn't petite like Clarice, the garments drowned her frame.

Mikhail took Edwina's arm and hustled her toward the bed. "Strip," he said, his voice harsh with the short order.

She lifted her chin, challenging him with her green gaze. "We are not having sex tonight. We're acquaintances, and that's all."

Mikhail released his breath, aware of how often he issued orders. His family and workers followed his edicts without objection. "No," he said, managing an even tone. "But you must take on my scent. Let me hold you until you sleep."

She searched his expression even as her brow puckered. "If you do anything other than that, I will geld you when you least expect it. At the very least, give me a memorable first time. Flying on an airplane with your men and the cabin steward outside is not the right time or place."

"Bloodthirsty woman." So much information to dissect in her statement. A sneaking sympathy crept through him. She hadn't known about this arranged marriage. That had been obvious. She'd been angry, shocked, and defensive about the money he'd advanced to her grandmother, but she'd believed him.

"Do I have your promise to do nothing to hurt me?"

She didn't trust him. His tiger released a snarl, and Mikhail wanted to growl at her doubts. Then he told himself she was right. He couldn't expect her to surrender with no fight or doubts or fears.

"I promise I'll hold you until you sleep and nothing more. You have nothing to fear from me. I want our marriage to succeed."

"I believe you," she said after a moment. "But I won't

be happy if you disparage my body. It's strong and fit and does everything I need it to. If I have faults in your eyes, keep them to yourself."

Mikhail gave a clipped nod. "You have my word."

She studied him a fraction longer and straightened to strip with quick, economical movements. There were no coy simpers or teasing twitches of her hips or thrusts of breasts that Clarice would've added.

He perused her when she stood naked before him. Her breasts were large, and her nipples pulled to tight nubs because of the air conditioning. She was right about her body, and if he compared her to Clarice, she held more flesh on her bones, yet she also had defined, sleek muscles and curves in the right places.

His tiger stirred, pushing against his control and urging him to scent her, to lick.

Edwina met his gaze. "Do I not get to see you?"

"Yes," he said absently, surprised by his shifter half. *This is a fake marriage. Temporary.* He reinforced his thoughts while he battled to hold his human form. His tiger wanted out. Perhaps he should show Edwina since his family often took their tiger forms at the private estate and out of sight of his grandfather. "Lie on the bed. If it is all right with you, I will shift to my tiger."

Relief poured across her face. She didn't want him to touch her, and that unexpectedly grated.

"Let me hold you first to exchange our scents." His instincts urged him to make physical contact in both forms. The urge to feel her breasts pressing against his chest was too much. She wasn't even his type, so this strange desire to experience the softness of her curves was way out of character. This could've waited.

He shrugged off his suit jacket and tossed it aside. Next came his footwear and his shirt. A tiny croak escaped her when his hands went to his belt buckle. A feeling of pride swept over him, but he kept a straight face and ignored his excitement, his attraction to her.

This feline woman had hidden depths, and despite her age and the way they'd met, she intrigued him.

An auspicious start to their marriage.

5

GODS, HE WAS INCREDIBLE to behold. Eye candy on steroids. She took mental photographs, her inner voice doing a *hubba-hubba* at each discovery. Tanned skin. Powerful muscles. The impression of size because the lack of clothes didn't diminish him. *Hah. No flab around the middle. Large all over...*

She and Suzie had peeked during the shifter runs they and their families attended. It wasn't polite, and they said nothing their parents might overhear. Privately, they'd discussed the varying body shapes and sizes of male equipment. Her feline purred and urged Edwina to rub against him, to seduce him.

Mine. Mine. Mine.

She battled her feline's raunchy desires and barely won.

Despite his age, Mikhail was a shifter in his prime and radiated strength and power, and curiosity had her fantasizing about testing those muscles with her tingling fingers.

He made a tiny chuffing sound, snapping her to attention. Luckily, she'd blanked her expression, or at least given it her best try. When their gazes met, his eyes flickered and glowed a deeper blue with a trace of gold. His tiger wasn't as unaffected as his posture and expression suggested.

He prowled the steps separating them and scooped her off her feet. With two giant strides, he reached the bed and placed her on the mattress. He followed her down before her tiny *eep* of surprise melted into nothingness.

His glowing gaze went to her mouth and dallied. "Can I kiss you?"

While he'd uttered a formal request, his gorgeous eyes shouted seduction. Her tongue slicked her lips while her mind shuddered, traveling a rutted road of disjointed thoughts. *He was asking her permission? With his strength and size, he could take whatever he wanted, even if he'd agreed otherwise.*

Ultra-aware of his hungry gaze, she gulped, gave a quick nod, and attempted iron control of her body. Her heart didn't listen. It lurched and gamboled like a playful puppy, running alongside her militant feline. Her breathing hitched. A fine tremor twitched her muscles, and every sense scaled virtual mountains, scrambling to get quality info on this shifter who wanted to kiss her.

His eyes never left hers as he leaned closer. A warm, earthy scent with hints of whisky and smoke filled her rapid inhalations. Chocolate and vanilla, maybe. Oh, such a decadent aroma. Time seemed to still, yet every rustle of the bedcovers and the hum of the plane's engines battered her ears.

When his mouth finally closed over hers, the intimate press of lips had her freezing. His tongue stroked against her skin, the roughness taking her by surprise. She gasped, and he took immediate advantage, kissing her with expertise. He embraced her with his solidness, his weight pressing her into the plush mattress. His kiss was unique, transmitting carnal messages, and her feline's purr was a constant mental accompaniment.

Edwina hesitated under this sensual bombardment, her confidence faltering. Should she trust her feline? Her human concerns? An instant later, she touched her tongue to his. An electric jolt arced through her, the shock of it disturbing. She gasped again, his kiss quickly overwhelming her senses until he became her focus. He tasted amazing. She caught the hint of smoky whisky and an underlying sweetness she found highly addictive.

When he lifted his head, her cheeks heated at his penetrating blue-gold stare. She'd kissed other men. Quite a few, if she were honest, so she had the experience to declare this was unequivocally the best kiss she'd ever shared. When Mikhail kissed her, she'd ceased to think, and for long, delightful seconds, she and her feline had been on the same page.

They'd wanted him.

His gaze drifted down to the curve of her breasts, and her mind darted to other activities she hadn't practiced yet. Taking on this shifter's scent would be a pleasure, although he might ruin her for other men. Thoughts and fears, hopes flashed through her mind at lightning speed. Silly, girlish dreams of happy ever after that she'd never have with her first lover.

The future...

It was murky, like the darkest winter night.

Trepidation replaced some of her feel-good mood. No! Best to take each day one at a time and focus on survival. Her grandmother might've landed her in this mess, but Mikhail had treated her decently. So far. She might find him attractive, but the situation could implode. What if he beat her, abused her, and nothing—no one—would stop him?

Edwina quivered and tried to calm her racing pulse. Then there was the other problem—the insidious urging from her feline. Her leopard wanted this man, wanted to rub against him and give herself to his care. She'd have to stay strong because there had been the odd moment when she'd wished for this too. It would be so easy to surrender.

Fierce need washed through her, fueled partly by her feline, but she tingled with desire too.

Her feline had half convinced Edwina that Mikhail would make them purr with happiness. His presence was imperative to their well-being. She peeked through her lashes and found him studying her. Her breasts prickled with an edgy fervor that made her want to wriggle and brush against him like a cat in heat. The thought popped into her mind, and a blush swept across her skin.

"You have experience."

The tone of his voice had her freezing. Her gaze jerked to his, and the faint accusation she spotted had her mouth firming.

"So have you."

She refused to apologize for the exposure she'd secured, and his implications jabbed at her temper. Edwina bit back her irritation and waited for his next salvo.

"You told me you are a virgin. Your grandmother assured me you were untouched."

"Double standard, much?" she said, with an overload of sweetness. *Pompous windbag.* The nerve of him expecting purity when she was positive he'd had many women. Then there was the fact he was accusing her of lying.

His nostrils flared, and he bared his canines, the sharpness of his mood reflecting in the firm set of his mouth. The bitter tang of his anger fragranced the air and choked her throat. A sliver of fear tap-danced down her spine. Had she gone too far? They traded glares, and she weakened first, glancing away. She silently cursed, miffed because he'd take this avoidance as a victory. A concession or even guilt.

The silence pulsed between them. The longer the hush stretched, the deeper the unease that assailed her. Her feline trembled, unhappy. Maybe she shouldn't have poked the tiger, but she was tired of everyone pushing her around. By marrying him, she'd exchanged her cage for another, albeit an expensive and luxurious one, judging by appearances.

She'd agreed to the marriage to save her family, as her grandmother had guessed she might. Valerie McClintock had planned and used her understanding of her granddaughter, her love for her parents to ensure

Edwina followed orders.

Yeah, she'd had no choice, but that didn't mean she'd let Mikhail disrespect her.

She'd fulfill the marriage contract with this sexy tiger and walk away to live the life she wanted for herself. Edwina tamped down the doubt that slinked into her mind. Her feline opposed this radical plan, and she understood. The man sported attractive qualities. A problem.

Mikhail sprang without warning. He pushed her flat against the mattress and kissed her. This kiss differed from the first. This one inflamed and punished. It was a kiss to show Edwina he was the boss. He ground their lips together and forced his tongue into her mouth. Initially, she fought and nipped his bottom lip. She tasted blood and heard him groan. Not one of pain or anger, but more of surprise and...

The kiss gentled, and she hesitated, unsure. Her feline released another loud purr as Mikhail's hands wandered, roaming down her arms, over her butt. Her pulse lurched, and she wasn't sure how to react since her limited experience took her only so far. Mikhail wasn't helping, although his anger had faded. Even as she thought this, he parted their mouths and swiped his tongue over her bottom lip. The rasp had her nerve endings jumping to attention, and she drew in an audible breath.

"Steady," he whispered, sliding his mouth across her jaw and down her throat. His teeth scraped pulse points and tendons, and she bit back a startled groan. So good.

Gods, she hadn't considered a physical relationship

until they'd reached the bed, fury at her grandmother driving everything from her thoughts.

He stilled. "What's on your mind?"

Rattled now, Edwina didn't bother to prevaricate. She loosed a truth bomb. "Everyone at our destination is a stranger. I have no one to count on if I need help. If you rage and kill me for mouthing off, that's it. I won't get to realize my hopes or dreams. You control everything." She scanned his face, his expression puncturing her run of speech.

The wretch was smiling.

"No need for humor," she snapped. "You understand my situation. If I displease you, no one will make you stick to the deal you inked with my grandmother or force you to honor your promise to let me leave after a year."

"You'd better obey me in everything," he said silkily.

"What does that mean?" Angry again, she glowered. "If you kill me, I *will* come back to haunt you. You'll regret messing with me. That is a promise."

"Noted," he said, drily this time.

"You can laugh at me all you like, but I'd make you pay."

He started to respond, but someone tapped on the door.

"What is it?" Mikhail snapped.

"Your grandfather is on the phone." One of Mikhail's guards.

"Why didn't he call me?"

"Your phone went to voicemail."

Mikhail's growl had the hair on her nape lifting. He must've sensed her unease because he stroked her upper arm as he cleared his throat. "I'll be there soon."

"He demanded to know where you were."

Mikhail sighed. "Two minutes." He separated their bodies, his gaze sweeping her breasts before he rose. "Sorry about the interruption. Try to sleep."

Edwina watched him pull on a pair of trousers and exit the bedroom. Her breath hissed out in dismay. This man had thrown her off-balance, leaving her uncertain of how to behave. At the first opportunity, she'd contact Suzie and tell her everything.

A yawn slipped free, and she rose to tug back the covers. She slid beneath and relaxed, exhausted after her event-filled evening.

She awoke to warmth surrounding her. A quick inhalation told her it was Mikhail, and she hadn't heard his return. His breathing was slow and even, so he must be asleep. Edwina swallowed as her mind slid to the mental images of his powerful body. It'd be easier if she didn't find him attractive. In the past, she'd appreciated a sexy body and moved onward with scarcely a blink. Mikhail had a presence that her feline refused to ignore, which meant she was doomed. He intrigued her. Dangerous because curiosity *had* killed the cat.

"Stop wriggling, or I'll assume you have something else in mind."

Edwina froze. "Ah, I'm awake now. I'll get up and get dressed. If you want to sleep longer, I can sit in the main cabin."

His arm tightened around her waist. "If you're no longer fatigued, we'll get back to what we were doing earlier. I got the impression you'd changed your mind about us having sex." The silkiness of his voice had that inconvenient awareness building in her chest again. *His kisses.* Her feline released an excited mewl, and heat rushed to Edwina's cheeks.

Mikhail twisted, shifting her body with comical ease. He pressed her flat to the mattress, holding her in place with his bulk. Seconds later, he kissed her. No tentative kiss, this, but a masterful one that consumed her. Fire licked through her veins as he nipped and rasped his tongue across her lips. A hungry noise escaped Edwina, and he laughed softly. Then his kiss turned sweet and coaxing, and soon she was drowning in desire and confusion. This man had the power to drive her crazy. His tongue ran down her neck while one of his hands crept lower to caress the upper swells of her breasts.

Fumbling boys had touched her before, only annoying her. Mikhail's hand skimmed with skill, with purpose. He brushed the back of his hand across one nipple, the jolt plunging to her core.

"Are your breasts sensitive?"

"They can be." She hadn't liked it when the males she'd met had paid more attention to her breasts than her as a person. Several times, she'd told men *she was up here*, not where they focused.

His mouth followed the path of his hand, the gentle rasp of his tongue prickling her skin. The tip brushed her areola, and the touch ricocheted down her torso, until resting between her thighs. Then his warm lips settled over her nipple, the powerful draw of his mouth making her cry out and arch upward in a silent demand for more.

Her legs stirred restlessly while she writhed beneath him. This man—his experience was evident. She gripped his shoulders, using them as an anchor while his breath caressed her neck and upper chest, and his mouth and tongue toyed with her nipple. That felt...amazing.

The wetness between her thighs increased with each firm pull on her breast. An edgy sensation filled her, threatening to overwhelm her, pushing at her desperation for more. Her feline arched under her skin, and to her consternation, claws formed beneath her fingernails.

Aware she was lying there and not doing anything, she ran her hand over his muscular back and gloried in the ripple of his muscles. A purr erupted from him when she repeated the move. It wasn't only her fighting her feline. He enjoyed strokes as much as she did. She continued to caress and smooth her fingers over his back and shoulders.

Mikhail switched to her other breast and gave it the same treatment. Unbidden, her thighs spread wider in a silent invitation. She might not have done this before, but she understood the mechanics. A faint giggle escaped her, and when Mikhail paused, she shook her head.

"This is amusing?"

"No. I'm...nervous," she said in a rush. Not the truth. She'd recalled the bookmark she and Suzie had owned. One that stated something along the lines of them not watching porn. *They read it like fucking ladies.* Which, bottom line, meant they knew sex mechanics even though neither of them had let their relationships progress past heavy petting. She could lie as much as she wanted, but her parents and grandparents smelled fibs. Literally.

"I see," Mikhail said.

How could he see anything? They were strangers. It would take days, months, maybe years before they understood each other.

Mikhail tugged a lock of her hair hard enough to cause pain.

"Ouch! What did you do that for?"

"You keep drifting off. I don't like my partners to zone out on me."

Edwina caught herself before she muttered something rude. She didn't offer excuses, but this entire evening was surreal. Marriage. Blackmail. Maneuvered by this man. The anger she'd tamped down rose to blast her again, and her feline released a silent snarl. Her gaze snapped to his.

"Ah," he said. "There she is."

Before she questioned him, he pressed his lips to hers. The kiss was forceful and compelling. He used expertise to seduce her, and it worked. She kissed him back, pressing against his broad chest and soaking in pleasure.

He moved down her body, touching her everywhere. Stroking her breasts, her belly, her hips. He settled between her legs and dragged his tongue along the crease of her thigh. A soft mewl escaped her, a sound of honest enjoyment because the shifter had skills. At least her first time would be memorable instead of the furtive fumbling of someone her age.

Mikhail lifted her with his hands beneath her bottom. Before the startled shock left her, his mouth was on her warm flesh, his tongue dragging the length of her cleft. Oh! Edwina shuddered and tensed as she anxiously awaited more. Thankfully, he didn't disappoint and teased her nub until her entire world converged on that needy spot. He caressed and licked, the rough rasp of his tongue igniting flames in her lower belly.

"Mikhail," she cried out.

He lifted his head, leaving her flesh throbbing, the cool air a painful balm against her aching sex.

"I like my name on your lips," he whispered.

He'd stopped to tell her that. Why? Why now? "Please don't stop. Action. Talk later."

There was a surprised beat of silence before he chuckled. "Interesting."

Once again, his response astonished her, but she remained silent. She reached for his head and forcibly guided it in the direction she wanted. Laughter shook his big body, but he didn't dally. He dragged his tongue over her flesh, and the prickling of her waiting orgasm sparked to life.

The bubble of pleasure grew and pushed for release. Under his direction, it increased to the point of pain until she shivered with raw need, with desperation. Shuddering, she arched her lower body higher. Her limbs quivered, but she thought she might die if he stopped. She didn't care about the others on the plane. She clenched his head with her thighs, probably half choking him but finding herself unable to worry. The spicy tang of arousal—her arousal—perfumed the air. That might bother her later, but not now.

Mikhail shifted his body and stroked her with fingers and mouth. He pushed one digit inside her and another until the savage throb became too much. The next flicker of his tongue had her crying out and starbursts lighting the backs of her eyes. She rode the emotional storm until the flickering pleasure faded, and she came back to herself. Her eyes opened, and she met Mikhail's blue gaze.

"Thank you," she said, admitting without words the power he held over her. If he'd wanted, he could've just taken her. She was vulnerable here, and no one would've stopped him.

He understood this, too. She saw it in his face, but he didn't gloat. Instead, he took her into his arms. He kissed her yet again, seeming to delight in this contact. Her arms crept around his shoulders, clutching him tightly while their lips tangoed. His legs twined with hers, and he clasped her firmly. It made her feel special. Treasured even when this was business.

The tenderness in his kisses had her heart beating even faster. Using his muscular thigh, he parted her legs.

"Are you ready?"

Her pulse rate went wild. Was she? Edwina had no idea but dipped her head in a nod.

"Are you on birth control?"

"Yes."

His eyes blazed, but he said, "Good."

Right. This marriage would finish at the end of one year.

He broke her chain of thoughts when he penetrated her. He slid inside her easily until he didn't. But before she protested, he drew back, and the sensation of him gliding inside her repeated. She relaxed a fraction, and this time, he pushed deeper. He didn't hurry or snap and snarl at her for wrongdoings, so she relaxed a tad more.

"Good girl," he murmured before sliding his tongue down her neck. His teeth scraped across the spot where leopard mates marked each other, and her entire body turned liquid.

Oh! She'd heard whispers from among the feline population, but the area had never felt sensitive to her. She'd decided, and Suzie had agreed, this marking spot was an urban myth. Yes, the mates had exchanged bites—evident by the raised scars—but turning into an X-rated area that would inflame if caressed hadn't seemed likely. Now, she understood, making her wonder if tigers would respond similarly.

No time like the present to conduct a scientific trial. She'd kiss and nuzzle Mikhail and learn how he reacted to her attentions. Before she put her thoughts into action, he slid from her and pushed home again, scraping against a place deep inside that lit her nerve endings. Clutching his shoulders, she gripped him and breathlessly waited.

Mikhail repeated the retreat and invasion, and the wondrous sensations intensified until she was awash with a coiled bliss that pulled tighter and tighter. She gasped, pushing up into his next stroke. She dug her nails into his muscular shoulders and rasped her tongue across the base of his neck, thrilling when he shuddered, and the smoothness of his strokes faltered. Next, she used her teeth, savoring the salt on his skin and his spicy freshness even as she strove toward pleasure.

He slammed into her, and the coil released, making her cry out. Edwina acted without thought, biting down until she tasted blood. Instinct drove her to lick at the wound she'd created, the entire situation taking on a dreamlike quality. He grunted at her bite but didn't stop stroking into her. He stilled, embedded inside her, his heart thudding loudly.

Edwina's entire body turned boneless, relaxed in the maelstrom of satisfaction. Total bliss. She had never undergone a magical release like this—all-encompassing—even experimenting by herself.

Mikhail held her close for an instant longer, and her eyelids drooped, contentment filling her and close to sleep. She was vaguely aware of him pulling away and gave a muffled protest.

"Stay, little one. Get some rest."

Little one. No one had ever called her that before, and as she drifted closer to sleep, she decided she liked it.

6

A KNOCK ON HER door woke her, and confused, Edwina took long moments to work out where she was and why she was naked.

"Half an hour until we begin our descent, Mrs. Lermontov. You need to get up now." The taps against the door came again, and it slid open. "Mrs. Lermontov, are you awake?"

"Barely," Edwina said.

"Take a quick shower, and I'll have coffee and breakfast ready for you in the cabin."

"Thank you." Edwina waited until the blonde woman retreated before sliding from the bed. Mikhail's scent surrounded her still, and she frowned now that she was marginally more awake. They'd made love—no, had sex to mingle their scents. It had been fantastic. Incredible. And if she were honest, she wanted a repeat. Sharing his bed would not be a hardship. Their age difference leaned toward the positive since his experience had made the event enjoyable.

Edwina stood, her muscles tender. She tottered toward the shower because his scent surrounding her made her uneasy and yet satisfied. How the two emotions existed together, she didn't know, but they were battling for supremacy.

She'd bitten him.

The memory thumped her over her head, and she froze while turning on the shower.

She'd bitten him.

Claimed him.

Oh, gods. This was a disaster. What she'd done... She couldn't take back. She'd marked him, and he hadn't mentioned her actions. Perhaps tigers differed from leopards, and they didn't bite their mates. Edwina slid under the warm water with a resigned sigh.

This was bad.

Terrible because it meant she had a permanent connection to him. Finishing their relationship at the end of the year wouldn't work now. *The mark.*

Tears stung her eyes. She'd made another misstep in a line of many, but this one was a doozy. No takebacks. Only death could break this bond with him.

Aware of the ticking clock, she hurried through her shower, using the unperfumed shower gel to cleanse herself. She scrubbed her skin hard, trying to remove his scent. Her feline half wasn't happy about this, but anger threaded through Edwina. She'd let her feline persuade her when all she'd craved was the freedom to follow her dreams. Edwina had refused to go from her parents' home directly to that of a husband. She'd wanted to live. Experience life. Make mistakes and achieve her goals. The last thing she wanted was to step into another cage, another set of rules. Protected and cosseted—what sort of life was that?

SHOCK FOLLOWED MIKHAIL'S SWIFT steps from the bedroom. He'd showered and changed into casual clothes before leaving Edwina to sleep. Luckily, his shirt had a high collar to hide Edwina's mark. His tiger released a throaty chuff of approval. The young woman was their mate. The information changed everything, and he'd need to alter his plans. Time to ponder that later.

He entered the cabin and took a seat with his friends.

Ivan lifted his gaze from a tablet. "Job done?"

Mikhail didn't trust himself to speak and merely nodded. What he'd thought to be one of the many steps to success had become more enjoyable than he'd envisioned. The sexual rapport between the two of them was a welcome surprise.

"Was it that bad?" Gregory held a coffee mug in his large hands. His chunky gold ring glinted and clinked faintly against the white china.

"No."

"Was she a sweet virgin?" Ivan asked, wriggling his bushy black eyebrows, his blue eyes bright with amusement at Mikhail's expense.

"I'm not discussing this," Mikhail said.

In the past, he'd been open regarding his sexual exploits. With his two friends, at least. The reporters exaggerated most of what appeared in the gossip pages. His mind drifted, and the bedroom incident came to mind. The instant she'd bitten him, he'd wanted to return the favor, every instinct screaming to claim her the same way. As it was, he'd had to fight his urges, barely controlling himself. If he marked her, he wouldn't have autonomy and the ability to continue his plans. His grandfather wanted him to marry the Ivanov girl. He'd taken care of that problem, but now Edwina had introduced a new set of difficulties to navigate.

"Was it worse than bad?" Gregory asked, a teasing note in his voice. "So awful that you shudder to remember the act, and the idea of repeating the sex is abhorrent?"

Mikhail released a curse and closed his eyes. His friends wouldn't let this go. Maybe he should tell them the truth. He inhaled, the breath steadying him since it hinted at her sweetness. He raised his hand and swept his collar aside, his thumb rubbing across the raised mark she'd left. Sensual awareness flooded him, every cell in his body throbbing.

Ivan noticed the mark first, understanding what it meant. He whistled, even as he leaned forward for a better look. "She marked you."

"Yes."

"Did you return the sentiment?" Gregory asked, no longer kidding around.

"My tiger wanted to, but I had to hold myself back. I almost knotted in her," he added.

Ivan issued a low whistle. "That's rare."

"Yes."

"You're true mates," Gregory added with wonder.

"Clarice is gonna be pissed," Ivan said.

"I don't intend to tell her," Mikhail said.

"She'll see your mark and grasp the meaning," Gregory said.

"Not necessarily," Ivan said. "Clarice is human. Marking isn't common with our friends, and although Clarice is aware of shifters and has shifter friends, they're not feline. Invent an excuse. An acceptable one if she asks questions."

"If Edwina is your mate, how will you touch Clarice?" Gregory asked, going for the practicalities as was his nature. "She's useful to have on your side for her contacts."

Mikhail scrubbed his hands over his face and groaned. "I thought marrying this girl would make my life easier. Instead, my entire plan has backfired, making my problems worse."

"You didn't mention your marriage to your grandfather when he called," Ivan said.

"Shush. No more of this discussion until we're alone. Edwina is coming."

She appeared in the cabin, her expression uncertain. The scent of coffee followed her, and some of Mikhail's tension dissipated. Breakfast would offer a distraction.

"Edwina, have a seat with us. Breakfast is almost ready. Did you sleep well?" he asked.

Her gaze went straight to his neck and the mark he'd concealed with his collar. Pink crept into her cheeks. Her throat worked in a swallow, and her steps slowed.

"Come and sit by me," Ivan said, his tone innocent while his blue eyes twinkled with devilment. "It's about time Mikhail introduced us to his lovely wife."

Mikhail barely restrained his snarl of displeasure. He didn't want any man close to her. Ivan got this and didn't care if he pushed Mikhail's buttons. Edwina perched on a seat, her subdued conduct making Mikhail want to curse. She'd acted brave earlier, but her behavior had changed since she'd marked him. Shock, most likely, since that was what he was suffering right now. He'd never thought of finding a true mate.

So many bloody complications.

Rissa appeared with a tray of coffee and pastries and set it on the small white table between them.

"We'll pour the coffee," Mikhail told her.

She offered a respectful nod and retreated to collect the rest of their breakfast.

"Ivan and I take black coffee. Gregory takes his coffee white," he said to Edwina.

Her hand trembled a fraction as she reached for the coffeepot, but as he'd hoped, the actions steadied her anxiety. The quiver retreated, as did her jumpy behavior. She settled in the chair properly and poured the coffee. Mikhail accepted a mug and took a sip.

"I thought we'd go straight to the house on our arrival. You can sleep, and we'll organize clothes for you," Mikhail said.

"I'd prefer not to sleep until nighttime," she said. "It's the best way to get my body clock in sync with the local time."

He inclined his head. "I'll be busy, but my housekeeper will show you around and organize clothes."

"Thank you." She handed Ivan and Gregory the plate of pastries before offering it to him.

"No, thanks."

She didn't take one for herself but sipped a white coffee. "You have a housekeeper."

A statement. He frowned. "Yes, and staff to maintain the grounds. I'm often away, and this makes my life less complicated."

"I see," she said.

One searching glance didn't illuminate him as to what she saw, but he let this slide.

Rissa arrived with cooked breakfasts, heavy on the meat. Edwina accepted her plate but picked at the food. He wanted to remonstrate and tell her she needed to eat, but he'd tossed a lot at her in the last twelve hours. He was bloody lucky she wasn't a mass of tears and tantrums.

Rissa cleared the plates and cups once he and the other men finished eating.

"Fasten your seat belts," Rissa reminded them before she retreated.

He and Edwina shifted back to their original seats and buckled in. Edwina scanned the view outside, although she wouldn't see much. They were landing at a remote airport, one close to his property, that allowed him to come and go with more privacy. Handy when he didn't want his grandfather to learn he was out of the country.

This time, he wanted to get his new wife home and

settled before he moved to the next stage of his plan. He gave a soft snort of derision. His plan had blown to smithereens when Edwina claimed him, and he'd realized exactly what a jewel he'd discovered entirely by accident.

He sucked in a calming breath, then swallowed hard because it smelled of her. His tiger stretched beneath his skin and rumbled out a lusty purr of pleasure. Mikhail tightened his control, refusing to let his tiger exert a say in proceedings. Responsibilities already overwhelmed him. His juggling skills were excellent, but fighting his tiger wasn't ideal.

"I didn't ask you," he murmured. "Most shifters don't enjoy flying. Are you all right?"

Edwina swung her green gaze in his direction. "Now you ask." She paused and wrinkled her nose. "Sorry. That was rude. Flying isn't my favorite thing, but I'm fine. It's always better once my feet are on solid ground."

He nodded, appreciating her silent peace offering. "I feel the same. Flying is necessary, but standing on an unmoving surface is preferable."

The wheels struck the runway, and the plane slowed before halting.

"We have a welcoming committee," Edwina said.

"What?" No one except his housekeeper had known they were returning this morning.

Rissa arrived with the men's suit jackets.

"Thank you," Mikhail said, thrusting his arms into his. The back of his neck itched insistently. He strode to the main door, waiting for it to open.

"Let us go first," Ivan murmured. "I don't like this."

Mikhail ceded to them and waited with Edwina.

"What's wrong?" she whispered.

"We weren't expecting anyone."

"Who is it?" She lowered her voice further. "Dangerous? The mafia or something?"

"Unlikely." His tiger relaxed, which meant so did he. Interesting, because his temper was legendary. He wasn't always patient or calm.

"Fuck," Ivan muttered.

That one word had his stress levels rising again, as did the look Ivan sent over his shoulder.

"Who is it?" Mikhail demanded.

"You'll see soon enough. You won't need a weapon apart from your wits and cool mind. No temper this time," Ivan warned and started down the stairs leading to ground level.

Mikhail hesitated before ushering Edwina forward. He cursed under his breath, understanding what Ivan had meant when he spotted Clarice waiting at the terminal building door.

7

THE WOMAN WAITING FOR them was stunningly gorgeous, with glossy blonde hair falling down her back. Her bright blue gaze never shifted from Mikhail, and her smile was dazzlingly white, her lips a vibrant pink to match the burgundy of her apparel. She was slim, and her clothes were classic and custom-fitted. Edwina identified that easily, and she owned not one designer outfit.

When they'd almost reached the terminal, the woman started running. She launched herself at Mikhail with a cry of excitement.

Edwina froze, her gaze drawn as the woman's pink lips pressed against Mikhail's. Her entire body shuddered, and the low growl of her leopard rumbled through her mind, her feline demanding action. That was their mate.

Ivan grasped her arm, and Edwina wasn't sure if he was keeping her safe or stopping her from springing at the woman cuddling her mate. *Mikhail was hers.*

"Steady," Ivan murmured in her ear. "Keep control and don't draw attention."

The stranger drew away from Mikhail and grinned up at him. "I thought you'd be pleased to see me."

"I am," Mikhail said in a low rumble.

The woman frowned and took another step back. "I thought you were away on a brief business trip." Her gaze settled on Edwina, her blue eyes slicing and dicing before smoothly shifting back to Mikhail. "Who is she?"

Mikhail's reply was inaudible, and Edwina didn't hear it, even with her shifter abilities. She strained for even a few words, but nothing. When she stepped forward, Ivan grabbed her upper arm.

"Let me go." Edwina tried to wrench from his grip.

"You need to trust Mikhail." Ivan spoke in an urgent whisper.

"Why?" Edwina snapped, jerking and gaining freedom this time. "We're practically strangers."

"You know him enough to mark him," Ivan replied softly, not shifting his gaze from the couple.

"A mistake." Shame and anger warred in her. Disappointment in herself as her grandmother's words haunted her. *You're an impulsive girl with no self-control. You never consider the consequences of your actions.* Never. *Instead, you leap into the flames and leave a mess for everyone to clean up.*

Her grandmother was right.

Tears stung her eyes, and emotions clogged her throat. She was a stupid girl. Marking a mate was irreversible. Anger flared in her then, burning through the tears and searing emotion that left her unsteady. Death could be arranged if he didn't get his hands off that blonde bimbo. A growl erupted, and Ivan gripped her shoulder. He frog-marched her from the main entrance and kept walking until she couldn't see Mikhail and the woman.

"Stop," he demanded, shaking her.

Edwina's head rocked back and forth. "She has her hands all over him." The words spilled free, uncensored. She wasn't invested in him. *She wasn't.* He was a stranger, using her to attain a goal so important that he'd traveled to Scotland to collect her. He might be her mate, but he hadn't made a return claim.

Her breath hitched, each hiccupped gasp difficult as if she were sucking through a straw. The truth. He'd fucked her so their scents combined to fool his family and everyone else who mattered to his plans.

She swallowed hard, but that knot filled her throat again, and her jaw ached from the tension and bitterness that suffused her. She was an idiot. Her shoulders slumped. "I'm tired," she managed, her voice thick. "When will we leave?"

"Soon." Ivan wrapped his arm around her shoulders and led her back to the central doorway. Mikhail and the woman must've entered the building, but Gregory was waiting for them, his expression blank.

"I hope you understand what you're doing," he told Ivan. "Mikhail won't like you touching her."

"He should've planned better. Clarice will create problems."

"Clarice?"

The two men exchanged a glance and ceased their chatter.

"Let's go," Ivan said.

They entered the squat building, and to her surprise, it was empty.

"W-where is Mikhail?" Edwina asked. Had he gone with that woman? Mortified when a whimper escaped, she angled away from them, bowing her head and letting her hair fall over her face.

"Hell," Gregory muttered. "Mikhail needed to see to something personal. He'll meet us at his place."

She rubbed away the tight pain in her chest. "I thought you were his security guards. Why have you let him go off on his own?"

"He's not weak," Ivan said. "He's smart and capable of protecting himself."

Edwina let them direct her toward the officials. Ivan produced her fake passport. She silently waited while the uniformed man scanned her face and documents. An instant later, he stamped it and ushered them through. Gregory led her outside. An icy blast swept over the open ground, and Edwina shivered. It was much cooler here in Russia than in Scotland, despite being mid-summer.

Even her surroundings were uninspiring. The land to her right held the scars of recent earthworks and heavy machinery, suggesting they were making additions to the airport. Cars filled the parking lot, most as old as the vehicle she and Suzie shared in Middlemarch.

Middlemarch.

A sigh gusted from her as she trudged after Ivan and

Gregory. She wouldn't mind returning to a New Zealand winter right now. It would mean this was nothing more than a horrid dream.

Car locks beeped, and Ivan opened a rear door for her. He waited until she was safely inside before he closed the door. Gregory loaded several pieces of luggage. Edwina put on the seatbelt, uninterested in the scenery or where they were going. Her mate had left with another woman. Willingly left.

Edwina gritted her teeth and held back a howl. What the hell did she do now?

MIKHAIL'S SKIN CRAWLED AT Clarice's touch. Her fingers trailing over his arm hurt, which was weird since Clarice had been his mistress for two years. His tiger shoved against his control, his snarls reverberating through Mikhail's mind. He had to bite his inner cheek, the jolt of pain helping him to exert authority. After paying the cab driver, Mikhail guided Clarice past the doorman in his bottle-green uniform to a bank of elevators. He pushed the button to summon the car and waited, mentally urging the machinery to hustle.

Gods, he had to get a grip on his thrumming emotions. It was Edwina, of course, but he refused to let Clarice know the woman meant something to him. All hell would explode if Clarice learned the truth. She was happy as his mistress and had even suggested he take a wife if he wanted to have children. One she approved of and who understood Clarice's position in his life. Nothing needed to change between them.

Clarice had introduced him to two different Ivanov cousins at the last party they'd attended together. He'd assumed that the wife Clarice envisioned for him wouldn't care if he kept a mistress.

Her encouragement irked him, his suspicions rising because his grandfather seemed determined to push him in the same direction. His father had struggled to make their business legal, and Mikhail refused to undo his hard work and dabble in crime.

His grandfather thought differently. Mikhail's father had died while trying to escape that life. The family company was solid. They didn't need to step outside the law to continue their success, even if his grandfather kept causing roadblocks and strife.

The elevator reached the top floor and opened to a short corridor with two doors.

"Clarice, I can't stay. I have urgent business to attend to at home," Mikhail said, pulling from her clinging embrace. He opened the door to her luxury apartment and ushered her inside.

"But I've missed you." She wrapped her arms around his neck. He shuddered at her touch, and she misunderstood the slight reaction, her pink lips tipping up at the corners. "You can stay for a while, surely. You have staff to take care of business matters."

He wanted Edwina, and that told him everything.

"No, not today." Never again. Not that he told Clarice because he didn't want to deal with the fallout. Stupidly, he'd thought to juggle both women without difficulty. He needed a different plan because the gleam in Clarice's eyes told him she had seduction on her mind.

"But I haven't seen you for a week." She pouted, but he no longer considered her habits cute. Instead, a curvy woman with green eyes enticed him.

"Clarice, I'm sorry, but I must attend to a business matter."

Irritation flickered across her face, an expression she would've hidden in the past. She'd always been sweetness and light with him, although he'd sensed she had a steel backbone.

"When will I see you? I want to go to dinner tonight and introduce you to my friends."

"Go on your own," he suggested.

"No, it's better if you attend with me," she said.

He understood then. She had more status and power when she was on his arm, and tonight was an evening when she judged his presence necessary.

"What time is the dinner?" he asked, mentally shifting his plans. He needed to keep Edwina under wraps until he'd spoken to his grandfather and had everything else ready in his business world.

"Eight," she said, smiling now that she'd sensed he'd acquiesce. "But they're having drinks from seven-thirty. I want to introduce you to friends visiting from Moscow."

Everything in Mikhail pulled tight, his suspicions coming to the fore again. A prospective bride? Or someone else wanting to muscle him back to his mafia roots. He wanted to avoid a scene. "Seven-thirty, it is. Should I pick you up or meet you at your friend's house?"

"Pick me up at seven-fifteen." Clarice placed her hands on his shoulders and stood on tiptoe to kiss him. His skin crawled, distaste filling him, and he had to steel himself not to jerk from her touch. He sucked in a breath, and her heavy Oriental scent struck him wrong. He struggled to fight his urgent need to retreat, his tiger releasing a silent snarl of protest when Mikhail held himself still.

"I missed you," Clarice said. "Perhaps you can stay the night?"

"Not tonight," Mikhail said, wondering how to finagle out of this mess without causing hurt feelings and tantrums. *Later.* He stepped back and contrived a wide smile. "I'll be here at seven-fifteen," he promised before she offered a protest.

Once the apartment door closed behind him, Mikhail strode to the elevator. The doors slid open, and he stepped inside, relieved to find himself alone. The couple from Moscow were worrying news because he suspected their identities. Bratva royalty, or at least as close as one came to nobility. They'd be high-ranked and want to extend their tendrils into his world. They'd take his contacts and control of everything his father had built, and he'd added to the business. Stopping a takeover would take power, and he wasn't confident he'd still be standing at the end of the battle. His grandfather had told him he could walk into a powerful Bratva position, but he wanted none of it, like his father.

He dipped his head to the doorman and continued outside before coming to a halt. He didn't have transport since they'd used the taxi Clarice had asked to wait. *Hell.* He might drop by his grandfather's home and organize for Ivan or Gregory to meet him there.

Mikhail didn't understand why his grandfather was determined to get his way. He'd kept from Bratva clutches for all these years and used his otherness and superior strength to repel attacks. Suddenly, his grandfather pressured him to change tack when they were successful and poised for greater success. The reasons were the key to this mess, but his grandfather remained mute about his rationale.

Mikhail set a rapid pace, striding down leafy avenues and catching glimpses of massive mansions behind high fences. Not one of these people understood the real world. They lived without fear or hunger and wielded the power that immense wealth offered them.

Mikhail had always wanted to help the workers who struggled to live and survive, and he thought he'd done a decent job. His workers stayed, and he didn't have the staff attrition that other businesses faced. Any positions they advertised filled rapidly. Mikhail wished he could help more people, and if his expansion plans succeeded, he'd offer more jobs.

He turned onto his grandfather's street and walked to the end house. He pushed the intercom to announce his presence. A security man appeared and allowed him entrance.

"I have informed your grandfather of your visit," the man said.

Mikhail's phone rang. He ignored the summons, but it

continued to ring. He glanced at the screen and frowned. "Ivan? What's wrong? Edwina?"

"No, it's the new worksite. A group arrived armed with bats, knives, and other weapons and attacked the building crew on site."

Fury blasted through Mikhail. "How many injured?"

"It wasn't as bad as it might have been. Victor was there with his assistant."

Relief flooded Mikhail on hearing this. "I'll call Victor. Why didn't Victor call me direct?"

"He tried. The call wouldn't connect."

Mikhail scowled at his phone. That made no sense. His phone had been with him the entire time and turned on. He thought back. He'd never received a call at Clarice's apartment—not in his memory. Was that suspicious, or did Clarice have a way of blocking phone calls? He was only a few streets from Clarice's apartment, so his phone should've worked. Something to consider and investigate later. He hit speed dial for Victor.

"Victor," Mikhail said as soon as the bear shifter answered his phone. "What happened?"

"A group of thugs came with demands for protection money. I told them we didn't require security and to fuck off before we handed them their arses. They didn't take kindly to my advice."

Mikhail pinched the bridge of his nose. Victor wasn't the most tactful person on his team, but he always got the job done with minimal trouble. "Anyone seriously hurt?"

"A few cuts and bruises. Andre didn't duck fast enough. He has a black eye. They got the worst of it," Victor said, sounding unperturbed. "They won't come around next month, not without reinforcements. These men misjudged us. We're not weak, nor will we cave to their demands."

"Do you need help?"

"I have everything under control. I'll call you or Ivan if we have further problems, but we're working with a full crew. There are plenty of bodies here should we require aid."

"Thank you," Mikhail said. "I'll check your progress in a few days."

"Will do, boss."

Mikhail hung up and went in search of his grandfather. He found him sitting on the terrace to appreciate the afternoon sun and the cool breeze.

"Where have you been?" his grandfather demanded. His gray hair was straight and needed a cut, but his brown eyes were as sharp as ever, even though his legs were failing him now. He no longer stood alone and required help to bathe and dress.

"I took some private time," Mikhail said calmly. His grandfather had always demanded a lot of him, especially after his father had died.

"I want to see you married before I die and the business settled. We must stick to the old ways." His gaze bore into Mikhail, his will strong even if his body was failing.

"Did you know the Bratva is shaking down businesses for protection money?" Mikhail asked.

"That's how I got my start. It's right that the tradition continues, and we support others."

"It's illegal, and my father—your son—changed how we do business. We fought to gain independence, and my father died defending our rights. You want us to return to that way because you're feeling nostalgic? I won't do it. Not for you. Not for my cousin. My people are better off now. They and their children are flourishing more than when you were running the company."

The old man glared because he couldn't dispute facts. He wanted his familiar world where he had his old friends and the same power and prestige he had when he was younger. His grandfather didn't understand that the traditional ways hadn't worked for most.

"I won't succumb to pressure from you. We're winning more and bigger contracts because people seek integrity and excellent workmanship. That's what we give them. We don't cut corners or overcharge for materials. Our buildings are winning awards for clever design and going green. Inquiries are coming in from surrounding countries who want us to build their offices and homes. This is the way forward."

"I want to see my friends before I die," his grandfather said. "I miss them. Your cousin Timofel understands this, which is why I have sent him to the United States to train with those who will help him to develop contacts and upskill."

Mikhail kept his expression impassive while relief surged inside him. His cousin was a pain in his butt, and Mikhail was tired of watching his back for the knives Timofel constantly wielded—actual and figurative. Timofel's absence was a blessing, and although he was curious about where his cousin had gone, he didn't ask questions. His cousin had buckets of attitude. He'd likely get himself killed if he didn't learn fast.

And they weren't real friends if they shunned his grandfather because the family company had changed how they did business. Mikhail had agreed with his father and backed him, even though he'd still been in his teens when the shift occurred. His father had lost his life doing what he thought was right, and Mikhail had fought hard when his grandfather had attempted to revert to the old ways.

"I promised my friend you would marry his daughter. I gave him my word." His grandfather was becoming querulous from fatigue. "You will marry her." His expression turned sly. "The notice appears in the newspapers tomorrow."

"No," Mikhail said. "That will not happen."

"It's too late," his grandfather said, his tone smug. "You can't get out of this marriage. I gave my word."

Mikhail cursed, and his heartfelt oath made his grandfather cackle.

"You're trapped now."

"I can't marry the woman because I already have a wife," Mikhail snapped. No sooner had the words left him than he wanted to bite off his tongue.

8

"WHERE HAS MIKHAIL GONE?" Edwina asked as they sped away from the airport, the building site giving way to an industrial area with massive warehouses. She caught glimpses of men in high-visibility vests, driving machinery and scurrying like conscientious ants.

"He has business," Ivan replied, and that was all he said. No details. No excuses. No clues.

"That woman didn't look as if her visit was business-related. Who is she?"

Ivan and Gregory exchanged a glance, their expressions telling.

Irritated, Edwina leaned forward between the seats, not intending to let either man get away with covering for Mikhail. "Girlfriend. Lover. Mistress?"

Neither man reacted, their expressions unreadable, and she stopped asking questions. Instead, she leaned back and watched the scenery. They departed the business zone and entered the confines of the town before leaving that behind and driving into the countryside. A crystal-blue lake came into view, and jagged mountains stood on the horizon, some with snowcaps. Lush fields contained cattle and horses, while in other paddocks, farmers had hay ready to harvest.

The drive took another forty minutes before Ivan turned onto a gravel road and pulled up in front of a gate. He used a remote, and the barrier slid open. Edwina wasn't sure what she expected—probably a mansion or something significant, worthy of a man with pots of money. Instead, they pulled up beside a single-level bungalow. It wasn't huge and luxurious but nor was it small. The gardens blazed with color, and it looked as if Mikhail used the outdoor area as extra living space, given the broad veranda and the wooden furniture clustered around what looked like a firepit.

"Home, sweet home," Gregory said, exiting the vehicle as soon as Ivan halted outside the door.

"You live here too?"

"Ivan and I share a cottage out the back," Gregory said.

Edwina clicked her teeth together to halt her questions. She had tomorrow to learn more. Right now, she wanted to retreat to a private place and fashion a plan. Mikhail was still her mate, even though he might not want her. She'd marked him, so the chances of leaving him were slim. Most people didn't go about mating this way. She exited the vehicle when Gregory opened it for her and followed the two men into an entrance hall big enough to fit a grand piano. Gleaming white tiles covered the floor, and a narrow wooden table held a vase of fresh yellow flowers. A landscape hung on the wall, depicting mountains, trees, and a lake.

"What would you like to do?" Ivan asked after ushering her into the first doorway on the right.

Edwina took stock. A reception room, beautifully decorated and magazine-shoot ready. The curtains danced with the breeze, and the fragrance of flowers filled the air. The chairs and other furniture appeared dainty rather than suitable for a man intent on relaxing in front of the telly.

She blinked. "Are you talking to me?"

"Yes," Ivan said. "You shouldn't sleep now."

Edwina shrugged. "No. I guess I'll check out the gardens and contact my friends."

A quick glance passed between Ivan and Gregory, one that told her speaking with Suzie wouldn't be part of the plan.

"Am I a prisoner?" She glared with accusation.

Gregory spoke first, his words rapid and conciliatory. "No, of course not, but it'd be best to check with Mikhail first."

"I'm a prisoner." She didn't have a phone either. "Am I allowed to get fresh air? I'm used to being outdoors, and I do better if I can exercise." When they glanced at each other again, she made a rude noise and headed for the terrace doors, which stood ajar. She stepped outside before either man offered another objection.

The scent of roses hit her first, and she lifted her head to inhale deeply. Next, the sound of a fountain claimed

81

her attention and her tension seeped away. Nature always helped her destress, but she wanted to speak to Suzie. Her friend would have words of wisdom and help her make a plan. She wandered deeper into the garden and trailed her right hand over a lavender hedge, the pungent scent rising to greet her. A bird sang somewhere to her left, but it ceased abruptly.

Edwina turned in that direction and recoiled when it darted right before her. She ducked back, almost tripping on a rock. Something whistled past her ear.

A curse colored the air from behind her. "Get down. Edwina, down now!"

Startled, she jolted in his direction. Ivan leaped at her, sending her flying. She struck the ground, the air whooshing from her lungs. Gravel burned her palms.

"Keep down. Someone is shooting," Ivan said in an urgent voice. "Stay down. Gregory saw where the shot came from. Give him a chance to catch the intruder."

Someone had shot at her? Why? The question whirred through her mind and repeated over and over. Someone wanted her dead? She'd only just arrived. She didn't know anyone except Ivan, Gregory, and Mikhail. Her thoughts stuttered and snagged on Mikhail. Did he want to get rid of her because she'd marked him?

"Does Mikhail want me here?" she whispered.

"Yes," Ivan said without hesitation. "Mikhail would never hurt you. He will protect you with every resource at his disposal."

And his men had immediately come to her aid. Edwina closed her eyes and inhaled to calm her racing pulse and doubts. Damp soil and greenery filled her senses while her knee throbbed from striking the ground. Warm blood trickled across her skin.

"Ivan." A sharp bird's whistle followed.

Ivan shifted off her and rose before extending his hand to help her stand. "Are you okay? He didn't hit you?"

"He?"

"Figure of speech," Ivan said.

Gregory joined them. "He went over the fence. We should get Edwina inside."

Ivan ushered Edwina indoors, and she heard Gregory speaking with someone else. An older woman with short gray curls and a concerned expression bustled over to her.

"You poor thing," she said, her English excellent and slightly accented. She wore a cotton blouse and black trousers that complemented her rounded frame. "Come with me, and I'll attend to your knee. It looks nasty."

It was sore now that the woman mentioned it. She wasn't sure what she'd collided with, but she'd ripped a hole in her borrowed sweatpants.

"My name is Rita," the woman said. "I'm so pleased you're here."

"I'm Edwina."

Rita nodded, the edges of her brown eyes crinkling. She had a regal air about her. It was the smart clothes, Edwina decided. She limped after Rita, who kept her steps to an amble.

What Edwina saw of the house interior impressed her. The textiles and pieces of furniture were elegant but not stiff, like the contents of her grandparents' home. The colors were natural, with a few pops of brightness.

"This is Mikhail's room," Rita said, standing aside to let Edwina enter first.

They were sharing? Curious, Edwina stepped into the masculine room. It was vast and full of light. White curtains fluttered at the windows, and Mikhail's scent permeated the air.

"The en suite is this way," Rita said.

Edwina's eyes widened because the bathroom suite was immense, with a massive shower big enough for four people. It looked as if there were several spigots. Luxury indeed, and she anticipated using the shower with pleasure.

"Have a seat there," Rita said, pointing to a stool in front of a mirror and a dresser.

Edwina sat and frowned down at her knee. Now that her shock and adrenaline had faded, her knee throbbed, and blood trickled down her leg. Her palms ached too, and she lifted them to study the damage. She prodded at a piece of gravel and winced.

"Let me do that," Rita said. She'd finished rifling through a drawer and carried over several items, including a pair of scissors. "It's best to cut your sweatpants off above the knee. They're past saving."

Edwina stretched out her legs to give Rita access. It was the work of seconds to snip off the partially ripped fabric.

"It's not too bad," Edwina said. "See, it's stopped bleeding already." Good feline genes were helpful sometimes. She didn't mention this because Rita smelled human, and she didn't know how much the woman knew about shifters.

Rita frowned. "It looks deep, but you're right. It's not bleeding any longer. How did you cut it?"

"I fell on the gravel. It was probably the way I struck the ground. Everything happened so fast," Edwina said. A shiver ran through her. Someone had shot at her, and she'd heard the bullet whizz past her head. It had barely missed her. Why, and what the hell had she stepped into the middle of? She needed to speak with Ivan and Gregory.

With Mikhail.

Rita cleaned the wound with minimal fuss. "You're right. It's not as bad as it looked. Iodine and a sticking plaster should do the trick."

"Edwina?" Rapid footsteps approached, and Mikhail appeared in the doorway. "Edwina, Ivan contacted me. Are you all right?" He crouched in front of her, concern etched into his handsome features.

She stared into his blue eyes, and her heart raced. He looked as if he genuinely cared, even though he'd left with *that* woman.

"I'll finish, Rita," Mikhail said. "We'll have drinks and a snack in the lounge in about half an hour."

"Of course," Rita said. "Everything will be ready when you're done here."

She left, and the atmosphere thickened between them. Edwina swallowed.

"I'm sorry I wasn't here," Mikhail said finally, breaking the silence.

"You didn't shoot at me."

"But someone shot you because of me and my actions,"

Mikhail said. "I didn't think they'd go this far."

"Who are they?"

"Bratva," Mikhail said. "That's my best guess. They're trying to pressure me into paying protection money and letting them take over my business interests." He sighed. "When my grandfather ran the business, he played the game their way. My father took over and cleaned house. He didn't like the way Bratva treated our people, and I have continued to steer clear of them. They're not happy with my decision."

"I don't understand. How can they pressure you into doing what they want? No, scratch that," Edwina said. "They strike at people you care about."

"Yes, and recently, I discovered my grandfather is colluding with them. He wanted me to marry into one of the Bratva families."

"But you married me," Edwina said, understanding everything.

"Yes."

"And now I'm in danger because someone saw us at the airport."

Mikhail sighed. "Unfortunately. I'm so sorry."

Edwina extended her hands and showed him her palms. "It's not your fault. Can you dig the gravel out?"

Mikhail held one of her hands between his and picked up the tweezers Rita had left on the dresser. "This will hurt."

"Yes," she agreed and sucked in her breath, a hiss escaping her as he dug out the first piece.

"You're different from what I imagined," Mikhail said.

"What did you expect? A spoiled young girl who executed your orders without issue? One who accepted her place."

Mikhail grinned without warning. "I didn't expect a mouthy woman who intrigues me. One with the heart of a lion."

"Leopard, if you please."

Mikhail chuckled. "But you are brave. Most women of my acquaintance would screech in alarm. They'd weep and throw themselves at me or take to their bed. Everything would be my fault."

"I'm a country girl. We're tough."

"So I'm learning. I made inquiries about a music teacher, and I'm afraid there is no one suitable in town, but what would you say to learning via the internet? I spoke to my grandmother, and she has a friend in London who will teach you. From what grandmother told me, you'd learn similar things to what your university course would cover. You'd have an hour's class three days a week and time to practice. If you wish to learn how to play the mandolin, I can arrange a teacher."

"You've organized that for me today?"

"It was the least I could do. Unfortunately, given the danger, I'll need you to stay around the house. You can go out, but I'm afraid I'll have to ask you to wait until bodyguards are available to escort you. I trust Ivan and Gregor with my life; they'll look after you with the same care I would."

"So I'm going to be a prisoner here?"

He sighed, and it was an unhappy sound. "It will only

be for a short time. That's the last of the gravel. Your palms should heal now." He stood and extended one hand. "Rita will have our drinks and snacks ready. Are you hungry?"

"Yes," Edwina said.

Mikhail took her face in his hands. His eyes glowed with an otherworldly glow, mesmerizing her. Her heart began a fast tattoo, banging against the wall of her chest. Her leopard stretched beneath her skin, and she leaned closer. An instant later, their lips met in a kiss that grabbed the breath from her. He teased her mouth, licked her lips, and stoked her pleasure. He cupped the back of her head, tangling his fingers in her hair. The lazy stroke of his tongue entranced her as he increased the assault on her mouth.

When he pulled back, her knees trembled, and she craved more. More of his mouth, his hands. More of his body pressing against hers as it had during their lovemaking on the plane.

"We'd better go before Rita comes looking for us." He clasped her hand and led her from the en suite. "You're welcome to redecorate if the rooms aren't to your taste."

"No, I like your house from what I've seen. I might add a few things, but I won't change much," Edwina said. "Is there a room I can use for my music?"

"Yes, there is a small reception room off the lounge. It overlooks the gardens and has good lighting. My mother's grand piano is in that room."

"Really?" Excitement filled her. A grand piano. "Is the piano in tune?"

"I had it tuned three months ago."

"Do you play?"

"Not me," Mikhail said. "I can appreciate music, but my talent in that area is sadly lacking."

"I'll be able to use it for my studies and to work with my friend." Pleasure at the idea of immersing herself in her music took some of the sting out of her day.

"Thank you," Mikhail said.

Puzzled, she studied him. "Why are you thanking me?"

"I've turned your entire life upside down, and you're making the best of what you have. Few women would behave with the dignity you have."

Rita arrived with a trolley of drinks, and Edwina's stomach rumbled at the savory scent of a meaty snack.

Mikhail chuckled, and she relaxed, not minding the humor at her expense.

"Let me feed you. You should've said you were hungry."

"I was too busy getting shot at." She watched Mikhail's expression turn dark and felt no guilt. "I dislike secrets."

"I'm older than you," Mikhail replied. "My life has traveled a very different path to yours. It will take us time to get used to each other."

Not very encouraging. Edwina sat in the chair Mikhail indicated, noting the seating area was away from windows and doors. "Will I continue to be a target?"

"Once more people learn of our marriage, I expect the danger will increase. My grandfather is unhappy with my decision to marry you. My link to a woman from outside the Bratva means his friends will see this as a further sign of our family's dishonor to the traditional ways."

"I know nothing about Russian gangs. Are they as bad

as they're portrayed?"

"In many cases, worse."

Another thought occurred. "Aren't you in danger too? Your business and your employees?"

"Yes."

Edwina appreciated his current honesty. Mikhail took a plate and filled it with a selection of snacks. He handed it to her, along with a napkin.

"What would you like to drink?" he asked. "We could have a glass of wine, or Rita has included a pot of coffee."

"Wine sounds lovely," she said. "Won't this situation be ongoing? There is a reason gangs are so successful."

Mikhail frowned as he selected food for himself. "I weary of this topic."

Edwina got the message, even though affront filled her. But she didn't intend to act the little woman who waited at home. She wasn't stupid enough to ignore his security measures but refused to be kept in the dark. This marriage would be a partnership for as long as it lasted. She didn't care if that wasn't how her grandparents or parents worked, or if Mikhail's country didn't behave in the same way. Saber Mitchell and his brothers had strong marriages, and their wives and mates were partners in everything. That was what she'd dreamed of once she'd wised up and ceased her self-destructive path.

"I am going out for dinner tonight, but I shouldn't be home late."

"Can I go with you?"

"Not this time," he said smoothly. "Maybe the next business dinner. This one is unavoidable, unfortunately."

Edwina narrowed her gaze on him. Every instinct told her that while he was telling the truth, there was something shady he didn't want her to understand. Subtext. She didn't even know how she perceived this. Some sixth sense.

"White wine?"

"Please," she said, not caring. This situation she'd found herself in had way too many currents beneath the surface. It simmered like a pot coming to a boil, which scared her. She hadn't allowed much to frighten her in the past—possibly because she'd been young and stupid. Now that she had a mate, everything had changed for her.

Gods, she needed time to think. Mikhail still only wanted a temporary arrangement, and maybe now that the Bratva had openly attacked her, their marriage no longer mattered. The bite of the shrimp savory turned to dirt in her mouth. She hadn't wanted any part of this marriage, but now that she was here, she didn't want to leave.

9

DESPITE THE SERIOUSNESS OF their conversation, Edwina impressed him. She might be unseasoned, but she was mentally strong and had a backbone. His tiger issued a chuff of approval. The young woman—his wife—had garnered their respect. Of course, she might be a pain in his backside in certain circumstances, but life with her would never become a tedious round of parties and shopping.

A sliver of guilt ran through him because he'd destroyed her plans. He reminded himself to speak to his grandmother again and organize the tutoring. He'd also remind his grandmother of her promise not to discuss this with anyone but him. Edwina's grandmother had run roughshod over her dreams, and he hated to shatter her fully.

As to who had tried to shoot her...

Anger pulsed through him, along with protectiveness. His young bride hadn't deserved that. Depending on the next few days, he might have to sequester her in a more private place that only his two trusted friends knew of. Staying at the cabin would allow them to run in their feline forms, and he liked this idea.

Aware of the growing silence, he settled in with small talk and found himself eager to learn more about her. "Tell me about the town you come from. My knowledge of New Zealand is scanty."

"Middlemarch is a small country town in the South Island of New Zealand. The South Island is more mountainous and gets more snow than the North. When I was growing up, the town seemed isolated and confining, even though we're close to Dunedin, a large city by New Zealand standards. During the last ten years, the local Feline Council has done heaps to attract women to the area because the population is more skewed to men. We have lots of different social events."

"Like what?" Mikhail asked, fascinated because tiger shifters stuck to family groups and were territorial. There wasn't much fraternization.

"The first function was the Middlemarch Singles' Ball, where unmarried women visited from Dunedin and nearby towns. It was a success, and several local men found their mates. Since then, we've had woolshed dances, parades, and fairs, a zombie run. Loads of unique events that draw humans and shifters to Middlemarch. The Feline Council also arranges runs for the felines and wolves who live in the area, and we have a plan for any time a human sees a leopard or wolf when they shouldn't. New arrivals and mates have set up businesses within the region, allowing the locals to work near home." Her brow puckered. "The Feline Council has achieved loads in a short time. The council also sponsored me and five friends to attend the gathering."

"Yet you wanted to leave," Mikhail mused.

"Yes, but I'd intended to make frequent visits home. Living in the city would be difficult, but New Zealand is small. It's easy to find wild spaces."

"We have beautiful countryside," Mikhail said, wanting to show her his favorite spots. He sighed. That would need to wait.

The grandfather clock in the hall struck five, and reluctantly, Mikhail rose. "I need to get ready for my business dinner. I won't be late."

"Where will I sleep?" Edwina asked, her gaze uncertain.

It made him want to embrace her. He didn't because physical contact would entice him to stay instead of leaving. "You sleep in my room," he said, his gaze meeting and holding hers. "That is our room now."

"You want to share with me?"

His tiger's growl echoed through his mind as he sought to exert his will. "It's a large room, and sharing is best for our scents to mingle." Her stricken face had him clenching his jaw. *Fuck.* That wasn't tactful or the best way to keep her onside. Another silent curse washed through him, and he attempted to rein in his frustration with Clarice, his grandfather, and the situation.

His decision hadn't changed. She was his mate, and he wanted her. Difficult when he'd kidnapped and dragged her to another country against her will. She was young and inexperienced and had been a virgin, and he'd behaved no better than the Bratva, taking without permission.

"You're welcome to explore any room except my office. That remains locked because of the sensitive business information in there. If I'm in my office, I don't mind you stopping in to say hello or ask questions, but if I'm away, the room remains locked."

"Understood," she said.

"I'll arrange a computer for your use and a more secure phone."

"Thank you."

"I'll see you in the morning." Mikhail kissed her cheek and retreated to shower and change. The instant he departed the room, it felt as if he'd left an important part behind. His tiger grunted, the harsh bark making his opinion clear. Mikhail ignored his feline, forcing his mind to plan how to approach this evening with Clarice.

Mikhail arrived at Clarice's apartment earlier than he'd specified because he wanted to speak with her. Initially, he'd thought his marriage would change nothing. Edwina, however, was a surprise, and the thought of touching another woman filled him with distaste. *Arrogant much.* His mouth twisted while his tiger chuffed in agreement. He'd behaved with condescension, but one time with Edwina had shown him the error of this attitude. Edwina was their one, and now they must prove their loyalty.

That started with cutting ties with Clarice.

Mikhail greeted the doorman and strode to the bank of elevators. He still hadn't decided on his approach when he knocked on Clarice's door. She'd given him a key, but he seldom used it, and now that he intended to sever their relationship, he didn't feel right about letting himself into her apartment.

The door opened at his first knock. Clarice stood in front of him, and he gaped at her appearance. Her hair sprang around her head in a mass of curls, her typical sleek locks not in evidence. She wore a silky white robe, and her legs were bare.

"You're here," she said.

Was that relief in her voice? He frowned at this deviation, every sense on guard. "Is something wrong?"

A choked sound emerged from her, and her eyes were tear-bright when she shook her head. Her gaze shifted to her clenched hands.

"I've had an exhausting day. I shouldn't have gone shopping this afternoon." She lifted her head, her lips curved in a smile that didn't reach her eyes. "I'm afraid I was rather lavish in spending your money. I sent the bill to you."

"No problem." While money was no issue to him, and he'd been generous in the past, he reminded himself to make it clear to those sending the bills that this was the last time. He would not be responsible for her future expenses. "I'm sure you'll look beautiful in whatever you purchased."

Her breath released in a hiss. "Let me finish dressing. I won't be long."

"No one will mind if we're a few minutes late," Mikhail murmured. "I'll wait in the lounge."

"Come and chat while I dress," she said, acting more naturally.

"No," he said, pulling out his phone. "I have business matters to take care of."

She hesitated as if there was something else she wanted to say.

Before she objected, he left, long strides taking him into her expensively furnished—at his expense—lounge. He glanced at the emails he'd downloaded at home but put his phone away, disturbed by her behavior. Because of business security, he seldom checked his email anywhere apart from at home or his office. Given the weird happenings in the last two days, it might be best if he didn't depart from security protocols. Ordinarily, nothing threw Clarice off course. Tonight, something had her rattled, and his gut roiled with misgiving.

Surprise filled him when Clarice hustled into the lounge. She'd restored her hair to its normal sleekness. Her silver gown seemed overly formal for dinner, but he didn't comment. "You look lovely."

She did a slow spin to give him the full effect. "You like?"

"A man would need to be blind not to appreciate your beauty." He meant every word, but an image of Edwina flickered through his mind. He preferred her curvy body and quick tongue to Clarice's extraordinary perfection. With Edwina, he sensed he could discuss anything—even a business matter—and she would understand and respond in kind. Clarice always kept topics light and never touched heavy conversation. Edwina was real, and he wanted to learn more about her to satisfy his burning curiosity.

With Clarice, he didn't care. He didn't dwell on her when they were apart.

And that told him everything—this break was an excellent idea.

Edwina was his future.

"Clarice, we need to talk."

"We don't have time for anything personal," she said with a coy smile, brittle at the edges. "If we don't leave now, we'll be late, and I'm eager for you to meet my friends."

"We'll have all evening," Mikhail said, not understanding her insistence. She'd never behaved this way before. "Where did you say your friends were from?"

"A town much closer to Moscow," she said. "It's the town where I grew up. We went to school together."

Mikhail took her arm as they exited the apartment complex. "What is the address so I can tell my driver?"

Clarice rattled off an address in an exclusive suburb, more herself now. It made Mikhail wonder if he was imagining things. He opened the door and helped her slide inside the sedan. He strode around the vehicle's rear and settled beside her while recalling a recent car ride with Edwina.

"Where are we going, sir?" the driver asked.

Mikhail gave instructions and sat back. "Tell me more about your friends. Why are they in town, and why aren't they staying for the entire evening?"

Clarice squeezed her silver clutch bag. "They're booked on a flight home in a few hours. If you hadn't gone out of town, you would've met them earlier."

"I see." An understatement. Clarice's behavior and this

dinner fuss were out of character. Well, he'd wait and judge for himself. Deciphering undercurrents was his specialty and made him an excellent entrepreneur. He'd read the room and determine his approach. "You said you went shopping after I saw you earlier?"

"After a quick lunch with my girlfriends," she said. "Was your business trip successful?"

Mikhail's smile was instinctive when he thought about Edwina. "Yes. Very."

She stared at him, and their normal easiness fell apart at the seams. Interesting. He didn't enjoy touching her anymore, and she no longer amused him. Mikhail checked his watch. It would be a long evening when he clamored to return to Edwina.

Their driver halted outside a large, gated community and opened his window to murmur into a speaker. An instant later, the gate slid open, and they drove through.

Mikhail glanced at Clarice and found her anxiously watching him. "Something wrong?"

"No, of course not."

But there was. He sensed it, and her anxiety rubbed his fur the wrong way.

Their driver pulled up outside an imposing mansion. Lights illuminated the entire building, and several luxurious model cars crammed into the driveway.

"I'll let you off here and find parking, sir," the driver said.

"No problem," Mikhail said.

"You want me to walk in these shoes?" Clarice asked in an icy tone.

"Where would you have us park?" Mikhail said, reining in his temper.

When the driver pulled up, Mikhail exited the car and circled the rear to open Clarice's door. He offered his arm, despite his tiger's rumbling protest. He'd act the gentleman for a few more hours.

The mansion's front door opened before they reached it. A woman stood there, dressed as formally and seductively as Clarice.

"You're here," the woman said.

Clarice smiled, but the gesture sat awkwardly on her mouth, and his instincts flared in warning. "I'm sorry we're late. The traffic was worse than we expected."

"Come in. This must be your Mikhail," the woman said. "It's nice to meet you finally."

Mikhail glanced at Clarice, who appeared faintly embarrassed.

"I'm proud of you," she blurted. "I can't help it if I want to tell everyone how happy you make me."

The woman ushered them into a room full of strangers. Mikhail had met some of Clarice's friends but spotted no familiar faces. More peculiar, Clarice had told him the dinner was with friends. Mikhail didn't like this and heightened watchfulness had him scanning the room's occupants.

"I'm afraid I can't stay for long," Mikhail said. "I have other commitments."

"Can't you change your plans?" their hostess asked.

"No," Mikhail said without hesitation or apology. "I explained this to Clarice before I agreed to accompany her here."

The woman's face grew hard before she slipped on an ill-fitting smile. "Let me introduce you to everyone. Would you like a drink?"

"A glass of water for me," Mikhail said. "Clarice, you'll have a glass of white wine?"

"Yes, please," Clarice said.

The woman's mouth firmed, and for fleeting seconds, she looked as if she'd tasted a sour lemon. "Of course," she said. "I won't be long."

"What's going on?" Mikhail asked Clarice in an undertone.

"Nothing," Clarice said, flipping her hair and tugging at her dress.

Mikhail's instincts prickled. "You were going to introduce me to your friends."

"They're not here yet," she said.

Mikhail's eyebrows rose in surprise. "You don't know any of the people here?"

"N-no."

Her diffident manner alerted Mikhail further. "Why are we here if these are strangers? That's not the impression you gave me earlier. You implored me to come, dragging me away from something important."

"What?" Clarice said, her blue eyes narrowing in more typical behavior for her.

"A family matter," Mikhail said smoothly, not wanting to place a target on Edwina's back. An unidentified trespasser had already tried to shoot her, and his grandfather was the only one he'd told about his marriage, apart from his two trusted friends. He was right to harbor suspicions because someone was spying on him.

"Here are your drinks," their hostess said, a silent male server bearing a tray with two glasses.

"Thank you." Mikhail handed the glass of wine to Clarice, who accepted it and took a healthy sip. When she'd finished, only half of the wine remained, and her right hand curled around the stem of the glass so tightly Mikhail feared she'd break it. He took his glass of water but didn't drink any.

Mikhail studied the guests and found many watching him and Clarice with varying expressions. He glanced at his watch. Another half an hour, and he'd leave with an apologetic excuse. He'd much rather spend time with his fascinating new wife and was hungry to discover more about her. Then there was the soul-deep urge to touch her, hold her, make sweet love to her. Cover her with his scent.

His mouth twisted. Caveman, much?

Several of the guests seemed familiar, but whenever he and Clarice drifted closer to them, the men directed their wives or partners to different clusters of guests. Despite the naturalness of the mingling, Mikhail's suspicions grew.

"Is your drink not to your liking?" Clarice asked.

"It's fine." Everything about this meeting shouted odd and peculiar, and Mikhail trusted his instincts.

They told him not to eat or drink here, so he intended to follow his intuition.

"You don't want to appear rude," Clarice muttered in a low voice. She seemed jumpy and constantly blinked.

"I'd like some fresh air," Mikhail said.

"No." Clarice balked, her face growing pale.

"Tell me what is going on," Mikhail snapped, grinding his teeth instead of shaking her.

Her gaze slid from his. "Nothing. This is merely dinner with friends."

"Which would make sense normally, but you don't know these people."

The sound of new arrivals had Mikhail snapping to attention. The man and woman standing with their hostess weren't familiar, but they studied him as if he were a fascinating specimen. His phone buzzed, and he pulled it from his pocket.

"Boss, it's Berto. Not sure what is happening, but they've posted dozens of guards. We should leave." The tension in his driver's voice prodded Mikhail into action.

"I'll come straightaway."

He stuffed his phone in his pocket and turned to Clarice. "I must leave now. Would you like to come with me or stay with your friends?"

"What's wrong?" Clarice asked, and her tone had renewed concern along with instinct humming through him.

"It's my grandfather. He's taken ill. Ah, there is our hostess." He crossed the room with long strides, and Clarice scuttled after him.

"Wait," she cried. "You can't leave."

"It's my grandfather," Mikhail said, lying without a blink. He should've obeyed his gut and stayed home instead of letting guilt sway him into escorting Clarice. "Clarice, I can't do this any longer. Our relationship has run its course." He paused, then led with the truth because he owed it to her. "I'm married and do not wish to cheat on my wife."

Clarice's gasp attracted attention. "You're married," she said, something more than shock threading through her words. It was distress and was that horror?

"I can't discuss this now. I'll call you tomorrow, but there will be no more cozy dinners or dates now that I have a wife." He turned away.

Clarice put on a burst of speed and gripped his forearm, her nails digging through his sleeve. "You cannot leave me here."

"If you hurry, I'll drop you at home."

"You have to leave?"

"Yes," he snapped, starting for the door, using his strength to tow her after him.

"Wait, my coat," she wailed.

Suspicion rose in him. "You're trying to keep me here."

"No," she denied instantly, but Mikhail saw through her rebuttal.

He jerked from her touch and headed to the main entrance. Clarice released a panicked cry. Someone had organized her to bring him here. This truth thumped him over the head as a beefy man dressed in a suit, his tie askew, appeared before him.

"You're leaving so soon?" he asked in a jovial tone. "We haven't had dinner."

"I have received an urgent message. One of my family members is ill."

Mikhail used his bulk and height to force the man to

retreat and exited the mansion with ground-eating strides. His steps faltered slightly on seeing the number of security men standing around. Their heads jerked in his direction, but to his relief, they didn't halt his departure.

A man in a uniform stepped in front of him without warning. "Sir, we must ask you to remain here while a VIP arrives."

"My driver is waiting for me," Mikhail said, aiming for pleasant. His words, however, emerged with a side of pissed arrogance. "I will be leaving now."

"Mikhail!" Clarice's panicked voice came from behind him.

Mikhail didn't bother looking in her direction because his sixth sense told him she'd maneuvered him into this situation. He brushed past the security guard, only halting when he heard the cocking of a gun. Mikhail froze and slowly turned back to the guard.

"I'm afraid I'll have to insist on you waiting, sir."

Mikhail burst into action, using his shifter speed. He was on the man and using his strength to rip the gun away before the guard reacted. He tossed the weapon deep into the garden and continued to where their driver had dropped them off.

"Mikhail!" Clarice wailed.

Mikhail jogged through the well-lit garden, more determined than ever to leave. Hurried footsteps after him had him breaking into a run. A shout rang out, but he ignored that too. Clarice had set up this meeting, and he had no idea why.

The horn honk had him veering in that direction since

he recognized the sound. His driver. He covered the remaining distance at a lope, the whistle of a bullet forcing a turn of extra speed from him. His driver revved the engine and took off before Mikhail was inside.

"What is going on, sir?" his driver asked as he almost ran over a guard who'd decided they might stop if he stood in the driveway.

"Clarice..." he trailed off, unsure of what to think. When he'd started dating her, he'd done a full security check, and she'd passed with flying colors. Nothing about her background had raised alarm bells. He'd trusted her, but tonight had been weird.

His phone rang, and he pulled it out, trusting his driver to get them safely away. The car was built to withstand bullets.

"Seat belt, sir," his driver said. "They're closing the gate."

They wanted to keep him here.

10

"CLARICE," HE BARKED INTO the phone.

"Mikhail, come back." She sounded close to tears.

"No," he snapped. "These people are not on the level. Whatever you've become involved in, I want no part of. I'm going home to my wife. Don't contact me again."

"B-but what about the apartment?"

That was all she was worried about? "I paid the rent until the end of the year. Live there or not. I won't foot the bill any longer. If you remain, you must pay the building owner."

"Mikhail, please return. If you cared for me, please do this." Desperation laced her tone. Fear.

"What's going on, Clarice?"

She sprinted to the vehicle, and her eyes were tear-stung and huge in her pale face.

Mikhail scowled. This wasn't Clarice. She never lost control.

"You must stay and meet my friends."

"Why?"

Clarice flinched and refused to meet his gaze through the window.

"Why, Clarice?"

She bit her lip and glanced over her shoulder. The fear on her face strengthened, and instead of replying, she tried to use her eyes to communicate.

Mikhail opened the door. "Get in, and I'll take you home."

"Gun!" his driver snapped, his gaze on the rearview mirror.

Mikhail leaned closer to Clarice, stretching out his hand even as the car sped up, the tires screeching against the driveway surface. Mikhail grasped Clarice's fingers and yanked her into the vehicle interior. He ignored her scream. Whoever these people were loyal to—the Bratva, most likely—didn't care about Clarice but had forced her to attend this dinner. That would explain her panic. He yanked on her arm again, and she tumbled into his lap even as another gunshot rang out.

Then they were shooting forward, and Mikhail swung the car door shut. Their speed increased as their vehicle hurtled toward the closed gate.

"Hang on," the driver shouted.

The scent of blood came to Mikhail. "Clarice, are you okay?"

"They'll kill him. They'll kill him," she whispered, her voice full of horror.

Seconds later, the car smashed into the gate. Metal

screeched against metal. Their pace reduced, and he and Clarice slammed against the front seat. If it weren't for his strength, Clarice would've gone flying. The driver gunned the engine again, and they were through.

"My son," Clarice said, her voice gurgling.

The scent of blood intensified. "Clarice, where are you hurt?" Now that they were speeding through the suburbs, Mikhail turned Clarice in his arms. Blood smeared his trousers and her arm. Cursing, he ripped open his jacket and tore off the bottom part of his shirt. He folded it into a pad and pressed it against the wound. Clarice moaned.

"You'd better drive to the hospital," he said to the driver. "The bullet has lodged in her upper arm. There's no exit wound."

"Is that wise, sir?" his driver asked.

"She's h... We can't treat her at my home," Mikhail said. "Very good, sir."

The car took a right and veered in a different direction.

Mikhail pressed the pad to Clarice's wound while he made her more comfortable on his lap. "Clarice."

Her blue eyes flickered open, and they held pain, conflict, and a dozen other emotions he'd never witnessed from her before.

"Clarice," Mikhail repeated. "Tell me about those people tonight. Who were they? How did you become involved with them?"

Clarice closed her eyes again, seeming smaller than usual. "They took my son. They threatened to kill him if I didn't follow instructions."

"What did they want you to do?"

"They wanted me to get you to the party."

"Why?"

"It's the Bratva. They want you. Your business."

"Then why didn't they shoot me? I'm never agreeing to do business with them."

"From what I deduced, they need your business expertise. Those in charge of the Bratva businesses can't do what you do."

He'd focus on that later, but this recent development meant greater danger for Edwina. He... He'd need to tell her because he refused to lie again. She'd had enough of that from her grandmother.

"Tell me about your son," Mikhail said. "You didn't mention you had a child." He and Clarice had been together off and on for three years. He'd liked her—still enjoyed her company when she didn't pull crap like this. "How old is he?"

Was the child his, and she hadn't told him for some unfathomable reason? No, hiding a pregnancy from him would've been impossible. Relief swept through him because he didn't want a child with anyone except Edwina. The young woman—gods, he still didn't understand how she'd swept him and his tiger into her heart. It was Edwina he wanted, and crazily, she returned the sentiment. She'd been brave to mark him when he'd cowered and balked at that level of commitment.

"My son is six years old," she sobbed. "They have him."

"Are you positive?" Mikhail asked, wondering why she'd kept her child a secret. "They might have lied to you."

Another sob broke from Clarice, and her entire body

shook. "Oh, no. They're not lying. I get a weekly report from the woman they hired to supervise him." Tears rolled down her cheeks. "They mean every threat. Last week, they told me they were tired of my lackluster results, and if I didn't follow their directions, they'd send me my son in pieces."

"Who are they?" Mikhail asked, except he already knew. He couldn't believe the depths they'd sunk to just to control him.

"The Bratva." Clarice pressed her fingers to her face and wailed.

"Who in particular?" Mikhail insisted.

He wanted names—people to aim at and destroy. His grandfather's business style and his father's attempts at reform had left an impact. He was tired of people pushing him to follow their path, their needs when he was simply a shifter, gifted with business matters, and unafraid of hard work. His grandfather's bully tactics didn't get the best from workers. A man or woman never excelled at their job if they were terrified.

"Clarice?"

"No, they'll kill my son."

A threat rose to Mikhail's lips, but he couldn't treat her like these criminals. "I'll tell you this—it's the truth, and it will hurt, but this is what your son's captives will do. They will kill your son, or not. These people without principles will do anything to achieve their goals. Clarice, your best bet is to tell me everything. *Everything.* I can't help if I don't understand the situation."

An image flickered through his mind of his wife as

he'd last seen her. Her pale face and strong determination as she'd told him she'd be safe with Ivan and Gregory. They'd protect her, and she'd kick anyone in the balls who got through his friends. Someone called Isabella had taught her how to defend herself, and Edwina had been an excellent student.

He and his friends had exchanged startled glances. His friends hadn't believed her brave talk. Mikhail hadn't been so skeptical because his new wife might be years younger, but she was a warrior in disguise.

Clarice wiped the tears from her face. "I know this, but what if they keep their word?"

"I'll do my best to find your son, but I require information." Another question came to mind. "How long have they been putting pressure on you?"

Clarice pulled a face. "They set up a meeting and instructed me to get close to you."

Mikhail's brows rose as shock punched him in the solar plexus. "That was three years ago." Slowly, he'd trusted her but never discussed business because he preferred to separate his business and personal lives. "Why didn't they act sooner?"

"Because they wanted to do their research," Clarice said in a tired voice. "You'd barely taken over the business. There were rumors about your intelligence and modern ideas, but the Bratva thought it gossip. Your family had never been a threat before."

"Who wanted to learn about me?" Mikhail prodded.

Clarice hesitated. "Konstantine Smirnoff."

Mikhail paused, his mind busy processing the

information. "Konstantine has a son. Pavel."

"Yes, Pavel is a disappointment to his father. He is not an intelligent man."

"I've heard stories that Konstantine is ill."

"Konstantine is dying and doesn't trust his son with his business."

"He wants to pressure me into taking over?"

"That wasn't his immediate goal. I assume his plan changed once he learned he was sick. He wants his legacy to continue."

Mikhail barked out a laugh. "I'd never agree to that. Never." He rubbed his chin, considering the angles. "If Konstantine calls you, give him my number and tell him to call me direct."

"Pride," Clarice said. "The man has an abundance of ego, and he hates to admit his son doesn't have the brains or the passion to hold everything. You won't change your mind?"

"No," Mikhail said without hesitation. "I refuse to do business with a man who'd use a woman and child. Clarice, you should've told me earlier."

"You would've helped me?" Scorn and doubt rippled through her words. "I've had an agenda and played you like a fish, yet you offer help?"

"Yes," Mikhail said.

When his driver stopped outside the hospital, Mikhail helped Clarice inside and waited until a nurse took charge of her.

His driver was waiting for him, leaning against the car's body that now bore myriad scratches along the doors and a sizable dent in the front.

"How bad is the damage?" Mikhail asked, wincing at the dinged panels.

His driver gave a Gaelic shrug, his mouth twisting as he met Mikhail's gaze. "The car is drivable. That's all that matters."

"Take me home, please."

"Yes, sir." The driver opened the rear door for Mikhail. Once seated, Mikhail called Ivan. "Everything okay at the house?"

"Yes."

"Good. Our problems are making sense now. It's Konstantine Smirnoff creating the chaos. He's sick and is dying. With his limited time, he's running out of patience."

"Smirnoff?"

"Yes, and Clarice was in this from the start. She has a six-year-old son, and they're holding him to ensure she behaves and follows orders."

"Bastards," Ivan muttered.

"Yeah, I'm on my way home. Should be there in half an hour."

Mikhail rang his grandfather, uncaring that he'd wake the elderly man. The phone rang eight times before someone picked it up.

"Who is ringing me at this ungodly hour?" a querulous voice demanded.

"Grandfather, it's Mikhail. When did you intend to tell me your best friend, Konstantine Smirnoff, was the one trying to jerk me around and force me into doing unpalatable things? The girl you insisted I marry is his daughter."

"Konstantine thinks you'll make a fine addition to his family."

"And because he learned I already had a wife, he shot at her to clear the path for his daughter." Anger released in his crisp words. His actions were no different from what Edwina's grandmother had done. Now he understood Edwina's anger and frustration. Old didn't mean wise—something he was coming to learn.

"I have no knowledge of that," his grandfather said.

Mikhail spat a curse and hung up. After a second, he dialed Ivan.

"What are you going to do?" Ivan asked.

"Speak with Edwina, tell her everything, and make a plan with her input."

Ivan's piercing whistle had Mikhail jerking his phone from his ear. "Enough from the cheap seats."

Ivan's laugh was rich and poked fun at him. One day with a new wife, and he'd changed his point of view. He tucked his phone away and leaned against the seat, closing his eyes. Clarice. What the hell did he do with her situation? Even though she'd lied to him, tried to maneuver him, he should help her. She'd been desperate—was still desperate to save her son—and he could hardly fault her for that.

"We've arrived, sir."

Mikhail jerked awake at the soft voice, surprised he'd slept.

"We're at your home," his driver said, maintaining a

healthy distance.

Mikhail blinked and surveyed his surroundings with one sweep of his gaze. "Thank you." He exited the vehicle and, with a nod at his driver, strode for the front entrance.

Gregory met him in the entranceway. "I understand you've had problems."

"Clarice and Smirnoff from the Bratva. He wants me to run his business because he can't trust his son not to wreck everything he has built."

"He doesn't have anyone else who can do the job?" Ivan asked, joining them both.

Mikhail shrugged. "Who knows how his damn mind works? I want nothing from the Bratva. My father died cleaning house, and he'd roll in his grave if I undid his work. Our people are happy and productive. They're prospering."

Ivan turned more somber. "We're lucky he has only attacked property rather than our people."

A rustle sounded to his right. Edwina. His heart skipped a beat while his tiger issued a welcoming purr. He didn't even care that his friends heard the betraying sound.

Edwina cocked her head. "Are you intending to meet in the foyer, or will you discuss matters in a lounge with liquid fortification?"

Happiness rose in Mikhail, and he grinned. Edwina wore a lilac robe and what looked like a pair of pajamas underneath. His tiger chuffed, this time in amusement, and Mikhail's grin broadened. She wouldn't be wearing those for long, not once they had privacy.

Mikhail crossed the distance between them with giant

steps and wrapped his arm around her waist. Momentarily, she leaned into him, and he savored her sweet, floral perfume. He nuzzled her hair, drawing her scent deep before he flexed his arm and guided her into the lounge. He stopped in front of a chair. "What can I get you to drink?"

"A whisky and water? Do you have a Scottish malt?" she asked.

"I do. Ivan? Gregory?"

"I'll have a whisky," Ivan said.

Gregory dipped his head. "Works for me."

Mikhail poured four glasses and added a dash of water to Edwina's. He carried two drinks to her and placed them on a round wooden side table near her chair. "Stand up," he said on reaching her.

She hesitated.

"Please."

Looking mystified, she rose. Mikhail plopped onto the chair and tugged her to sit on his knee. She fought him for an instant.

"Please," he murmured for her ears only. "I need the physical contact."

Edwina slanted him a glance, then relaxed. "What has happened?"

Mikhail explained the evening's events to Edwina, Ivan, and Gregory. Everything. He told her about Clarice and didn't gloss over the fact he'd liked the woman and had initially intended to continue their relationship. That had changed once he'd met Edwina, but he'd owed Clarice an explanation.

Edwina barked out a laugh.

"Have I amused you?"

"It's funny you thought you were using her services when she had an agenda the entire time."

"I wish she'd confided about her son," Mikhail said. "I only spent a few nights a week with her, but there was never any evidence of a child."

"Who is his father?" Edwina asked.

"Not me," Mikhail said without hesitation. "The boy is six."

"*Who is his father?*" Edwina asked. "Is he part of the problem?"

"Clarice refused to tell me. She cried. Whoever threatened her told her they'd send her son back in pieces."

"Bastard," Edwina snapped. "Do they want you to oversee the business? Has she told you the entire truth?"

"I'll need to research and ascertain their financial status," Mikhail said. "I'll start that in the morning."

Edwina sipped her drink. "Now that you understand their aim, what will stop them from picking off your family and friends? That's what I'd do."

"If they hurt someone I care for, that won't make me work for them. They won't get what they want by pushing their usual tactics," Mikhail snapped.

"They don't sound intelligent enough to work that out," Edwina said. "I presume they're the ones who shot at me? How do you intend to stop them?"

"As yet, I don't have a plan. Once I research their finances and understand their power structure, I might have a better idea. The last thing I want is an all-out war. If Smirnoff and his family go down, another multi-headed monster will take his place. Someone with an eye on the main chance."

"You could always agree and clean house from the inside," Edwina said thoughtfully.

Mikhail's arm tightened around her waist, momentarily blindsided by the radical but intelligent idea. "Perhaps," he said. "That might take the sting out of their plans."

"Request a meeting with the head honchos," Edwina suggested. "After you do your research, of course. It'd be better to go in prepared."

Mikhail glanced at Ivan and Gregory. Both men displayed approval and wore grins. "I'll think about it."

In answer, she let out a loud yawn. "Sorry. I'm tired. It has been an eventful day."

Mikhail set his glass aside and lifted Edwina to her feet. "Let's go to bed. We'll see you in the morning."

Neither Ivan nor Gregory commented until they'd left the lounge, but Mikhail caught their soft laughter. They liked Edwina, and he'd won a tremendous prize when he'd forced her to marry him. A woman such as Edwina at his side was gold.

11

Slightly bemused, Edwina strolled at Mikhail's side. His honesty had disarmed her, although she'd hated hearing about the other woman. At least he'd spoken the truth, not sparing his anger and frustration on learning Clarice had been playing him all along. These people who wanted Mikhail's help—stooping to kidnap a child and threaten the mother couldn't end well.

Mikhail reached for her hand, his thumb rubbing lazy circles on her skin. Every part of her zeroed in on the sensations radiating from his touch. A purr rippled in her mind, and Edwina faltered over whether to laugh or cry. This mating business had more complications than the intricate puzzles her father loved to challenge his mind.

"You've had a lot thrown at you today," Mikhail said. "I want to assure you I've changed my mind about continuing as a single man." He glanced at her as if judging her reaction.

"That's reassuring," Edwina said, not hiding her sarcasm. "You expect me to act with decorum and remain faithful, yet you'd pursue business as usual? I'm not stupid. I would've learned of your behavior, and the discovery would've made me extremely unhappy. Our marriage might have a limited term, but this isn't the eighteenth century. I expect respect." Edwina ground her teeth together, trying to corral her anger. He was bigger than her, stronger, yet he didn't scare her. This realization cooled her wrath, and she checked his reaction to her outburst.

"I understand," he said in an even, controlled tone. "I was furious with my grandfather for trying to maneuver me into following his wishes and didn't think my plan through as I should've. Not an excuse, but an explanation."

"My grandmother is constantly pushing my buttons. Her justification is that I'm young and stupid and running wild, but most of us learn from mistakes. My grandmother never gave me a chance. I'd take a bet she always planned on our marriage. They've manipulated us."

Mikhail gave a muffled curse. "I dislike your grandmother."

"She won't care," Edwina said. "She behaves like a ruling queen and always has. I doubt she'll ever change."

"What do you want to do about her?"

"I haven't decided yet." As they entered Mikhail's bedroom, she said, "I don't wish to discuss her any longer. What do you intend to do tomorrow?"

"I'll meet with Smirnoff and learn what he wants."

"Take me with you." It was an impulse, but the perfect way to lighten a possibly tense situation. "Smirnoff won't be expecting that. He'll see a young and inexperienced woman if he is anything like you. He'll underestimate me. Does he know you're a shifter?"

"Most people I have dealings with aren't aware," Mikhail said.

"I'm a leopard shifter. I'm strong and an asset to you."

"Someone shot at you this evening." He tugged on the hand he still held and turned her to face him. "I could've lost you before our marriage has even had a chance."

Edwina shrugged, but her pulse raced, as did her mind. Hope filled her at his words, but she stuffed it down to concentrate on the Smirnoff meeting. "I'm tougher than I look."

"Did you get clothes?"

"A few things."

"If you come with me, you must dress smartly and stay in the background. You would need to remain silent." His lips twisted while his blue eyes sparkled with humor. "Is that possible?"

Edwina rolled her eyes. "With the right incentive."

Mikhail laughed, the smile creating a dimple on his right cheek. His eyes glowed a deep lake blue, and her breath stalled as their gazes connected. Held. Her fingers tingled, and she reached for him. He took the hint and wrapped his arms around her. She pressed her cheek against his chest and breathed in his scent, at peace with everything in her world. She didn't understand how or why, but Mikhail felt like home. The mark, perhaps. All she knew was she no longer had the urge to batter him over the head for changing the course of her life.

Thoughts of escape and revenge had lessened, at least regarding Mikhail. Her grandmother, not so much.

Mikhail pulled away. "It's getting late. We should go to bed."

Tension ratcheted up in her at the idea of intimacy. Yes, they'd made love—had sex once, but... Gods, she'd marked him, which made this relationship messy. The fleeting idea of faking a yawn came to mind, but she discarded the thought. Stupid. Silly. Childish. If she wanted him to treat her like an adult—a partner—she needed to act maturely.

"If we get into that bed together, I won't want to sleep." Her words emerged, laden with tension and a hint of longing. Oh, yeah. She badly wanted to repeat the experience. This time, she'd learn his body. She'd had time to consider, time to decide exactly how and where she wanted to explore. The answer—everywhere.

His head cocked, and she sensed his surprise before his mind turned the corner she'd nudged him around. Sensual intent stamped on his expression, his posture straightening, focus fixed on her. Oh, she loved an intelligent man.

"What did you have in mind?"

Okay, he wanted her to express her desires. Fair if embarrassing. Given their initial meeting and the blackmail, honesty between them was a necessity.

"I want to explore your body, leading to sex." Heat crept into her cheeks, but she held his gaze despite her discomfort. This feline was her mate, and while the future appeared murky, they had now. "Live in the moment instead of worrying about how we arrived at this point and what might happen tomorrow."

"Edwina," he whispered, his eyes shifting to a deeper, more complex blue-gold. He wrapped his arms around her, pressing her to his chest. She sank into his warm strength, and it was akin to coming home after a bad day. Perfect. After a long moment of savoring his wild scent and the comfort of his hard chest, she lifted her head. An instant later, he kissed her.

The kiss started gently before gathering momentum and sweeping Edwina into a maelstrom of pleasure. Her hands crept up to grip his shoulders, holding him to her. Their tongues danced together then he pulled back to study her with those sexy feline eyes of his.

Mikhail's slow smile had a different heat writhing through her. "Let's get these clothes off you." He unfastened the lilac robe to stare at the pale blue flannel pajamas.

"Sexy," he said, his lips twitching.

"Warm," she retorted. "It's cooler here than Scotland."

He laughed, and it was deep and joyful. A natural sound a man might make if he was relaxed. It warmed her heart, and she hugged the emotion tight. She'd make it her mission to have him repeat that tone often.

"Can I remove this warm attire?"

"I would like that." Shyness struck her then, which was silly. She raised her chin a fraction and forced herself to project confidence. The longer she held the smile, the more naturally the curve fit her mouth.

This shifter male wanted her. If he hadn't, he would've placed her in one of the empty rooms, and there were dozens because she'd explored the house during Mikhail's absence. Second, he would've rejected her brazen suggestion. He'd done neither.

He flipped open buttons with expertise, his gaze on her breasts bringing heat to her face again. Shocking, considering she hardly ever blushed. He slipped the sleeves down her arms and tossed the garment aside.

"Beautiful," he said in a husky voice.

"Did you see my photo before you met me?"

"I did, and it was a recent one, but seeing you in person is different. You looked grumpy."

"Ah. My grandmother and I are similar, I fear. We're not patient, so photos taken under those circumstances wouldn't show my best features."

"Are you feeling resentful toward her?"

"Are you angry with your grandfather for pushing you in a direction you don't wish to go?"

"Yes."

"Likewise," Edwina said, temper roiling, her feline pushing at her control. Her canines sharpened, and her claws lengthened beneath her fingernails. "I'm furious at my grandmother, and I'm not sure how I'll react when I see her." She focused on her breathing, a technique that always helped her to calm and regain control. "I don't want to discuss my grandmother. We're alone. We have an enormous bed." She lifted her head and winked. "We should take advantage of this opportunity."

Mikhail chuckled, but not for long. He scooped her off

her feet and carried her to the bed. He placed her on the mattress and followed her down, caging her in his arms.

"You're amazing," he whispered. "So strong and not at all who I expected."

Before she replied, he kissed her again, demanding and with intent. He framed her face with his hands and kissed the stuffing out of her until desire and urgency consumed her. His hands skimmed her body. It felt as if he was strumming every pleasure point until she writhed beneath him, desperate for progression. So frantic. Hungry little noises escaped her, and he parted their mouths, ending the kiss. He smiled down at her, his beautiful eyes twinkling with satisfaction.

"I don't deserve you," he whispered.

"What?" she shrieked with mock horror. "You want to give me back? Surely not."

He laughed and kissed the tip of her nose, the exuberant sound bringing a grin to her. "We're staying right where we are until need forces us to leave." His mouth twisted, some of the joy leaving his expression. "Probably in the morning."

Edwina turned his gaze to hers by placing her hands on his jawline. "We'll worry about everything tomorrow." She used her strength to roll him onto his back and pounced, laughing as she did so.

"What are you doing?"

"It's my turn to explore. That's fair. I haven't had the opportunity, and I should take advantage of the freedom."

He relaxed, the usually harsh angles of his face absent. He was a handsome man with no spare flesh. She straddled his legs before running her fingers over his shoulder and pectoral muscles. Firm flesh resisted the press of her hands, and she hummed under her breath. "Nice."

He twinkled at her. "I thought you intended to explore."

"Oh, I do."

She wriggled back until the hardness of his cock prodded her backside. "Ah," she said. "Undeniable masculine interest."

He chuffed out a breath, the exhalation containing humor. "Waiting."

"Yes, of course." Edwina stared at the acres of tanned skin, the sculpted muscles. "It's difficult to decide where to start."

"Everywhere, and I suggest you hurry because I have limited patience."

Edwina nodded. She leaned close and licked across the mark she'd placed on his neck. His gasp delighted her, and she toyed with the raised flesh. Mikhail shuddered, his fingers closing on her biceps. His muscles coiled as he flipped her. She stared up at him and pouted. "It was my turn."

"You were taking too long." His husky voice had turned to gravel, influenced by his tiger. "Mine," he said, and this time, she shivered.

How had this happened so fast? Mere days ago, she'd understood her path and what she wanted to do with her life. Her plan hadn't included this handsome, mighty tiger.

Her mate.

Gods. She wanted him to mark her so badly.

"Why are you shaking, little one?" He stroked a fingertip across her cheek, and her eyes flew open. She hadn't even realized she'd closed them.

Edwina swallowed and tried to use her words. "I want you." She cringed inwardly because those hadn't been the words she'd wanted to say, even if they were the truth.

"That I can do," he said after long moments of blatant masculine appraisal. "Now, where should I touch first? What would I enjoy most?" He tapped his chin with his fingertip.

Edwina stared, unable to see the stern tiger shifter she'd first met. She was learning he had a playful side. Despite some disappointing him, he was protective and cared deeply for his people and his family.

"Ah!" He winked at her, or at least she thought that was what he intended. He blinked both eyes, and she gaped at the boyish charm that radiated from him even as she realized he couldn't wink. "It occurs to me that since you're my wife, I don't need to choose. I can pace myself and do everything."

He kissed her, forcing back her words. The kiss held a large serving of tenderness that turned her gooey inside. So many facets to this man. So many layers. She could explore him for years and still find quirks to intrigue her. The kiss deepened, distracting her from her thoughts. So much better to feel and enjoy.

By the time he lifted his head, every part of her quivered and prickled, primed for more. Her pulse thrummed in her veins, and she desperately wanted him to finish this seduction and make them burn.

"What to do next?" That playful tone that mesmerized her came again, and his gaze settled on her breasts.

She wanted to scoff because ever since she'd reached her teens and developed, men had stared at her boobs. Men liked to grope her, and she guessed she should be used to it. While she wasn't averse to him touching her, disappointment edged into her.

The fingers of his right hand trailed down her neck and across the upper curves of her breasts. He dampened his left forefinger by sucking it into his mouth and caught her gaze simultaneously. His moist finger traced circles around her nipple, his blue eyes turning dark at the tremble that washed through her.

"That's nice." Nothing less than the truth because his touch fired her nerves, and she stirred restlessly, needing him to hustle.

"Nice," he mused. "Nice is a nothing description. I can't have you calling this *nice*."

A sharp pain arced through her as he pinched her nipple between finger and thumb. The prickling stab raced down her body when he repeated the squeeze with a slight twist and coalesced in her sex. Oh, boy. She had not understood the concept of painful pleasure. Hadn't understood it would send such deliciously agreeable sensations twisting through her body. He tugged this time, a sharp pull that hurt yet was strangely arousing.

Their gazes met, and his blue eyes twinkled with otherworldly power. He was entirely in control and understood what he was doing to her. The age difference between them had given him this experience, and while twinges of jealousy at the unnamed women in his past got to her, she pushed them away because, *hello!* She was the recipient of his amassed experience and wouldn't tolerate other women in his future. She frowned. Did she want more than the allotted year? Her feline did because she'd taken control and marked the tiger.

"Stop thinking so hard, little one." He pinched her nipple again and moved, repositioning himself between her legs. He parted her thighs with quiet insistence, and Edwina let him, although she swallowed when he stared at her aroused flesh. Mikhail leaned closer and inhaled her scent, giving an appreciative sigh. His tongue was rough as he licked her. He parted her legs farther and lifted her to his mouth.

She cried out as his tongue encountered her clit, the stirring arousal bumping up a notch.

He glanced up to stare at her, his nostrils flaring. "You taste of honey and spices. Everything delicious and decadent."

Edwina quivered, breathless in a world that had suddenly paused. She waited, the moment drawing out until she wanted to yank on his ears and force him to action. Anything. *Now.*

"Would you like my mouth or my cock?" he asked, breaking the silence.

"Both."

He chuckled, his playful smile appearing briefly before retreating. "I want to feel your body gloving mine, to test how wet you are for me."

"The night is only so long," she reminded him.

"True." Once again, he moved fast, rising upward and fitting his cock to her. He pushed against the slight resistance, and she held her breath, losing herself in his sensual gaze. Mikhail drew back and re-entered her, and she savored her flesh parting for him. He repeated this, impaling her deeper each time until he could go no farther. Her sex throbbed around him, not with discomfort but with a thrilling awareness of what would come. This man, with his experience, was turning her brain to mush.

"Please move," she said, and when he didn't obey fast enough, she tried using her internal muscles to clamp his cock more tightly.

His low growl suggested her plan was working fine. He kissed her with urgency rather than tenderness. Mikhail crushed her mouth under his and kissed her until she gasped for air, then withdrew and plunged back into her, hitting every pleasure point. He rocked into her repeatedly until she sobbed, striving for the sweetness beyond, the explosion of bliss that awaited her.

"You feel so fuckin' good on my cock," he growled. "I want to do this for hours and then repeat it. Clench my cock again."

She followed the order without hesitation, glorying in his feline grunt and the tightening of his facial muscles.

"Yeah, like that. You are so fuckin' perfect. Too good for me, yet I don't want to let you go." He pulled back and shafted her deeply, the strokes faster and harder. Edwina had no experience to compare the lovemaking, but surely sex didn't get better than this. Her body sang with his deep drives, wandering hands, and mouth.

"More," she whispered, instinct driving her to lick his mark until lust consumed her. Mikhail pulled back, and this time, his thrust perfectly aligned.

Her entire sex tingled, and she held her breath as the feelings expanded and pulsed, then leaped outward, darting down her legs and up her torso. Even her breasts prickled as the lightning spasms overwhelmed and seduced her. She groaned, gripping Mikhail's shoulders as an anchor. She writhed in pleasure, and Mikhail shouted as he rocked his pelvis forward. He remained embedded in her, his cock throbbing. Edwina gave him a sleepy smile but tensed when a sharp pain struck her deep inside. Her breath whooshed out, and Mikhail gave a startled grunt.

"Hell," Mikhail muttered and gave his hips an experimental twist. His gaze darted to her, his expression thoughtful. "We seem to be attached."

"How?" The tug had felt strange, and now the initial sharp pain had subsided she craved sleep. Her eyes closed, and she tried to open them again. They immediately closed.

"It's nothing bad," he said, although he didn't sound confident. "I've heard of this happening, but it never has to me. Go to sleep, little one."

12

EARLY THE NEXT MORNING, Mikhail held a sleeping Edwina in his arms, his mind racing for answers. Why had she marked him when she hadn't wanted to marry him? Fear had stopped him from asking questions, from letting his hopes rise. He'd known she was his mate, but given the circumstances of their marriage, he didn't feel he had the right to claim her when she'd had plans that meant so much to her.

And now—now she might be in danger because of him.

He could send her home and collect her once he resolved this mess. That might work. He'd have to sneak her out of the country...

He'd need someone trustworthy to go with her. Mikhail cursed softly because neither Ivan nor Gregory would willingly leave while he was in danger.

"Your brain must be overheating," a soft voice mumbled.

"I thought you were asleep."

"Your thoughts are deafening."

Mikhail chuffed out his humor. This slip of a girl made him laugh. She challenged him, unafraid to stand up to him. She was perfect.

"You might be safer if I sent you home to your Middlemarch."

"No." Edwina glowered at him. "No, that's not happening."

"Take up your university place."

"No, not with what is happening here. I refuse to act the selfish wife who thinks of only herself. I can help you."

Mikhail's brows rose. "How?"

"I've already suggested a meeting with this Konstantine Smirnoff. Some place neutral. Maybe dinner in a hotel restaurant or something like that. Call him this morning and organize the meeting at short notice. Don't give him time to organize his people. If he argues, tell him it's for your safety and his."

"I'm not interested in returning to that lifestyle. I saw what it did to my father, my mother."

"I understand. Perhaps you need to tell him that to his face. Tell Konstantine your reasons for rejecting his offer."

Mikhail finally uttered the thing that had haunted him for months. "If I don't do what he wants, he'll destroy everything I care for and value. My remaining family. My business and employees." He paused. "You."

"There must be some way to stop him." She frowned but reminded him of a tousled angel with loose hair and naked breasts. She didn't understand the tempting picture she made—all pink and bare, with her serious expression. "You mentioned your businesses have had problems."

"Yes. And when Konstantine dies, and his son takes over, the problems will intensify. His son will want to prove a point."

"That's he's a worthy successor?"

"Yeah."

"What about relocating?"

"I considered this, but my employees are settled here with their families. They rely on their wages, and I couldn't throw them to the Bratva."

"Put a hit out on them," Edwina said. "On the father and son. Do it when you're out of the country or in another town. At a function with dozens of witnesses."

Mikhail's mouth dropped open, and he pressed his lips together to halt his gaping. "A hit?"

"Yeah. Get rid of the problem with ruthlessness. Hit the major players. They wouldn't expect that from you, not if you're known for your integrity. It would be revenge for your father's death."

"A hit," he said slowly, considering the idea now that his initial shock had subsided. Edwina was right. Smirnoff would never suspect him when he'd always avoided physical trouble. But could he live with himself afterward? That was the question.

He glanced at Edwina and found her watching him, much like a scientist regarded an interesting specimen.

"What do you think?"

"You're a bloodthirsty wench, and it's a turn-on." The truth spilled from him since he was still grappling with his surprise.

"If you went that route, you could take over Smirnoff's men and women and force them to go honest. I bet you'd give them a better, safer life than what they face now."

Once again, surprise stabbed him, along with fascination. This young woman had intelligence and smarts far beyond what he expected from someone with her lack of life experience.

"Well?" Her brows rose in emphasis to her question. She held up her left hand and counted by tapping one forefinger against another. "One, you arrange a meeting and listen to what he wants. Two, you take me with you because I'll look innocent and harmless, but I'm excellent at noticing things. Three, even if you don't like his plan, tell him you'll consider it to stall him to give yourself time to formulate a new strategy. Ask for his reasons and learn as much as you can about his operation. Search for weaknesses."

"I've already done that. He's bleeding money because his son and cronies are skimming. I'm unsure if Konstantine knows."

"Would the son's friends come into line if the son was no longer a factor?"

"I'm not sure." Mikhail nodded, his mind busy now as he saw that, although radical, Edwina's suggestion might work. "I'd intimate I'd take over, and if Konstantine's son was out of the way before I did that, I might manage plausible deniability."

"True, you'd need to plan carefully and keep innocents from the line of fire. Four, you'd arrange the hit and remove the key people presenting problems. I'm sure Smirnoff has other enemies who are eying his territory. Five, you leave Konstantine alive and take out his son and his friends. That way, people might not even consider you a suspect. Not if you're in talks with Konstantine. Some might presume he had his son taken out." Edwina counted the last points on her fingers, then grinned. "What do you think? I watch too many thriller movies?"

Mikhail placed a smacking kiss on her lips before pulling back to return her grin. "You're a bloody genius. As much as I hate the idea of bloodshed, that might be the only way."

"Someone tried to shoot me. They had no compunction about removing me from the equation to get what they wanted," Edwina said. "You have a reputation for honesty, and you value hard work. It will be why your employees stay in their jobs and turn up for work each day."

Pleasure seeped through Mikhail. Her praise, after his grandfather's constant complaints, was a welcome change. He held out his arms. "We need more sleep," he said, settling back under the covers. "I'll finesse the plan later this morning."

"*We* will refine the plan. This is my life, too. You dragged me into it, and now it is mine—at least for the next twelve months. I deserve the chance to fashion my life. I insist," she added with a harsh tone in her voice.

"I don't want to place you in danger."

"Someone took potshots at me today. They might try again. I should stay close to you, Ivan, and Gregory, and if that means attending meetings, then so be it."

Mikhail chuffed. This new wife kept one step ahead of him. He imagined chasing her when he was his grandfather's age, and the idea didn't repel him. Her solid core of determination, added to a brain that functioned at top speed, made her an asset. She'd already shown she refused to sit around and attend ladies' luncheons. Music was her priority, but she also intended to participate in his world.

"You can attend our discussion, but I want you safe," he added. "I'd like to keep you alive and learn more about my new wife. So far, each nugget I uncover intrigues me more."

"That's a good thing?"

He laughed again because he'd never relaxed with Clarice, not like this. "It is. Your grandmother might have maneuvered you, but I won big time. Go to sleep. I need your beautiful brain at full capacity if you're attending my planning session."

"A cup of coffee and toast, and I'll be firing on all cylinders."

"It's a deal," he said, drawing her closer. His tiger released a loud purr that echoed through his mind. Mikhail smiled against her neck, well-pleased with his wife. His mate.

Mikhail called Ivan and Gregory as soon as he and Edwina woke again. "We have a plan."

"If you want to toss in breakfast, we can come now," Gregory said.

"Done," Mikhail said.

"Ten minutes," Gregory said. "We've just finished in the gym."

Mikhail hung up, absently accepting the cup of coffee Edwina pushed in his direction. "Thanks."

"Are Ivan and Gregory together?"

His gaze snapped to Edwina. "What?"

"Are they a couple?"

"No!" Mikhail blurted. "What made you think that?"

"They're always together."

"I spend time with them, but you didn't assume that about me."

"No, you're my husband, and your working parts don't seem to have a problem with mine," Edwina said sweetly.

Mikhail spluttered, and she broke out in a chortle. Ah! She'd been teasing him. "Our fathers were friends, so we spent time together as kids. Our friendship started then. Have a croissant."

"I've already had one," Edwina said. "I'm not exercising much and need to watch what I eat."

"You can use the gym in the basement. Ivan, Gregory, and I use it when we have time and can't go for a run in our feline forms."

"Are you certain your enemies don't know you're feline shifters?"

Mikhail frowned. His grandfather didn't since Mikhail's father hadn't trusted him with the sensitive information about his wife. Smirnoff would've used her and Mikhail to his advantage if he'd learned the truth. No, this was one secret best kept close. "I don't think so."

"An added weapon in this battle," Edwina said.

The door opened, and Ivan and Gregory strode inside. The housekeeper bustled in with platters of bacon and eggs, and the two men took seats and started eating.

"It's like watching feeding time at the zoo," Edwina said, wide-eyed.

Mikhail spluttered, and his men froze. They stared at Mikhail before shifting their attention to her.

"What?" she asked.

"He's laughing," Gregory said, his face still slack with puzzlement.

Mikhail blinked, his cute version of a wink. "Wait until I tell them the plan we've devised."

"We?" Ivan asked, his brow furrowed.

As one, the two men stared holes in her.

"At the risk of sounding like an echo—what? Why are you staring at me?"

Mikhail chuckled and stabbed his fork into a bacon rasher.

The men's eyes goggled even more.

Edwina snorted and picked up a slice of toast. "Men are a mystery to me. The more I learn, the less I understand."

"I'm an open book," Mikhail said.

Ivan's and Gregory's gazes pinged back and forth like they were watching a tennis match.

Mikhail's blue eyes gleamed, and Edwina hid satisfaction. He wasn't the same severe and determined feline she'd met in Scotland mere days ago. He'd relaxed and appeared happy.

Edwina tested her emotions and discovered her anger had dispersed. Oh, she'd still rip into her grandmother when she saw her because she was not a chess piece for the matriarch to shift around her personal game board. Her grandmother was not the boss of her, even though she might've fluked into finding a shifter male who fitted Edwina perfectly.

Edwina popped bacon into her mouth and enjoyed the salt and crispy meat hit. Nothing better than perfectly cooked bacon. Mikhail had an excellent housekeeper, and Edwina appreciated her expertise.

Mikhail placed his knife and fork on his plate. "This is the plan Edwina and I discussed," he said, filling in Ivan and Gregory.

"Ballsy but clever," Ivan said. "Where will you have your meeting?"

"It needs to be at a place with ties to none of you," Edwina said before Mikhail answered. "And you need to ensure that monster returns Clarice's child. Once that happens, you can get them somewhere safe."

All three men stared at her this time.

"The child is innocent, and as much as I'm not happy learning about Clarice, it doesn't sound as if this was her fault. We need to take them out of the equation."

Mikhail nodded, the sensual gleam in his eyes making her shift in her chair. Edwina pushed carnal thoughts away and dealt with her traitorous body. She could go for a few hours without dragging her husband to bed. She glanced in his direction and bit back a smile when he double-winked at her.

"What have you done to him?" Ivan blurted.

"Nothing," Edwina said.

"Stop teasing my wife," Mikhail said. "Suggestions for meeting places. We need more than one, and given that Smirnoff has the boy, we'll insist the meeting occurs today."

Edwina nodded. "That might make it look as if Clarice has successfully persuaded you to do as he wants."

"My thoughts exactly," Mikhail said. "Okay, fire suggestions at me. I'll call Smirnoff when we have four or five neutral properties."

"Are you going to tell your grandfather?" Ivan asked.

"No, he has been interfering and trying to shunt me in Smirnoff's direction. He can't see that the new way is safer for the family, and we have staff who are loyal to us. I prefer to keep him out of negotiations because I don't trust him."

Edwina topped up everyone's coffee while the men tossed suggestions back and forth. Once satisfied with the shortlist, Mikhail pulled out his phone and the business card Clarice had given him.

"Everyone remain silent, no matter what he says. Your feline hearing should mean you catch everything."

Edwina nodded, curious about what a Bratva leader would sound like. She wasn't kept waiting long. A harsh voice answered Mikhail's call.

"Smirnoff," he barked.

"This is Mikhail Lermontov," Mikhail said. "We should talk."

"Ah, Lermontov, I've been waiting for your call." Smug satisfaction oozed into the room.

Edwina's eyes narrowed, but she remained silent like the other eavesdroppers.

Mikhail tensed. "I believe we should meet today."

"Come to my estate," Smirnoff said, that satisfaction still ringing through his voice.

"No," Mikhail said, and rattled off the short list of properties they thought might suit their purpose. "I prefer to meet in a public venue. Each of the places I mentioned has more privacy. They should suit our purposes."

Smirnoff picked the coffee shop close to Clarice's apartment, which surprised Edwina, but perhaps it was a sign.

"Excellent," Mikhail said. "Please bring Clarice's son with you as a sign of your goodwill."

Edwina marveled at his even tone. He sounded as if he was conducting a business meeting and had no interest in the outcome.

Smirnoff paused, and she could practically hear him weighing his options. "I would expect something in return."

"Why?" Mikhail said without hesitation. "From what I hear, you're the one who wants something from me. You should do me a favor to show your sincerity."

Smirnoff paused again. Finally, he capitulated. "I'll bring the boy."

"Alive," Mikhail said.

"What kind of monster do you think I am?" came the silky voice. "Two this afternoon. Don't be late and do nothing stupid." He hung up.

"That went about as well as we expected," Mikhail said.

"Can we trust him?" Ivan asked.

"Not as far as we could kick him," Edwina said. "He

sounded like a slimeball. I didn't like his manner."

Ivan drummed his fingers on the tabletop. "What will you do with Clarice? Now that she has played her part, she's not safe. He doesn't need her any longer."

"Wait until we know something more," Edwina said. "Once you have her son and they're reunited, you can decide where to send her."

Gregory stared at Edwina. "Don't you want to scratch out her eyes?"

"I don't like it, but she was trying to protect her son. I doubt we'll ever be friends, but I can empathize with her."

Gregory turned to Mikhail. "You lucked out, my friend."

Mikhail caught Edwina's gaze, his smile full of satisfaction. "I did."

13

DURING THEIR DRIVE TO meet Smirnoff, Mikhail worried about everything that might go wrong. He glanced at Edwina, his gaze drifting to their linked hands. He couldn't believe he'd claimed this remarkable woman as his wife. His perfect partner. Not once had she complained about her needs and wants when most women might remain bitter at having their dreams wrested from them. Instead, she'd tried to help him with his problems. She'd given him so much, and he...

He should've talked her out of attending this meeting. It was a dangerous move, and Smirnoff would have his team standing by, hoping to gain the upper hand.

According to rumor, Smirnoff wanted Mikhail's help so his life wasn't in danger. But Edwina wasn't necessary to the crime boss, and Smirnoff wouldn't think twice about ordering his men to get rid of her. If someone hurt Edwina, Mikhail would struggle to control his tiger.

"Will you stay in the car?" Mikhail tried again.

"No, my presence will give you an advantage. He won't expect a woman at the meeting."

Gregory snorted. "Smirnoff believes women are only necessary in the kitchen and the bedroom."

Edwina's plump lips made a moue of distaste. "He should tell my grandmother that. She'd take great pleasure in puncturing his ego. I promise to stay in the background and will sit at another table. He might not even realize I'm your wife, and if he does, tell him your plans changed at the last minute, and you need to drop me at your house in the city. You have one of those, right? He won't realize I can eavesdrop. Besides, if Smirnoff sticks to his word, you might need me to calm the boy. If you have to deal with him, it will split your focus."

"A compelling argument," Ivan said. "The boy will respond better to a woman."

"You hope," Edwina said dryly. "I'm used to small children, and they can be difficult."

"All right," Mikhail said. "Although if something happens to you, I will spank you myself for talking me into this damn fool plan."

Edwina flashed him a warning glance. "You could try."

Mikhail released a feline growl, and Edwina grinned as she slid from the vehicle. Early days yet, but she thought she'd enjoy marriage. He'd softened toward her, although the future was murky. A twang of pain darted through her chest, and she pushed her unwelcome thoughts away. She'd deal with the future once Mikhail straightened out this mess. Then, they'd focus on their relationship. That she'd marked him, she ignored. Claiming Mikhail was a mess she'd need to sort out by herself.

The cafe was quiet when they entered, with only four customers. Mikhail scanned the room and escorted Edwina to a table by the window while she inhaled in pleasure, savoring the sweet scent of chocolate and caramel. Their gazes met in silent communication, and she gave an imperceptible nod of approval. Sitting here would give her a view of the area outside the cafe, plus she was close enough to the private rear booth where Mikhail intended to conduct the meeting. From here, with her feline senses, she should pick up most of the conversation, even if Mikhail and Smirnoff weren't visible.

Mikhail left her alone and retreated to the booth with Ivan. Gregory had stayed with the vehicle and was watching the street. He'd call Mikhail once Smirnoff arrived and be ready for a quick getaway when required.

"Maybe I should've brought more men with me," Mikhail said.

"We discussed this," Ivan said. "This is a public place. More men would draw attention. We don't want law enforcement to turn up because we can't trust that Smirnoff hasn't bought them off. Each of us can handle ourselves. Trust in us, and we'll get through this meeting."

A brief period of silence ensued, then Edwina heard a faint murmur that she struggled to discern, before a waitress wearing a black dress and frilly white apron approached her table.

She spoke in the local language, and Edwina frowned. "I'm sorry, but do you speak English?"

"Da," the woman said, her pen poised and dark-brown eyes intent beneath straight bangs. "What can I get you?" She smelled of sugar and spices.

"A pot of tea, please, and something sweet to eat. What would you recommend?"

The woman rattled off several items, but her thick accent made it difficult to understand.

"Can you show me?"

The woman gestured at a large glass cabinet full of pastries and cakes, and Edwina rose to follow. She pointed at each item and spoke the name.

"Thank you," Edwina said. "I'll take this one." She attempted to mimic the woman and made a hash of it, but the woman noted it on her order pad and darted behind the counter. She disappeared through a doorway, and Edwina meandered back to her table. "I have no idea what I ordered, but it looks delicious."

"You're intelligent, kitten. You'll learn the local language and our ways in no time."

A phone rang. "Yes," Mikhail said. "All right."

Ivan slid from the booth and took up a position nearby. He'd hear most of their conversation because of his feline nature.

The doorbell tinkled, and the waitress emerged from the kitchen. She froze for a second before she pinned on a bright expression and continued toward Edwina's table. Her hands trembled when she set the teapot, cup, and saucer before Edwina. Tea sloshed on the tabletop, and she apologized, whisking it away with a cloth.

The waitress's throat bobbed as she glanced at the four

men who strode through the door and loitered at the entrance, their gazes full of tension.

Before the waitress greeted them, Ivan approached, his hands visible, and said, "Sir, Mr. Lermontov is waiting for you in a private booth." He gestured toward the café's rear and dipped his head, looking so subservient Edwina barely restrained her gasp. It made her realize the unusually close relationship between Mikhail, Ivan, and Gregory. She hadn't considered the rareness of the association until she spotted the clear boss-employee vibes between Konstantine Smirnoff and his men.

Aware she needed to stay quiet and not attract attention, she poured milk into her cup and added tea. She studied the passersby in the square outside and acted as if she was resting her weary feet after a day of shopping. They'd even made some quick purchases on the way, so she had her two glossy bags from women's fashion stores as props.

The waitress arrived with a delectable-looking cream cake covered with a drizzle of chocolate, and she smiled her thanks.

Her distinctive accent was one thing they hadn't considered, and what if Smirnoff spoke in Russian rather than English? Not everyone understood English—she'd discovered that fact already while shopping.

From her peripheral vision, she caught Smirnoff's abrupt hand signal, presumably for his men to search the cafe for signs of trouble. This made sense since Mikhail and Ivan had quickly scanned the occupants before approaching the rear booth.

Mikhail stood and showed himself. "There's me and

one of my men." His actions implied Smirnoff was behaving with overkill, and the man knew it because his features tightened, and his lips disappeared in the flat line of his mouth.

He was older than Edwina had guessed, and when he walked past her table, she smelled the sickness on him, the decaying flesh. He was tall and, during his younger years, probably a fit man with an upright stature. Now everything about him sagged, and his black designer suit hung on him. Yet power still radiated from him, and the men with him remained attentive.

He murmured something in Russian, his quick gesture telling Edwina more. He wanted them to remain within hailing distance yet give him the perception of privacy.

"Where is the boy?" Mikhail asked.

"Outside in the car," Smirnoff said without hesitation. Edwina believed him.

"I want to see him," Mikhail countered.

"He'll get in the way."

"Your men can look after him or mine can," Mikhail said. "I'd like to reassure myself of his health."

"I haven't hurt him."

"You've scared him, taken him from his mother. He'll probably experience nightmares for years to come." Mikhail's voice was without inflection, but Smirnoff's brows rose, anyway.

"I'd heard you are generous with your staff." Smirnoff was mocking Mikhail, but her mate didn't react.

Edwina poured more tea and used a fork to cut a mouth-sized piece of cake from her slice. Hmm, it was delicious and melted in her mouth. She idly watched two women stop outside and glance at the cafe as if they intended to enter. A man approached them and spoke rapidly. Seconds later, they scuttled away without a backward glance.

Interesting. Smirnoff had come with a retinue of men. Would they try to kidnap Mikhail and force him to work for them? Heck, anything was possible. Tension slid through her, and her second bite of cake didn't taste as magical. Her muscles locked up, and she swallowed hard, her throat working as the lump descended to her stomach. Every muscle in her body hardened, and she fought the impulse to leap to her feet and inflict damage on these arrogant men who sought to use Mikhail and his talents.

"Very well," Smirnoff said, jerking his head toward Ivan. "As a show of good faith, I will release him to your man here."

Two obvious tourists stopped outside the cafe, conversed quickly, and entered. Humans, since they didn't seem to notice anything off. The male and female pair stopped at the counter and asked for coffee and cake. Like her, they did the pointing thing, but their entrance seemed to relax Smirnoff's men rather than ramp up their tension.

"Yuri, get the boy and deliver him to Mikhail's man."

Ivan glanced in Mikhail's direction and must've received a nod because Ivan headed for the door.

Yuri, a large man who had squeezed his frame into a store-bought suit, lumbered from the café with Ivan on his heels. He headed straight for a vehicle parked across the other side of the square. On reaching the car, he spoke to the man sitting in the driver's seat before going to the rear door and opening it. He leaned forward and must've said something because a small blond boy slid from the vehicle. The kid trailed the giant with unwilling steps, and when he stopped, Yuri turned around, and whatever words he uttered had the boy hustling. Yuri strode to Mikhail's vehicle and must've told the boy to stay there because the kid sank to his knees by Ivan and didn't move. Ivan scowled when Yuri retreated and squatted beside the child.

Edwina muttered under her breath and picked up her teacup to stop herself from letting loose with a foul curse. She and Suzie had grumbled about life in Middlemarch and how their grandmothers held all the control, but her parents loved her, and if she had severe problems, she approached Saber Mitchell or his family to seek help.

This kid had no support, and it raised her ire.

"I'm here, Smirnoff," Mikhail said. "What did you want to discuss?"

"That's Mr. Smirnoff," a male voice snapped.

"Leopold, it's fine. Please take a table near the door. Order tea and cake and try to blend." The last held an unexpected shimmer of humor. "Mikhail and I need time to discuss things in solitude."

Nothing more was said while Smirnoff's men relocated, giving him and Mikhail greater privacy. Edwina attempted to eat more cake but had lost her appetite. She pushed the plate aside and concentrated on her tea.

"You're a challenging man to contact," Smirnoff said. "Even your grandfather didn't know where you were last week."

Edwina scowled into her cup. Why did he want to keep abreast of Mikhail's whereabouts?

"I didn't realize my life was so interesting to you, but since you asked, I traveled to discuss a project with a new client. I work on more than one project at once."

"Clarice didn't know," Smirnoff mused.

"She isn't my girlfriend," Mikhail said in a tight voice. "She was someone I saw casually, and we attended a few events together. I went to parties with other female acquaintances, too."

"But Clarice seemed to be your favorite."

"She is out of favor now," Mikhail said.

"Yet you ensured you gained custody of her son."

"She didn't deserve to get dragged into this mess. I owed her at least that."

Smirnoff said nothing, merely allowing the silence to lengthen. Mikhail didn't bite but waited him out, and Edwina suppressed a snigger. Smirnoff might be older, but Mikhail had learned the rules of negotiation. It made her curious about the discussions with her grandmother.

"You're a cool character," Smirnoff said.

That was admiration in his tone. Edwina heard it clearly, and she was certain Mikhail heeded it too.

"Please tell me what you want. I'm a busy man," Mikhail said.

"I want you to take over as head of my...business."

After a lengthy silence, Mikhail said, "Won't your son expect you to hand everything over to him? Isn't that what you have been training him for?"

Quiet fell again, growing to a point shy of extreme

SHELLEY MUNRO

discomfort. Finally, Smirnoff said, "I love my son, but he's not a good man. I have made mistakes since I took over the business from my father, but I have expanded and built the concern into a legacy to be proud of. My son lacks the same talent and resents taking orders from me. I don't want to see the business dwindle into dust while I'm still alive to see the decline."

"What makes you believe I can do your business justice? We have a different business ethos. I'm sure your son will object and create difficulties. Isn't there someone else you trust to take over?"

"My second-in-command does not gel with my son. Giving him control would lead to inner conflict. You're strong enough to hold off my son and anyone else who tries to steal the role. Mikhail, I've watched you since you were a child. You have strength and grit, and you inspire loyalty in your people. That's difficult, but you do it without effort. Your grandfather is proud of you, and justifiably so. You're an asset to him."

More silence ensued, and Edwina imagined Mikhail's thoughts. He'd fought with his grandfather to run the business his way and continue on the path his father had set them. His grandfather had wanted to return to the old ways, and Mikhail had fought his grandfather's orders. He'd been young when he'd taken over, and it couldn't have been easy.

"My grandfather has nothing to do with my business."

Smirnoff barked a rusty laugh, his amusement clear to Edwina, although she couldn't imagine a smile fitting smoothly on his thin, sickly face.

"No," Mikhail said. "I have a journey I wish to travel, and it doesn't include rejoining the Bratva. I disagree with your practices. My staff works for a fair wage. They give their loyalty because they respect me. That regard will die if I change directions."

Smirnoff sighed heavily. "I thought you might say that."

"I don't see any advantages to me," Mikhail said smoothly. Calmly.

"What if I sweetened the pot and offered you my daughter? If you married her, you would gain a helpmate who understands the life and would offer loyalty and beauty. She's a virgin."

"I already have a wife."

Silence fell yet again, and Edwina guessed there was shock too.

"Who? Is this recent?" Smirnoff didn't wait for a reply. "It doesn't matter. No marriage is forever. Easy to remedy."

Every muscle in Edwina's body clenched. His words had been as casual as a man swatting a fly. He'd get rid of her to clear the path for his daughter.

"Thank you for the great honor, but I find my current wife entirely to my liking," Mikhail said. "I would be extremely unhappy if anything happened to her."

No mistaking that tone for anything but dangerous. A warm sensation whooshed through her chest and encased her heart.

"When did you marry? Why the secrecy? Your grandfather didn't mention you'd wed."

"It's recent, and I haven't had time to introduce my wife

to my friends. I find I'm selfish and want to keep her to myself."

"As I say, your grandfather never mentioned a marriage. Where were you wed?"

"If that's all you need to discuss, I'll leave."

Edwina drank a mouthful of tea and rose, winding between the tables. She ignored the suggestive gazes of Smirnoff's men and approached the counter. "I'd like to pay my bill, please." It was best that she left before Smirnoff so he and his men didn't realize she was with Mikhail. While she might miss some of the conversation, she was confident Mikhail would keep her in the loop.

Luckily, Mikhail had given her cash earlier, and she pulled out the purse she'd borrowed from the housekeeper. "Thank you," she said on accepting the change.

One of Smirnoff's men stood and approached her, his intent visible on his handsome face. One of the remaining men said something, but his friend ignored him and continued toward her. Edwina headed for the door, but the man grasped her upper arm and dragged her to a halt.

Easy to deal with. Edwina let him drag her closer and raised her knee with a quick jab. The man let out a pained croak and released her as he folded in on himself. Edwina swept past and out the front door before his friends blinked and Mr. Gropey recovered enough to exact punishment. She didn't look back and didn't make the mistake of heading straight for Mikhail's vehicle. Instead, she skirted the perimeter of the teashop and walked around the corner, where she waited and watched for any suspicious behavior.

Her pulse raced, but she was unhurt and hadn't caused enough of a stir to garner attention from Smirnoff or Mikhail. A slow grin spread across her face because she'd dropped the guy, all thanks to Isabella's self-defense training. She wasn't stupid enough to think a second time would go the same way, but she'd done well and couldn't wait to tell Suzie.

14

MIKHAIL HEARD THE KERFUFFLE—THE pained groan and the resulting sniggers. Nothing shifted in his expression, but his feline perked his ears and gave a growl that echoed through Mikhail's mind. If someone had hurt her, he wouldn't be responsible for his actions.

He immediately cast out every sense but couldn't discern if Edwina was in danger. No, she would've shouted, screamed, or raised the alarm if she hit trouble. The front door opened and closed. When no further sounds disturbed the peace, he shifted his focus back to Smirnoff.

"You have said nothing to make me change my mind. While I'm honored, I decline."

Smirnoff contemplated Mikhail but didn't reveal his thoughts apart from the faint widening of his eyes. Surprise? Surely Smirnoff hadn't thought he'd jump at his offer. Hadn't the man done his research? Had he been arrogant enough to expect Mikhail to jump when told or at least ask how high?

"Your grandfather told me you'd change your mind." Banked anger simmered in Smirnoff now, a hint of the ego that made him God in his world.

"My grandfather is not the boss of me. I thought everyone understood that."

Smirnoff's lips twisted. "I must insist. Accept my offer or face the consequences."

Mikhail silently fought his agitated feline and kept his mouth shut to conceal his canines. He could've taken out Smirnoff before his men did a thing, but he hadn't because that would leave a power vacuum, and the city's residents would feel resulting ripples for months. "Are you trying to blackmail me?"

"If you don't take over the business, I will make it my mission to take out this mysterious wife of yours—the one no one has seen. And once I've done that, I'll start with your family." His voice grew harder, his temper riding him now. "You will take over from me. You have six months to learn the ropes and exert control."

Alarm rushed through Mikhail. He hadn't seen this coming, and he should've. *De-escalate.* His mind worked at warp speed while he worked out the best way to wriggle free of the impending trap and keep everyone safe.

"I have your grandfather," Smirnoff added in a silky voice. "If you don't do as I ask, he won't leave his current whereabouts under his own steam."

"You're friends."

"Your grandfather thinks so," Smirnoff said.

Everything in Mikhail went icy cold. He cleared his throat, and even his feline paused, waiting. Mikhail firmed his control and ordered his cat to stand down. They needed a strategy. "How long have you been planning this?"

"Since I watched you take your father's floundering business when you were scarcely more than a boy. I love my son, but he takes after his mother. He's stupid and venerates himself. He never considers angles and strategic decisions. You've impressed me. You have integrity, which is rare in my world."

A derisive snort escaped Mikhail. The man was talking about principle and honor? As if he admired it when the old bastard had several rather significant character flaws. He'd threatened Edwina, his family, and even his grandfather. Mikhail wasn't sure what to make of that because his grandfather wasn't weak-minded, despite his age. Surely, he wasn't stupid enough to trust Smirnoff? He knew what the man was capable of, what he'd done over the years to obtain his goals.

Mikhail stood abruptly. "I'll give you my decision in two days."

"One," Smirnoff countered. "Clock is ticking."

Mikhail stalked off, his mind whirring. Unfortunately, Smirnoff had trapped him like a tiger in a cage, but somehow, he'd turn this situation around.

The son would be an enormous problem.

He'd discuss strategy with Ivan and Gregory. Edwina, too. The spot between his shoulder blades itched, but he kept striding through the café.

A whoosh of sound, then the sharp prick on his neck, had him halting in shock. He yanked at the dart and pulled it from his neck to gape in disbelief. "You shot me."

"Time is a liability for me," Smirnoff rumbled from behind him.

Mikhail's limbs wobbled. "So you thought to take me by force? How will that inspire loyalty?" His tongue thickened, his words slurring. His legs went from under him, and he struck the floor, none of his muscles obeying the frantic orders from his brain.

Darkness blurred his vision, the light reducing to tiny pinpricks. His last thought before he surrendered was that Smirnoff might've outplayed him today, but he'd be damned if the man forced him to act against his will.

15

EDWINA WAITED AT THE corner of the building. Ivan had seen her exit the café and stride away with only a glance and a head jerk as she'd gestured she'd wait out of sight. He'd wait for Mikhail, then they'd drive past to collect her on the way home. The minutes ticked by, and she risked a phone call to Ivan.

"Mikhail hasn't finished his meeting," he said, noticeable tension coloring the words.

"What aren't you telling me?" She clenched her hands into fists, every part of her sensing this wasn't sterling news.

"Not long after you walked out, two other tourists fled at a run. I didn't see what happened, but they left and wasted no time disappearing."

"I'm going back inside."

"Mikhail would cut off my balls if something happened to you," Ivan said. "Let me or Gregory go inside."

"Smirnoff will know you. While he might've noticed me, he won't automatically suspect my motives. I'll tell the woman at the counter I've lost my pendant. I'll make a fuss. They won't suspect me of anything except being a dim-witted tourist. Get ready to leave in a hurry." She was on the move and darting around the corner of the red brick building before Ivan offered an objection. But she wasn't stupid either.

She swept into the cafe and walked straight to the counter. "I've lost my pendant. It has sentimental value and... You haven't picked it up, have you?" She made her voice sound breathless as if she'd been running and was in a flap. "Oh, you haven't cleared my table. I'll search now."

She allowed herself to scan the cafe interior, and everything in her cried out in shock. The hulking men who'd loitered had gone. She raced to the booth where Mikhail and Smirnoff had sat, which was also empty.

She spun back to face the woman behind the counter. "What happened to the men who were here? Never mind," she snapped when the woman gave a helpless shrug and pantomimed, not understanding.

Edwina ran outside and straight to the waiting car. "They've gone. All of them."

"There must be a rear door," Gregory said.

Edwina nodded. "Which of you has the best sense of smell in human form? "

"Me," Ivan said.

"You might question the woman inside. She is pretending we have a language problem."

Ivan took Edwina's arm, and they entered the cafe with

more aplomb and intent this time. Ivan spoke to the woman, his tone sharp when she was slow to answer.

Edwina made herself useful and discovered Mikhail's scent among the others. It ended at the counter, and her mind jumped ahead. She turned to Ivan. "Mikhail's scent ends here, but that might be because they lifted him. I can't smell blood, so that's a plus."

Ivan barked at the woman, and she flinched, fear flashing across her face.

Edwina didn't understand what he said, but she got the gist.

The woman started crying, and impatient, Edwina stalked around the counter and into the kitchen, where she spied a rear door. Despite the woman's protests, Edwina jerked open the door and stared outside.

"Did they take him out this door?" she asked the young girl, chopping vegetables at a counter.

Tetchy at the girl's ponderous attitude, Edwina growled deep in her throat. The girl's hand tightened on her knife, and she backed away. When Edwina took half a step toward her, she blurted, "They carried an unconscious man through that door. I don't think he was dead, but he couldn't walk unaided."

"Thank you," Edwina said, working hard to control her anger. Smirnoff and his underlings had taken Mikhail. While she and Mikhail had known this meeting was a risk, they'd had to halt Smirnoff's pressure to get Mikhail to follow his orders. She strode to the door again and inhaled, testing the air for scents. Yes, they'd taken Mikhail since she caught a hint of his wild tiger fragrance. She also recognized Smirnoff's essence, which held a medicinal tang and an underlying decay. The man wasn't lying about his ailing health.

"Are you able to pick up their scent?" Ivan asked in a low voice when she stomped back to join him.

"They took him out the rear door. Where does Clarice live? We need to interrogate her because she might have held back information when Mikhail questioned her. We have her son to return to her, anyway. She needs to disappear once we've spoken to her. Any suggestions?"

He flashed a grin before he spoke. "We have a pilot on call. You're right. She should leave the country. We can ask her where she wants to take her son. She might have a family."

"Let's do this. This Smirnoff is an idiot, trying to change Mikhail's mind this way."

She and Ivan retraced the scent trail and burst outdoors. Every inhalation contained a hint of Mikhail until they reached the curb.

"They loaded him into a vehicle," Ivan said.

"We should've thought of something like this."

"Yeah," Ivan said. "I hope Smirnoff keeps a close eye on Mikhail. He's expecting his son and the rest of those high in management in his organization to let him replace them with an outsider. While Smirnoff is alive, they might play the game, but the minute he dies, there'll be war."

"I get that. Why can't Smirnoff?"

"The guy has an ego."

They reached the car, which Gregory had running. She slid inside to find Clarice's son curled up in a ball in the footwell. His pale face was wet with tears, and sympathy welled in her. The poor kid.

"Hey, sweetie. Are you okay?" His fear was palpable, and her inadequate comfort only made him hunch into a tighter ball. She'd noted the bruise on his cheek, and he was way too thin. "Why don't you come up here? We're taking you home to your mother."

The boy stared at her as if he thought she was telling him a tall story. Then she wanted to thump herself over the head. He probably didn't speak English.

He studied her for several beats longer. "Mama?" he whispered.

"Yes," Edwina said. "We're taking you right now."

He uncurled his thin body, and she spotted more bruises on his skinny arms. That anyone would do this to a child had her temper flying, and she made a silent promise. When they retrieved Mikhail, she would take great pleasure in exacting revenge on Smirnoff.

"Mama?" he asked, surveying her as if he didn't believe her.

She couldn't blame him.

Edwina wished she'd thought to buy an extra cake or something for him to eat since he appeared undernourished.

They drove down quiet streets, and Gregory stopped in front of an expensive apartment.

"I'll take the boy," Ivan said.

"No, let me. Clarice might answer my questions more readily if it's two women, and I have her son with me."

"Keep your wits about you," Gregory said, distinct

worry in his features. "We can't trust her."

"I'm aware, but she deserves to have her son back. She must've gone through hell. Let's go, kiddo." Edwina slid from the vehicle and held out her hand for the boy. "Do you have a name?" she asked when he cautiously crawled from the footwell.

He stared at her with big brown eyes. Edwina pressed her lips together because she didn't want to scare the kid. But the man—Smirnoff—deserved his death. Who the hell persecuted a child to get what they wanted? It was despicable, disgusting, and a lot of other things besides.

"Which apartment?" she asked.

"The penthouse," Ivan replied, his expression blank.

Edwina guessed what he was thinking. Mikhail and Clarice had happened before she'd come along. She'd kissed other men and done more with some of them, so having a hissy fit would be hypocritical. Infidelity after their marriage was a different story, and she would create merry hell if she learned of this type of betrayal.

Once the boy exited the car, she held out her hand again. He hesitated for so long she was about to let her hand drop when he clasped her fingers. She crossed the road, angry all over again at his noticeable limp. If she were Clarice, she'd take the boy to a doctor for a complete physical check.

"Let's find your mother," she said. "Are you hungry?"

"Yes," he said in a whisper.

"You don't need to be frightened any longer," Edwina said. "You'll be with your mother." And hopefully safe, although she couldn't guarantee that part. None of them were secure while Smirnoff was alive.

When Edwina arrived in the apartment lobby, a doorman materialized from a wooden booth. "Do you require assistance?"

"Yes, is Clarice home? I believe she lives in the penthouse apartment."

"I'll call her," the doorman said, his English accented. He picked up a phone. "Whom can I say is here to see her?"

"Edwina and Alex. Alex is her son. Can you ask her if we can go up, please?"

The man's eyes widened a fraction as he dialed a number. He spoke to Clarice in Russian and held the phone away from his ears when she shrieked. He hung up, his expression pained.

"The elevator is over there." He pointed, and Edwina led Alex in that direction. The doors opened to her touch, and they stepped inside the car.

The ride was short and fast, and she spied a blonde woman waiting as the doors slid open.

"Alex!" she exclaimed and sprang forward, wrapping the child in her arms, weeping, and laughing simultaneously. One of her arms was heavily bandaged, but it didn't seem to bother her.

Edwina exited the elevator and stood quietly while Clarice greeted her son and cried over him. The boy clung, his stick-like arms clutching his mother. Finally, Clarice drew back.

"I need a word," Edwina said, hoping the woman spoke English.

"Of course. Where... How did you get my son?" she asked, leading them toward an open door.

The apartment was gorgeous—luxurious and feminine in shades of rose and silver grays. The modern furniture was expensive and lovely. Edwina assumed Mikhail had paid for this, but she shoved the thought away. None of her business.

"Mikhail met with Smirnoff and made your son's release a condition."

Clarice gaped, her eyes awash with tears. "He did that? For me?"

"Because it was the right thing to do," Edwina said. "Alex is a kid. It's not fair to involve him in this mess. We suggest you take your son and leave. Is there somewhere safe for you to go? Somewhere that Smirnoff won't find you?"

"I want to stay here. Mikhail—"

"Mikhail won't change his mind about you," Edwina said, girding herself against the blast of jealousy that struck her.

"Who are you?" Clarice demanded.

"Mikhail's wife," Edwina said sweetly. "Leave here and make a new life for yourself and your son. Mikhail will be busy, should you try to contact him."

Clarice's chin lifted, and it looked as if she might argue.

"Stop," Edwina snapped, raising her right hand to emphasize the order. "I'm telling you now. Mikhail is unlikely to alter his opinion because he can't trust you."

"Smirnoff kidnapped Alex from his school. I had no choice. They would've killed Alex if I hadn't followed their orders."

"And now they have Mikhail," Edwina snapped. "Leave

or not. I don't care, but you won't see Mikhail again. Should someone abduct Alex a second time, we won't offer help. We have enough problems without you adding to them."

"Mikhail wouldn't do that to me. He wouldn't force me to leave." Clarice allowed smugness to play across her red-painted mouth.

Edwina snorted. "I believe he told you he won't pay for the apartment any longer. Protect yourself and your son. Take him to a doctor and find a place where no one knows about your past. Where would Smirnoff take Mikhail?"

"Probably to his country estate," Clarice said. "I believe that's where he held Alex."

"Thank you." Edwina made for the door.

"I... Thank you," Clarice said, sounding as if she hadn't wanted to express gratitude to Edwina. "Thank you for returning my son."

Edwina gave a clipped nod and stalked to the elevator. A few minutes later, she joined Ivan and Gregory.

"That woman is delusional if she thinks I'll allow her near Mikhail again," she muttered when she slid into the rear.

"I thought she might try that," Ivan said.

"I told her Mikhail had a wife, but that didn't seem to impress her much. She might discount my advice to leave, but if she cares for her son as much as she claims, she'll travel far away from the Smirnoff family."

"She has always behaved as if her beauty gives her the power to take whatever she desires," Ivan said. "I admire her beauty, but I don't like her."

"To be fair, she loves her son, and her betrayal was understandable. But yes, I gained the impression she was out for herself." Edwina leaned against the seat, fear writhing in her chest. "Will they keep Mikhail alive? He'll refuse to help, and Smirnoff's son won't accept this slight."

"He's a canny man, but he has misjudged the situation," Gregory said. "Mikhail will need to keep his wits about him because the son is a bully and a hothead. He doesn't like to work, yet he covets the money and prestige the family business offers him. He won't want to lose his position."

Edwina rubbed at her tired eyes. "We need to break Mikhail out of there as soon as possible. Tonight. The longer he's in their clutches, the more dangerous it will be. Will anyone else have the layout and security details? Or does Mikhail have the floor plans or access to them?"

"You have a cool heady, missy," Gregory said.

"My falling to pieces won't help anyone," Edwina said. "I'll have plenty of time to crumple after we've made a plan to retrieve Mikhail."

"Mikhail's grandfather is familiar with the estate," Ivan said.

"All right." Edwina paused. "We should check with Mikhail's grandfather and learn what he knows of Smirnoff's plans."

Gregory did a U-turn and headed in a different direction. "We'll check on the old man before we return to Mikhail's estate."

"Has Mikhail told him about me?" Edwina asked.

"Mikhail told him he'd married, although I doubt he

171

believed this marriage occurred," Ivan said. "He has always wanted Mikhail to return to the fold and blames his son for the break from his friends."

"Well, it's time to introduce myself," Edwina said.

Ivan and Gregory shared a concerned glance before Ivan addressed Edwina. "Can we visit the old man with you? You might need our backup."

Edwina's eyes narrowed at the faint quiver of Ivan's lips. "Something you're not telling me, boys?"

"He lacks respect for women. No man of his generation has time for strong women," Ivan said, his words chosen with care.

Edwina snorted. "Right. Well, let's see what happens when he faces me."

16

Edwina wasn't sure what she'd expected, but it wasn't this frail old man who looked as if a strong wind might send him aloft. He sat on an upright chair, the arrogant tilt of his head and the distaste digging into his features suggesting he still considered himself the family boss.

He surveyed her intently, his brown eyes narrowed and alert. Another thing shocked her even though Mikhail had told her. This man held not a drop of shifter blood. Not even a hint.

"What do you want?" the old man demanded.

Okay, so no small talk. Worked for her.

"Your friend Smirnoff kidnapped Mikhail," Edwina said.

The man surveyed her with distaste. "Who are you?"

"Mikhail's wife," Edwina said. "Smirnoff intends to force Mikhail to do his bidding."

The old man cackled. "The boy is stubborn. Takes after his mother. I told my son he was a fool to marry someone from another part of the country—no matter how beautiful and fascinating. He didn't listen. Look at the mess now." He didn't wait for Edwina to comment. "At least he is with Konstantine and in his proper place. The boy will thank me once he is in charge."

Edwina doubted that, and another thought occurred. Crap. She hoped that whatever they'd drugged Mikhail with wouldn't impede his tiger or worse. On the plus side—it took a lot to flatten a shifter. He'd likely awaken more quickly than a human.

"Mikhail doesn't want to run the Smirnoff empire. He has one of his own," Edwina said. "Is he at the estate out in the country?"

"You won't get close enough to rescue him. If Mikhail is smart, he'll accept his fate. He'll marry a woman of his station who can aid him in his duties." He sniffed, his nostrils flaring. "A woman with more class than you."

"Wow, that burns," Edwina said. Mikhail might decide many things, but she'd have something to say if he tried to ditch her. He was her mate, and she'd claimed him. Mikhail would marry another woman over her dead body.

"You refuse to help us," Edwina said.

"Mikhail is in his rightful place." The old man sneered. "He is the heir to the empire. Get out and return to the hole you crawled out of. If you go now, you'll stay alive."

"You threatening me, old man?" she asked.

"Leave before I call security," he snapped. "Mikhail was mad to chain himself to someone like you."

Words tickled the tip of her tongue, but she reined them in. The old man didn't want to hear anything she told him, would never approve of her. Fine, she'd rescue Mikhail without his help.

"Let's go," she said to Ivan and Gregory.

They piled into the vehicle and drove away from the house.

"Mikhail told me his grandfather was a human, but I expected a hint of scent from him spending time with shifters," she said. "Some sort of awareness. Why didn't you explain how dangerous he is to Mikhail? He'd use his grandson in an instant."

"It was a test," Ivan said with a heavy heart.

"What sort of test?" Edwina's tone was snotty, and she didn't care. They were past secrets and distrust. She was a shifter with as much to lose as Mikhail, Ivan, and Gregory.

Ivan sighed. "Mikhail's father was a human, and his mother a full-bred shifter. They were mates and tried living without each other. It didn't work. Alexi knew his father would try to take advantage of the shifters, and he promised his wife he'd keep her secret. Mikhail's grandfather disapproved of the marriage and ignored his son until Mikhail's birth. Around that time, Mikhail's grandfather became too ill to manage business affairs from his bed. He was furious when he learned Alexi had turned his back on his Bratva roots. Alexi made no secret of wanting out. It caused hard feelings within the family, but Alexi stuck to his decision, and his wife supported him."

"What happened when Mikhail started shifting? How did they keep the secret from the old man? He doesn't strike me as stupid."

"Mikhail isn't dense, either. Alexi and Sasha trained him from an early age. He understood he must guard his tongue while in his grandfather's company. His family on Sasha's side helped to train and mold him into the man he is today."

Mikhail had confided little about his mother's family, but he had mentioned a grandmother. "The grandmother who helped arrange for Mikhail and me to meet—she is definitely a shifter?"

"Yes," Ivan said. "Most of Mikhail's workforce are shifters or others. We have a few humans, but they have worked for the company for a long time and keep our secrets."

A plan formed in Edwina's mind—probably the only way to grab Mikhail. She didn't expand on her idea but twisted and turned it in her mind and poked at it for weaknesses. "Should we worry about the drug they gave him playing havoc with his shifter?"

"Yeah," Gregory said. "At least they don't want to kill him."

"Yet," Ivan said with a grimace.

Edwina shoved at her plan again. "Mikhail's grandfather is old and frail. What sort of leverage will they use when he dies? He won't last forever."

Ivan snorted. "Who knows how their minds work? Smirnoff is desperate for his legacy to survive. I mean, how the hell do they expect to control Mikhail? Or force him to do something he loathes with every particle in his body?"

"Smirnoff might rule the Bratva, but no one said he

didn't possess the crazy gene," Gregory said.

MIKHAIL WOKE WITH A hell of a headache and no clue about his location. Despite instinct shouting something was wrong, he remained still and cast out his senses, gathering information. The last thing he remembered was...

Hell, he had nothing.

He batted back his panic and attempted logic. When he heard nothing except his pounding heart, he cracked open his eyes.

He lay in the center of an enormous bed, crisp cotton sheets beneath him. Navy blue. Once confident he was alone, he lifted his throbbing head and took stock. A sheer curtain billowed inward, buffeted by the breeze drifting through the open window. The sweet fragrance of flowers, the freshness of greenery, and a faint hint of furniture polish wafted through the air. His stomach released a demanding rumble. Food. A meaty richness filled his next breath. He turned his head to spot a tray bearing covered plates.

A sense of unfamiliarity emerged as he observed his surroundings. Where were his books? His wallet? His sunglasses? Alarm surfaced in him, and his breaths quickened, his pulse racing.

Mikhail willed his whirring brain to focus. His name... His name was... He frowned. How could he not recall his name?

An image of a massive tiger flitted through his mind, and his scowl deepened. What was wrong with him? Why was he in this room? His mind stalled, no further answers forthcoming. He swallowed to moisten his dry mouth and pushed to a sitting position. He wore navy blue trousers and a pale blue shirt with no tie. A watch encircled his right wrist. It was late afternoon.

Someone knocked on the door and entered before he decided how to act. *Attack.* The weird tiger in his mind pushed the order through him, but his limbs behaved like heavy weights when he tried to maneuver. He backed up, every muscle tense, his mind racing with questions, with a trace of panic.

His visitor was a woman, but he didn't recognize her. Straight, honey-blonde hair framed her oval face, and her wide, almond-shaped brown eyes sparkled with vitality. She blinked on seeing he was awake and flashed him a bright smile.

"Mikhail, darling, you're awake."

Darling? Mikhail? Okay, that was one question answered. He edged away when she came at him, her arms outstretched. He'd never met this woman. Maybe her eyes were familiar, but nothing else about her jerked his memory into gear.

"Who are you?"

She froze, those brown eyes of hers widening. Surprise washed over her face. A hint of shock.

"Mikhail, I'm your wife. How are you? Papa told me you were in the motor vehicle accident, but the doctors thought you'd be all right." She burst into a flurry of movement, approaching him again. "Let me see your head. Papa said there was a slight bump above your right ear. Nothing more. Should I summon the doctor again?"

"No," Mikhail said, an edge of fear striking him. *No doctors.* "I feel fine."

"But your memory." Her expression told him she didn't believe him.

He didn't recall an accident. He shot a glance at the woman. What was her name? He searched his mind, and nothing...

"How long have we been married?"

"Six months," she replied without hesitation.

The striped beast in his mind growled, the sound audible, and he blinked. No, the growl had come from him, not the tiger. He focused on his wife. This woman smelled different—wrong—and this unsettled him. He caught a trace of flowers, acrid cleaning liquids, and lavender from her clothes. A touch of soap and sunshine perfumed her hair.

"Mikhail, perhaps we should cancel tonight's dinner if you're not feeling well. Of course, we've invited people to celebrate Papa's birthday, and some have already arrived. Papa is excited, and he's accepted you as a son-in-law. We've been waiting for his approval." She winged him a look he couldn't decipher. "Papa was against our marriage, but you won him over. I'm proud you've worked to win his trust." Without warning, a sob tore from her, and Mikhail's heart twisted weirdly. He hated seeing her upset. Worse, he had no damn clue what her name was. Perhaps he should've asked when she entered the room. Now it was awkward.

He frowned at her bowed head. "I have a headache, but I'll be fine once I shower. A tasty meal and an afternoon nap, and I'll be in fighting condition for the dinner."

Her smile was instant, broad, and relieved before fading. "Are you certain?" She worried her bottom lip. "My brother says you want to cause trouble for Papa's big day. To hear Pavel talk, the accident was your fault."

"Your brother is a dick." Mikhail racked his brain, and nothing about her brother came to mind.

This room wasn't familiar. The entire situation screamed wrong, yet an explanation for his apprehension eluded him. He wanted to ask questions, but his teeth clacked together, instinct propelling him to caution. He'd wait until he learned more and would piece the clues together soon enough.

He indicated his crumpled clothes. "Should I have a shower now, or should we go for something to eat and drink? I'm thirsty."

The woman smiled, relief clearing her expression.

Was it because he wanted to leave his room or for another reason? Wait, why weren't they sharing a room?

"We should go now," she said.

Mikhail opened the bedroom door before glancing at the woman. Her name still escaped him, but he might work it out if they encountered other people. Hell, where were they? He offered his arm, and bright approval lit her face.

Relief, yet tension, too.

Yes, something else lurked beneath the murky surface,

and he'd understand it—once his brain unscrambled.

Mikhail let the woman guide him, interpreting each subtle move of her body, his instincts helping him. He inhaled but angled his head away, ostensibly to scan his surroundings. He searched for anything that might scream familiar. Sights, smells, or sounds.

Disappointment struck him when they reached a lounge. Still nothing recognizable. Glasses clinked and the low hum of music and chatter filtered to him when they paused in the doorway. The conversation stopped, and the group of mainly women stared at them. Mikhail offered a polite nod before surveying the room.

Everywhere, in every direction, soft fabrics and polished surfaces screamed wealth. Statues stood tucked in alcoves, and his shoes sank into the thick woven carpet with each step. Simple and elegant and beyond the means of most people. Mikhail instinctively understood this.

Once they entered the lounge, the woman—her name still a mystery because it hadn't leaped magically into his memory—glided away to ring a bell. Almost instantly, a servant arrived, pushing a trolley.

"Will you take your tea by the window or the conversation pit, Miss Bridget?" the woman asked. She was neat in her black uniform, with her soft brown hair swept into a knot at the back of her neck. She hovered while waiting for Bridget to decide.

Bridget.

The name wasn't familiar, nor was the stonking big engagement ring and wedding band on her left hand. Surely, he'd recall the ring since he'd given it to her. Not even the slightest memory of a kiss or an embrace came to him. He was a man. He liked sex; if he were involved with a woman, he'd want to touch and kiss her. She'd smell like him. If he cared for her, she'd imprint on his soul. They wouldn't resemble strangers. His gaze darted to the rings on her right hand and lingered while his mind chased in circles.

A new arrival claimed his attention. A man who was shorter than him. He had piercing brown eyes and brown hair so dark it would appear black in some lights. The man bore a sullen expression, bringing instant wariness to Mikhail. Even the strange tiger roaming his mind bristled, which reinforced the emotion writhing inside Mikhail. *Take care.*

While the man wasn't familiar to him, Bridget's cheeks lost color upon seeing him.

"Pavel," she said, her tone neutral. "Papa didn't mention you were visiting."

Mikhail remained silent, watching their interaction.

"I wanted to say hello to you and your husband," Pavel said smoothly, yet icy disdain radiated from him in contradiction to his words.

Bridget's hands trembled before she clasped them together. Pavel spotted her distress, and his mouth curved upward.

Mikhail crossed the room to join Bridget. "Since more people are arriving, we'll take our tea over there," he said, gesturing at a grouping of chairs and a large coffee table.

"Yes, sir." The servant wheeled the trolley over to the area.

If Mikhail wasn't mistaken, the servant disliked being in the same room as this Pavel. A man to watch, then. He hated men who preyed on women, using them while considering them far beneath him. Mikhail paused, not knowing where his thoughts came from but instinctively accepting them as truth and part of his fabric.

Another two men entered the room, one much older and stooped, fatigue weighing down his shoulders. Mikhail inhaled to catch his scent and frowned. This one smelled familiar—that biting aroma of sickness. His face was almost gray as if he had overdone things today.

His gaze swept the room, alert and watchful despite his physical fragility. "Ah, my daughter and my son-in-law. My son, too, joining me for afternoon tea. How lovely." His gaze rested on his son for the longest time.

Mikhail sensed the underlying current. All was not well between father and son, but they played games and pretended the opposite.

They sat around the conversation area, and Bridget picked up the teapot. She poured tea for her father and brother before glancing at him. "Darling, did you want tea, or should I ask the kitchen for a cold drink?"

"Tea will be fine."

She bit her lip, which seemed a habit around him, and gave a jerky nod. Her hand trembled as she poured milk into a cup and added tea. She handed him the cup and poured another for herself, adding a slice of lemon instead of milk.

"Papa, would you like something to eat?"

"One ham sandwich," her father said, making her smile

with approval.

"You can get me sandwiches and pie," her brother ordered.

"Can you not get them yourself?" Mikhail said. "Let your sister relax and enjoy her tea instead of waiting on you."

Pavel spat a curse under his breath. Mikhail didn't hear what the man said, but his father, seated closer, had no problem. He barked an order in Russian, ordering him to pull in his head.

Mikhail ignored them and grabbed a plate. After considering the treats, he placed a jam tart and a sandwich on a plate. He handed it to Bridget. She appeared startled but accepted the food.

"Thank you," she whispered.

"No problem." Mikhail helped himself to a plate of food. His stomach gurgled loudly. "My apologies," he said when everyone stared at him. "I'm hungry."

"Eat," the elderly man said. "It's gratifying seeing a healthy appetite."

Mikhail ate a sandwich in two bites and reached for another before picking up his tea to take a sip. He paused because he didn't take his tea or coffee with milk. He didn't react but stuffed the information away to mull over later. Shouldn't a wife know how he took his tea? And shouldn't she be more comfortable with his presence, his touch?

Something wasn't right, and he needed to learn why this place and these people were foreign to him. Despite the rings, Bridget didn't seem a comfortable wife.

He wasn't sure what game these people played, but

they'd learn he was a worthy opponent.

17

BACK AT THE MANSION, Edwina, Ivan, and Gregory settled in the lounge on black leather seats with a crystal decanter of Scottish whisky sitting on a mahogany coffee table between them. Late afternoon sunlight spilled through the open terrace doors, and nearby, a bird sang, its lilting notes filled with happiness.

Edwina sipped her drink, fidgeting and having a hard time sitting still. She should appreciate Mikhail's fine, expensive whisky with its notes of oak, peat, and smoke, but her mate was in the clutches of a madman. She set her drink down with a clink and jumped to her feet, giving in to the urge to pace. "They're not aware of Mikhail's shifting ability. His grandfather doesn't have a clue. That gives us an advantage. Where is he?"

"I vote for Smirnoff's country estate," Gregory spoke without hesitation, his brow etched with a crease of lines. "It's close to the city but secluded enough to imprison someone."

Ivan scowled. "Yeah. That affords them privacy to keep Mikhail out of sight yet use him to their benefit."

Edwina stalked across the room and plopped down to drink more whisky. "Smirnoff won't hurt Mikhail, will he? Or his family?"

"The guy is as nutty as my aunt's fruitcake," Ivan replied. "He'll use any lever necessary."

"We need to confirm Mikhail's location," Edwina said. "Once we learn his location, we can plan a rescue. Is there someone we can count on to help with an extraction? I'd ordinarily suggest limiting the rescue to us, but if they've injured Mikhail, we'll need outside help."

"We work with a security company if we require muscle. Mikhail has helped them in the past. They owe him, although normally, he wouldn't require them to return the favor," Gregory said.

If she'd been at home, she'd call on Saber Mitchell, on the two local cops, on Gerard and Henry, who worked in security. They would've done everything possible to retrieve Mikhail. "Don't you have a Feline Council to help?"

Both men gawked at her as if she had two heads.

"I'll take that as a no, then. Why not?" she asked, at a loss. Even the wolves who'd moved to Middlemarch contributed to the council.

"Tigers are solitary animals. We don't play nice together," Gregory informed her. "This made it impossible to unify, not that we tried hard."

"Then how are you friends with Mikhail?"

"We met as boys. Our relationship hasn't always gone smoothly," Ivan said. "Even now, we don't agree with everything Mikhail does—abducting you, for one—but he has spearheaded worthy schemes for his employees and those who live in this town. He has earned our loyalty."

"What about me?" Edwina asked in a faint voice.

Gregory's face lit, and his blue eyes twinkled. "We like you. You're gutsy and brave and nothing like the woman we'd imagined. Mikhail had better behave, or one of us will steal you away."

"Huh." Edwina's breath hitched, taken aback by the praise when everyone in her family typically shouted at her. The only people who'd ever given her a chance after her screw-ups were Saber Mitchell and London Drummond.

"Mikhail is your mate," Ivan said, expanding on Gregory's words. "None of us expected this might happen. You shocked him when you marked him. He envisioned a short, temporary marriage before you separated again."

A growl burst free, unbidden, and Edwina glowered at both men, but she didn't cower them, their grins merely widening.

Gregory lifted his hands in a surrender signal. "It's as amusing as hell because Mikhail thought he'd get a wimpy bride afraid of her shadow. He didn't count on you."

"Thank you," Edwina said drily.

"It's a compliment," Gregory said. "We have a chance of rescuing Mikhail because of you."

Edwina pulled a face. She drank more whisky. *Oops!* Her glass was almost empty. She needed to slow down and keep her wits about her. "What do you mean?"

"You're mates, destined to be together. You marked Mikhail." Ivan beamed at her. "Mikhail will get around to returning the favor. He's worried he's too old for you and your differences are too great. You were doing an outstanding job of persuading him otherwise. You challenge and force him to see you as more than a woman to use for his ends."

"Stop right there," Edwina snapped.

Gregory chuckled. "See. That's what we mean. You don't take crap. You're willing to fight for whatever you want and tell us to take a hike if we upset you. We're not used to that."

"We need a plan," Edwina reminded them. "The only plausible first step is to check out Smirnoff's estate in feline form during the early morning hours. Smirnoff has decent security since he's head of the local Bratva."

Gregory leaned back in his chair, his whisky cupped in his big hands. "From what I hear, he has excellent protection."

"Right," Edwina said, determination filling her. "We must gather information before we proceed. The security team you suggested, are they human or shifters?"

"Shifters," Ivan said. "One or two of them shift into birds of prey."

"Perfect." A minute later, she spoke to a gruff man and gave him the basics. She made an appointment to connect, not daring to accept anything at face value. She'd meet this shifter and use her gut to determine his trustworthiness. Ivan and Gregory assured her he was reputable, but they were discussing Mikhail's life. If something went pear-shaped and he died in the crossfire, she'd never forgive herself.

"Tomorrow morning at eight," the man confirmed. He didn't act surprised or angry or even amused at her request to meet in person. He behaved with courtesy, something she appreciated.

The following day, after little sleep, Edwina sat in the rear of an SUV. It wasn't their everyday vehicle because now, more than ever, it was better to fit in rather than stand out.

"Mr. Roscoe," she said, extending her right hand in greeting. He wasn't feline but something else, and he measured her in return. His eyes were a pale gold and sharp. The way he cocked his head reminded her of a bird, but he was a large man and towered over her. She tried to guess his shifter type. Maybe eagle? But he was so big. She wondered if Ivan and Gregory knew and kicked herself for not asking.

"Mrs. Lermontov." His handshake was firm and professional.

"I'd like my friends to listen to our meeting," she said. "That way, I won't need to repeat everything."

"Of course." He gestured them into a windowless meeting room.

She stepped inside, and the sole decoration was a simple wooden table and several chairs, their legs scraping against the tiled floor as they moved to take a seat.

"Can I get you coffee?" Roscoe asked.

"Please," she said.

Once they settled, coffee at hand, Edwina plunged straight into the problem. After meeting Mr. Roscoe, her qualms faded. His powerful, masculine presence and towering size gave her unwavering confidence.

"Konstantine Smirnoff is dying. He wants Mikhail to take over his business rather than his son, Pavel. Mikhail has refused many times, but Smirnoff wasn't willing to take no for an answer. He arranged a meeting, and we presume he drugged Mikhail before spiriting him away. We suspect Mikhail is at Smirnoff's country estate, although we haven't been able to verify this."

"You'd like us to confirm his presence and extract him if he is there?"

It was best to make her intentions clear. "I'd like to participate. I don't have experience in situations like this, but I'm smart and can take orders. My skills run to a little hand-to-hand combat training. I won't get in your way, nor will I create problems. I need to see for myself what is happening so we can stop the Smirnoff family from creating future obstacles. Konstantine Smirnoff might be dying, but he's mentally strong and determined. I refuse to let him succeed; otherwise, Mikhail and his father's efforts will have been for nothing."

Mr. Roscoe contemplated her with shrewd eyes that missed nothing. "You seem a resourceful woman. Your accent is stronger in person. Antipodean?"

"I'm from New Zealand, and this is my first trip to this side of the world. Before this, I led a rather sheltered life."

The man flashed her a quick grin of approval. "I've done business with Mikhail over the years. This marriage took us by surprise. He seemed happier..." He trailed off, suddenly uncomfortable.

"Playing the field. That is his past—if he knows what is good for him," she added, her tone much darker and edgier.

Mr. Roscoe leaned back in his chair, the wooden frame creaking under his bulk. "I have several operatives available to monitor the estate tonight. Did you need to be part of this initial reconnoitering?"

"No," Edwina said. "I thought I'd get my hands on a set of estate plans and determine a way to enter. A more productive use of my time."

Admiration flashed in him, although the emotion was so brief, she might've been mistaken. "I'll contact you as soon as we learn anything."

"Thank you. It doesn't matter how late the hour." Edwina rose before turning to Ivan and Gregory. "Was there anything I've missed?"

"Payment?" Ivan asked.

Mr. Roscoe sent Edwina a sly glance that had her spine straightening. "No payment. Instead, I want Edwina to work for me."

"Me?"

"Yes, with training, you'll make an excellent addition to my team."

"I'm studying music," Edwina said. "I've dreamed of it ever since I was a child."

Roscoe slowly nodded, his golden gaze lingering. "I'd be willing to employ you on a part-time basis."

"I'll consider it," Edwina said.

Ivan groaned. "Mikhail won't agree."

"We'll have a discussion." Edwina glared at Ivan before turning her ire on Gregory when he released an almost silent snigger. "Just as soon as we rescue his arse from Smirnoff."

Once they arrived back at Mikhail's home, she, Ivan, and Gregory went into planning mode.

"What is the best way to obtain a copy of Smirnoff's house plans? Are they on public record? Who would have a copy?" she asked.

"My cousin works for Smirnoff's architect," Gregory said. "He told me he designed the house. He was proud of his work and miffed for not receiving credit."

"Will he help us?" Edwina asked.

"I think so," Gregory said. "The management likes to cut corners, and Rome disapproves. He's biding his time while he searches for a better job."

"Right, that's your task," Edwina said. "We need to speak with someone on Smirnoff's staff, someone we can trust to give us accurate information and perhaps confirm Mikhail is at the estate."

Ivan frowned. "I don't know of anyone offhand, but I'll put out feelers."

"Perfect." Edwina booted up the laptop Ivan had procured for her. She had no contacts but was skilled with computers and discovering information. If there was anything useful to find online, she'd uncover it soon enough.

18

MIKHAIL SLEPT FITFULLY, HIS gut writhing with a warning of incoming danger. Nothing eventuated, and his low-level adrenaline had no way of dispersing, leaving him restless and edgy. He'd excused himself early from dinner, the atmosphere at the table thick enough to slice with a knife. Pavel, his brother-in-law, had glowered for the entire meal while Bridget jumped every time he'd paid the slightest attention to her. The others at the dinner table—relatives of varying degrees—had gawked throughout until he'd quivered with awareness and not in a healthy way. It was a rare specimen in a jar sensation, and he'd loathed every second.

His father-in-law showed off his perfect teeth and made Mikhail inwardly twitch. The others had smiled too, but not with the same wattage. Mikhail didn't need to be a mind reader to understand that whacked dynamics filled this family.

His family now.

He'd eaten his roast beef slowly, surreptitiously waiting for everyone else to eat each food type before he consumed his plate's contents. He took the same care with the water and the glass of red wine a server had poured for him because every instinct inside him cried danger. Mikhail spoke when spoken to and listened, gathering information to make sense of later. Instead, his mind muddled even more and drifted.

A woman's face flitted through his thoughts. She wore a teasing come-hither smile, and seduction radiated in every slow flutter of her hands and sway of her hips. Every fiber of his being told him he was familiar with this woman, yet he couldn't place her face. Did he have a mistress or a girlfriend on the side? The mystery woman evoked a profound reaction in him, emphasizing the brokenness of his marriage—the strangeness of his relationship with Bridget. Questions ate at him throughout his meal.

"How are the birthday preparations going?" Smirnoff asked his daughter. "Do you require more help?"

He'd asked Mikhail to call him Konstantine, and that jovial request had filled Mikhail with wariness. He distrusted this man. Something about Smirnoff screamed at him to run. But his head throbbed, and the lump on his skull was still sensitive, the persistent pain clouding his ability to reason clearly. The imaginary tiger—because who pictured a tiger all the time—lurked at the forefront of his mind with the woman, fretful and bristling with foreboding as if he'd become prey instead of a hunter on the prowl.

195

Smirnoff's daughter fiddled with the ring on her left hand—the one he'd supposedly given her and didn't recall. His quick glance took in the massive stone, and he barely held back his sneer of disgust. An obscenely large diamond, it was in-your-face massive. It was the ostentatious ring a gold digger would love to show off, flaunting its exquisite gleam and sparkle. The jewelry didn't fit his fiancée, who seemed nice enough—quiet and biddable, well-behaved and polite, trained for social situations, and a credit to her parents.

The mystery woman popped into his mind again. This time her animated features radiated attitude and temper. Interest filled him as he prodded his memory while the tiger issued a low purr. The man beside him jolted, sending him a wide-eyed glance and edging away. Hell, not as quiet as he'd assumed. Mikhail silently chided the strange tiger. His senses were working, but a strange disconnect blindsided him, and that made him ultra-cautious.

"Everything is on schedule, Papa." Bridget's voice held a quiver, a tic of nerves, drawing Mikhail from his musing. This woman didn't fit his vision of a wife. The feistier woman drifting into his memories brought more comfort and a trace of lust and wistfulness. He didn't want an amiable wife. He wanted one who stood shoulder-to-shoulder with him and fought at his side. One who loved him yet wasn't afraid to tell him when he was behaving like an overbearing dick. And for someone with a hole where his memories should be, he had many wants.

"Good to hear," Konstantine said. "We will run over several business matters in the morning. I need your help with a project."

He directed this at Mikhail, who nodded acceptance, despite not wanting to stand between father and son. It was apparent Pavel resented Mikhail's presence. He was brightness and sunshine in front of his father, but the moment the older man left the room, he made no secret of his hatred.

Mikhail would never display his soft belly to this man. He recognized the streak of cruelty in him and the avarice glowing in his eyes. The son wanted ownership of everything his father had earned. Easy to see his weaknesses, his greedy nature.

Mikhail would avoid Pavel and his associates and watch his back in their company.

"What time?" the son asked. "I should be there."

Konstantine smiled, but the emotion didn't reach his eyes. "Ah, but I have an important job for you. I need you to check the progress at the Plaza build and hire a crew to break ground on the Ignor project."

"I can do that." The son straightened, the resentment fading from his florid face. He'd be handsome if he controlled his drinking. Mikhail had watched the inroads the man had made on the whisky bottle. He had a decent tolerance, which suggested he drank to excess.

"I want a report of your progress tomorrow night or the next morning. This project must stay on track. That means you'll need to hire an experienced crew and push them to get the required results."

"No problem." The son ate the remaining part of his meal with gusto, but Mikhail noted the flicker of relief in

Konstantine. The son didn't, but Mikhail didn't make the mistake of underestimating him. A cornered rat fought viciously.

Now, hours later, Mikhail wondered exactly what Konstantine wanted of him. He stared into the darkness, facing the window, cracked open to let in the fresh air. Whatever it was, his decision weighed heavily on the older man.

A creak in the passage outside his bedroom had Mikhail's senses alert. He froze, hearing nothing but the tiger snarling, the inaudible sound one of warning. Mikhail slipped from his bed and hesitated before stuffing his pillow under the covers and making it seem as if he were asleep. He didn't analyze the instinct, merely following intuition before sliding deep into the shadows.

The creaking came again, this time right outside the door. Mikhail watched the handle go down and the door open. A figure dressed in black, a hood concealing their face, hovered in the doorway. Mikhail's mouth thinned. Of course, it was as cliche as it sounded. He was in the midst of a soap opera and, worse, had no freaking clue how he'd managed the feat.

Mikhail watched, listened. Waited. He analyzed with each of his senses and came up with a possible identification. Pavel or perhaps one of his friends. A knife appeared in the figure's right hand, the silver blade catching the light shining through a skylight.

Okay, one question answered. They weren't here to discuss the coming day. The figure crept toward the bed. He inhaled cautiously, casting out his senses for information.

His mouth dropped open, and it wasn't to open his receptors to better gauge the scent. It was the shock. Disbelief in his conclusion.

The figure halted for a long moment before a burst of speed took them to the bed. They raised their weapon and plunged it into the pillow with a harsh grunt.

"Wife, are you looking for someone?" The astonishment and bewilderment at the discovery of the intruder still rippled through him.

She whirled, yanking up the knife in one seamless action. He flicked on the light, not to see her better, but so there was no misunderstanding from her side. He wanted her to see his anger.

She glanced from him to the bed and back.

"Still very much alive," he said drily, "but my pillow is a goner."

Her moan of distress didn't move him. He wanted answers. He deserved them, dammit.

"Care to explain why my wife is trying to murder me in my bed? I can't recall doing anything to upset you, and surely if I had, your father or brother would've come after me?"

A tear rolled down her cheek. "I don't want a husband."

"Then divorce me. There's no need to resort to violence."

"I can't," she snapped and roughly swiped at her damp cheek. "I tried to talk papa out of this idea. Marriage to you."

Mikhail scrutinized her, wary in case she carried a

concealed weapon. "You must've accepted my proposal."

She laughed, the sound holding bitterness and not a shred of humor. "My father wants you to run the business. He admires your strength, and your principles are important to grow his legacy. He has always admired intelligence and business nous in others. Males, at least. Who does he think was doing all the grunt work, the backroom admin and cogwheel stuff that makes a business work? It wasn't his stupid son. No, it was me. I'm qualified with a degree in accountancy and business, but all I'm good for is marrying and popping out grandchildren. Males, of course."

Mikhail studied the passion on her face. The determination. Clearly, she wasn't lying about her talents, and her fury made sense if she was working to support Konstantine in his sickness.

"Why didn't you tell me? I'm a reasonable man and value each person—male or female—for their skills."

A derisive snort escaped her. "You're a man. You want the same as my father—for me to have children to secure your legacy. I'm a possession rather than a partner."

"If you kill me, your father will settle you with the next entrepreneur on his list. Or, say you get your way, and your father listens, doesn't that place you in your brother's path?"

"I can deal with my brother." Her top lip curled with distaste.

No respect between siblings, for sure.

"You should leave."

Suspicion crossed her face, turning it hard and

impassive. Interest rose in him because she'd played her part well. She'd acted frightened and cowed, but right now, she was the opposite and radiated attitude. She was her father's daughter, full of determination and grit, willing to go after something she wanted, even if it meant killing him.

"What will you do? Will you tell my father?"

"I'll give it some thought."

"You can't tell anyone." Urgency stamped her face.

"Should've thought of that earlier."

She continued to study him, her mouth pressed flat and indecision radiating from her. His wife wanted him dead. Interesting times.

Footsteps in the passage outside grabbed his attention and instinct had him turning off the light.

"Someone's coming," he whispered, his gut telling him that these footsteps didn't bode well.

She glided into the shadows on the opposite side of the room. Mikhail cocked his head when he heard something else, but this sound was outside. A large bird had settled on the windowsill and peered through the glass. The raptor took to wing a beat later and vanished into the darkness.

Mikhail shifted his attention back to his loitering visitor, unsurprised when they paused before carefully opening the door and pushing their way inside. This person—also dressed in black—strode forward without hesitation. They were bigger. *The brother*. How the hell had he landed in this nest of vipers? He pushed at his powers of recall, but it was like bashing against a brick wall. His life seemed to have begun in this house.

Mikhail switched on the light. "Something you wanted?"

The son whirled, the knife in his right hand larger than the sister's. Hatred flared on Pavel's face.

Yeah, things were gonna get nasty.

He wondered what the sister would do. Would she hide or attack him, too? They both wanted him—

The son sprang, knife extended. Only Mikhail's reflexes saved him from a nasty gash in the gut. He jumped back, balancing lightly on his feet. The tiger roared, and the sound tore up his throat and escaped. Pavel faltered and fell back, his eyes wide.

"Get out," Mikhail snapped. "Both of you."

"I'm the one with the knife," the son said, his tone snooty.

The daughter slipped from the shadows, skirting them both on her way to the door.

"What are you doing here?" the son demanded.

"Saying goodnight to my husband," she said coolly before exiting.

"Leave," Mikhail thundered, baring his teeth at the son.

Pavel retreated half a step before he halted and straightened his shoulders. A sneer formed on his lips as he raised his knife. The light reflected from the silver blade. "Why don't you make me?"

Mikhail huffed. These people were irking him. They'd both visited him with murder on their mind.

His murder.

Only Konstantine wanted him here. "Get out before I use my fists."

"If I were you, I'd watch your back," Pavel spat, but he spoiled this threat by tripping over his feet, such was his haste to put distance between them.

"And if I were you, I'd worry about my safety." Mikhail's tiger—since it seemed determined to remain in his mind—gradually relaxed when Pavel exited after his sister. Mikhail closed the door and tugged a heavy dresser across the entrance. He wanted a decent warning of any further nocturnal visitors.

19

THE TAP-TAP-TAPPING OF EDWINA'S shoes against the tile floor echoed off the walls as she anxiously marched the confines of the house while waiting for the shifter team's findings. It might take a while. Exhausted from prowling for the last hour, she retreated to her bedroom and flopped on the bed. The white ceiling wasn't doing a great job holding her attention, but she must've dropped off to sleep at some stage. Her phone rang in the early hours.

She switched on the bedside light and grabbed her phone. "Yes."

"We've located him. He's at Smirnoff's estate," Roscoe said.

"Fantastic. Can we meet later today and plan to hit the Smirnoff estate pre-dawn tomorrow?"

"Sooner is best, although they'll be expecting us. If they're not, they're idiots."

"Can you meet me at Mikhail's estate?"

"Ten this morning," he said in his gravel voice. "I'll meet you in the forest bordering the estate, in case someone is watching Mikhail's property. In the car park at the start of the walking trail. One thing, though. Mikhail should've recognized me or at least signaled. He didn't."

Edwina frowned. "What does that mean?"

"Uncertain. I'm skilled at reading people. He seemed comfortable enough, but I suspect his memories aren't intact." He paused as if weighing his words. "They've either continued to drug him or whatever they gave him originally is still active in his system."

When he didn't say more, she didn't push.

She'd learn the truth soon enough.

AT A FEW MINUTES to ten the next morning, Edwina left the estate with Ivan and Gregory. They'd decided to walk to the meeting point, and all wore active gear to give the appearance of an exercise outing. Ten minutes later, they arrived at the trailhead and took possession of a bench seat with perfect visibility of their vicinity.

"Is everything working smoothly with Mikhail's business affairs?" Edwina asked once it was clear Roscoe hadn't arrived yet. She hadn't asked since they were juggling so many balls after Mikhail's disappearance.

"The new building site had six men turn up and try intimidation tactics while I was there speaking with the supervisor," Gregory said. "When their jibes didn't work, they resorted to physical violence. I helped the supervisor chuck them off the site."

"Did they have weapons?" Edwina asked.

"Knives. One had a gun. I knocked it out of his hand before he did any damage," Gregory said.

Ivan's eyes narrowed with distaste. "I'm sick of these petty problems. It's time to arse-kick and let those in charge understand we won't take this crap. Do you know where they came from? Who was paying them?"

"They left before we grabbed one for questioning. I figured it was Smirnoff or his son."

"What if it's the son causing problems, hoping this will make Mikhail act against his father?" Edwina asked. "Or perhaps his grandfather is stirring and causing the issues. The old man is sly enough to knife Mikhail in the back."

Ivan cracked his knuckles. "It's not Mikhail's cousin. He truly has left for the US. We should arrange a tail for the son. Mikhail has tried to avoid Bratva business, but they're determined to cause chaos. Maybe we need this confrontation to stop our problems."

"Perhaps it's time to show those in charge we have teeth and claws," Edwina mused. "If we do it the right way, regular people won't witness the showdown. Those creating our problems will see otherwise and think twice about poking at shifters."

"You mean to do this so that if people blab, others will believe they're loco," Gregory said.

"Exactly. It could be done, and that might be enough to stop them messing with us," Edwina said. "Although it might be too late with the Smirnoff family. It will depend on how messed up Mikhail is when we retrieve him." After this was over, perhaps they'd go somewhere private with a beach and sunshine—where they were alone and could get better acquainted.

Her life had upended overnight, changing her point of view.

She loved music—always had, but Mikhail had become important despite the short length of their marriage. Finding a mate—the person who completed one—caused plans to change, at least from her observations of friends and acquaintances in Middlemarch. She mightn't have fought so hard if she'd understood this truth. And now was not the time for this daydreaming. It was time to focus and save her mate.

"It's a suggestion," she said. "Let's listen to Roscoe and let him voice his plan. We'll go from there."

Roscoe arrived. He paused at the edge of the shadowed forest, did a quick scan, and headed in their direction. "Good morning." He dropped onto a second bench facing the car park, acknowledging them with a curt nod.

"I spotted Mikhail early this morning, and others on my team sighted him walking in the garden." He tapped his fingers on his knee with a quick one-two beat. "I've worked with Mikhail for ten years. He noticed me, but there was no spark of recognition. Someone stood in the bedroom with him, so he might've been keeping shifter secrets private."

Edwina tried to ignore this intelligence, stuffing back her feline's testy growl. "You don't think that's the case."

"It's hard to say if they've kept him drugged or the drugs have had an adverse effect, or he might've adopted a strategy. We won't know until we speak with him."

"Will you be able to get close?" Ivan asked.

Edwina clenched her hands in her lap, battling concern. "We need him out of there sooner rather than later. Tonight."

"That's the plan," Roscoe said.

"I'm going with you," Edwina said.

"Us, too," Ivan said.

Roscoe nodded. "I thought you'd say that."

THE MOON LIT THE sky and the barrier surrounding the Smirnoff estate, the stillness of the night broken only by the gentle creaking of tree branches against the boundary fence. Scouting the area was simple, but avoiding the guards was crucial.

Leaving Mikhail in Smirnoff's clutches wasn't tenable. They had to rescue him before Smirnoff caused more damage to Mikhail and his business.

They left their vehicles parked at the end of a dirt road, a distance from the estate. Roscoe had told them they'd used this road and gone on foot to the estate, encountering no difficulties the previous night.

"How will we get through the fence?" Edwina asked, keeping her voice low.

"There's a spot at the rear of the property where the gardeners are redoing the landscaping. This has made a gap under the fence where it's possible to crawl under in animal form." Roscoe grinned. "My men tell me it's an electric fence, and touching it produces a decent buzz."

Edwina wrinkled her nose. "Sounds like fun."

"You want to rescue Mikhail?" Roscoe asked in a mild voice.

His group of six men, wolves and felines, stood apart, their expressions impassive while they waited.

"He's not safe here." Edwina read their narrow male minds. None of them approved of her presence, assuming she'd be a handicap. She made a mental note not to slip up and create problems.

"Let's shift and move out," Roscoe said. He already had two bird shifters in position to act as watchmen.

Edwina hustled to the rear of the vehicle and stepped behind for privacy. She stripped without ceremony, her mind on the mission ahead. They had this one chance to execute their plan. Failure tonight was not an option.

20

MIKHAIL STARED AT HIS closed bedroom door, confused. His heart was racing, and the headache he'd experienced since he'd woken after his illness returned like a skulking predator. He pressed a hand to his heart and massaged the racing organ while trying to take deep breaths.

After several slow inhalations, his pulse rate slowed, and the adrenaline from having his life threatened subsided. The strange tiger stalked back and forth, a restless creature in his mind. The pain levels remained about the same, but he was becoming used to the vise-like grip on his head.

With another glance at his door, he sat on the edge of his bed. His wife wanted him dead rather than working to strengthen their marriage, and she wanted control of the business. His brother-in-law wanted him dead because he wanted to run his father's mafia empire. Mikhail's mind kept sidetracking to the faint memory of the other woman—the mystery one, and every time he pictured her, his head throbbed harder. A low growl echoed through his mind, and Mikhail's muscles locked tight. What the hell? When long moments passed, and nothing happened, the tenseness seeped from his muscles.

Mikhail let out a weary sigh, overwhelmed by the situation. Earlier, Smirnoff had closeted him in his office and showed Mikhail various parts of the business. The knowledge Smirnoff gave him wasn't rocket science. Any competent man or woman could control the company. All they needed was common sense and initiative. The hard part was keeping every ball in play, but once he was more familiar with the different parts of Smirnoff's business model, the juggling would become second nature.

Smirnoff had explained his reservations about giving his son control of the business. His son disagreed, but that wasn't Mikhail's problem. But why hadn't Smirnoff considered his daughter for the position? A woman could run a business. The illegal activities and the people committing the crimes on Smirnoff's behalf might prove challenging to control. However, given how the daughter had tried to kill him, she possessed the mental toughness to run the show. According to Bridget, her father was a chauvinist.

While he was happy enough working for Smirnoff, doing so held a sense of wrongness. He prodded at his moral compass.

Yes. The illegal nature of Smirnoff's enterprise bothered him.

If he had his way, he'd reduce those activities and

focus on the legal ones. The warehouse stocking car parts and the motor vehicle side rather than the drug running and intimidation racket that brought in vast amounts of money each year for his father-in-law. Mikhail didn't like the blood money aspect of the business, the broken families when drugs grabbed hold, and the bullying of innocent business owners who merely wanted to earn enough to live. He searched his memories, and nothing jumped out to explain why he felt so strongly about the illegalities.

Not that he'd mentioned his misgivings since Smirnoff had puffed up with pride while describing the various business sectors. His grandfather and father had grown the firm, and he'd done the same. His challenge was to add to the business scope, and Smirnoff was confident of Mikhail's success.

Then there was the son. Pavel wanted to change the current situation. *Understatement.* Smirnoff had warned him of Pavel's resentment at his decision, but Konstantine hadn't given Mikhail advice on how to deal with his son. Maybe he thought Mikhail would kill him if he presented too many difficulties. Mikhail hadn't liked to ask.

The daughter was cunning, and Mikhail needed to watch his back. The brother and sister weren't the only ones who wanted him gone. Mikhail had overheard some of Smirnoff's security guards talking about him and the likelihood that lieutenants in Smirnoff's business would reject Mikhail's insertion into the company.

Restless and still in pain, Mikhail reached for the bottle of tablets the doctors had prescribed. Funny, he didn't recall any of the accident that had laid him out for over a week before he regained consciousness. Smirnoff had told him he'd hit his head hard, which was why he was experiencing head trauma. He was lucky he hadn't broken any bones and had escaped lightly. It could've been much worse.

Mikhail hadn't liked to mention a tiger now stalked his mind. He swallowed two pills before pulling on jeans and a T-shirt. He'd go outside and wander around the gardens. The fresh air and gentle exercise were the only things that helped the restlessness that plagued him. Maybe he was going mad? Then there was the woman.

The stiff jab of pain to his temple had him squeezing his eyes shut. He gasped, trying to ride the agony gripping his head. The low, furious growl that echoed through his mind didn't help his battered brain.

Mikhail rose, his foot colliding with a hard object. "Fuck," he muttered and fumbled for the bedside lamp. He squinted against the surge of brightness and the onset of shooting agony in his head.

Hell, when would his brain return to normal? Even a slight improvement would be a relief. He waited long seconds for the gnawing ache to subside before discovering the object he'd kicked was Bridget's knife.

He scooped it up and grabbed a hand towel from the en suite to fashion a sheath. Not a bad idea to take the knife with him, given the number of people who wanted him gone from this estate. He made a tie to attach the blade to his belt and walked at a snail's pace while breathing slowly to regain his equilibrium.

He opened his door and peered down the passage to check he was alone. His wing of the mansion seemed quiet, but he wasn't about to announce his presence to anyone monitoring his movements. He slipped through the shadows and out a rear door he'd discovered three nights ago. When sleep eluded him each evening, he watched the security guards and memorized their paths as they patrolled the estate gardens.

Mikhail waited until a guard passed the shadowed spot where he lurked. When he could no longer hear the man's footsteps, he strode rapidly across the night-dappled ground, avoiding the worst of the well-lit areas. To his right, an owl hooted, its mournful cry sending goosebumps across his skin. He paused for another guard to stalk past when he reached the tall pines. The man only gave the area a perfunctory scan. Undoubtedly, he wanted to return to the hut where they took their coffee breaks and played with their phones. They did a shoddy job, but Mikhail didn't mention this to Konstantine. Once Mikhail took over was soon enough.

He'd spent his wakeful hours during the night clocking them doing their rounds and picking holes in their efficiency. They barely checked the property perimeter, instead keeping close to the house. They never varied their routes nor switched up the times of their rounds. Whoever was in charge didn't run training or keep watch over his subordinates.

Mikhail enjoyed the challenge of switching between different tasks in his organization. It was the way—

His organization?

Mikhail seized that thought and pushed at it, but nothing happened. The ache in his head intensified as he struggled to recall the elusive information just beyond his reach. He pressed his fingertips into the sore spot and worked in small circles, slowly easing the throbbing. Mikhail inhaled the cool, fresh air, savoring the green fragrance from the trees, the more earthy soil, and the release of tension in his brain. He'd try to remember later because this seemed important.

With a last scan to check for guards, he left the shelter of the trees and traversed the grassy patches between the rose beds. A frog croaked in the pond he passed, although he didn't spot it. Night insects clicked, a cacophony and music to his ears. A vast improvement on the piano recital he'd had to sit through after dinner.

He followed a gravel path once farther from the house and danger of discovery. It led to a grassy meadow and a meandering stream. The tension in his shoulders released as he enjoyed the cool breeze against his bare arms and face. It had been an excellent idea to escape his room, that house, the risk of visitors bearing knives. He snorted, still unable to believe both siblings wanted him dead.

He'd almost reached the stream when an eerie sensation crept up his spine. He halted and cast out his senses while surveying the vicinity. The insects ceased chirping, and it was as if everything around him held its breath. His nape prickled harder, and self-preservation had him sliding into the nearest shadows.

A flash of black in his peripheral vision had him turning that way. It took him a second to focus, to work out what had drawn his attention. An animal, but it was acting with as much caution as him. More movement, and he finally registered it was an enormous cat.

He tried to make sense of the sight.

Not only a big cat. A black leopard.

Even as the thought crystalized, the animal inched closer, its gaze intent. Mikhail swallowed hard, his mouth dry as the creature scarcely blinked.

The chuff—a feline sound—in his head had him wincing. Of all the times for his imagination to embrace tiger stuff. Undoubtedly, he was a hop, skip, and jump from Crazy Town.

Without taking his attention from the animal, he reached for the knife still attached to his belt and slid it free.

The animal kept low and slithered close, its bright green eyes fixed on him. The tiger popped into his thoughts, and he shook his head to clear it. A mistake. The pain had him cursing, nausea sweeping through his stomach. Swallowing rapidly, he retreated, his heart slamming against his rib cage.

Instead of jumping him, the cat halted. Sat on its haunches. It cocked its head, and he swore humanlike intelligence flashed in those green eyes. The animal released a grunt that emerged faintly inquiring. The vision of a tiger paraded through his mind again. *Crazy.* Was the black cat his imagination?

Another grunt came. The same head tilting. The leopard edged closer.

"Stay away," Mikhail said, his voice shakier than he

wanted.

He hesitated to make more noise, given he was determined to avoid detection by the security guards. His gut told him Smirnoff would disapprove of Mikhail skulking around the garden like a thief in the night.

And his bloody mind was wandering. Crap, the beast—imaginary or not—was edging nearer.

He slashed out with his knife, the sharp blade slicing through the air. The creature jumped back with a pained hiss, and Mikhail smelled the blood, saw it on the steel.

"Who's there?" a gruff voice demanded.

The leopard melted into the shadows and disappeared.

"Who's there? Show yourself, or I'll shoot," the gruff voice repeated.

With adrenaline still coursing through his veins, Mikhail cleared his throat. "It's Mikhail. I couldn't sleep, so I came outside for fresh air."

"Hold your hands up where I can see them. I want to view your face."

Edwina spat out a curse as a dull ache reverberated through her side. Mikhail hadn't recognized her. She was sure he hadn't been pretending. He hadn't inflicted a severe wound, but the acrid sweat of his anxiety had blanketed him. He'd thought she intended him harm.

The shriek of a bird wheeling overhead yanked her from her troubled recollections, and she picked up the pace. The signal to abort. An unexpected whoosh of body odor had her stiffening before she stepped onto the forest path. She crouched, heart thudding while a guard stopped to pull out a cigarette. He lit it before meandering onward.

Edwina didn't move, trying to ignore the smarting on her side. The metallic scent of blood filled each of her breaths, but she hated to shift and survey the damage now, especially with guards wandering the forest. There hadn't been this many earlier, and she wondered if something had happened or if one of them had alerted the guards to intruders.

Once the guard left earshot, she slipped onto the path and headed to the meeting point. At least she'd confirmed Mikhail's presence, but his lack of recognition worried her.

He hadn't seen her in her feline form but knew what she was. He should've recognized her scent. She had no idea what this might mean. Perhaps Roscoe had seen more from his aerial position.

It took Edwina longer than she'd expected to reach the rendezvous point. Her side stung relentlessly, and her breaths came in hoarse pants. She crawled under the fence with difficulty and staggered, almost toppling, before she reached the sanctuary of the trees.

"What took you so long?" one of Roscoe's team said with a trace of impatience.

Edwina gazed at him with bleary eyes. His words registered, but her brain refused to compile a reply. It was all she could do to focus on her shift. Her transformation was sluggish, and her legs refused to hold her once she became human. They folded, and her butt hit the ground. Gasping, she remained where she was, unable to summon the energy to rise.

A huge hawk landed on the ground and shifted.

Roscoe scanned the group, his dark hair ruffled. "Who's bleeding?"

"Me," Edwina said tiredly. "Mikhail got me with his knife. I didn't think my injuries were too bad, but my legs have the strength of spaghetti noodles." She struggled to stand and failed. "You'll need to help me."

Roscoe reached her in two giant steps. "Let me see."

She lifted her arm, uncaring she was naked. Roscoe's calm and competent manner went a long way to ease any embarrassment she might've experienced.

The knife slash ran across her ribs and down to her left hip. Roscoe's probing fingers had her choking back a pained gasp.

"Did the knife or Mikhail smell wrong?" Roscoe asked.

"No. I mean, I didn't notice anything unusual. I was more surprised Mikhail didn't recognize me," she said. "He backed up and pulled his knife. I didn't think I was too close and underestimated his reaction. It was stupid, but his behavior shocked me. I don't know if he was pretending not to recognize me because a guard appeared or if he has lost his memory."

"Hmm," Roscoe said, rocking back on his heels. "You'd better help Edwina dress, and we'll take her to a medic. The injury smells peculiar, a sign the knife blade carried poison."

"Poison?" Gregory parroted.

Ivan helped her to pull on her clothes, and she appreciated his circumspect manner.

"The wound isn't deep, but Edwina's blood has an odd odor, and the flesh is red and swollen. She's healthy and, given her shifter abilities, should heal rapidly. The wound isn't healing at all," Roscoe said. "Let's move out."

"He didn't recognize you?" Ivan murmured, keeping his voice low.

"No. It was strange. They're all humans here on the estate, so do you think whatever drugs they gave him have affected his feline?"

"I don't know," Ivan said. "You're his mate. He should've instinctively reacted to you or understood you're a shifter. We'll have to try again or intercept him when he leaves the estate."

Edwina shuffled between the two men, the throbbing from the cut on her ribs echoing through her body. She hadn't wanted a mate, but now the man acted as if she didn't exist, not even sparing her a glance. She should've been happy about this situation, but it hurt like hell.

Go figure.

21

THE FOLLOWING DAY, MIKHAIL spent most of the afternoon with Konstantine running through their figures and the nuts and bolts of their business operation. Konstantine hadn't mentioned Mikhail's nighttime walk, so he figured the guard hadn't blabbed and had accepted his explanation. Some deeply held instinct told him he needed to learn about the security protecting the outside area. He had no clue why but trusted his impulse and intended to walk again tonight.

"Are you listening?" Konstantine demanded. "I don't have time to repeat everything."

"I heard every word," Mikhail said. "You're explaining your company structure."

"Yes, well," Konstantine said, his temper appeased. "It's time for a break. Organize coffee."

Mikhail obligingly rang the kitchen for coffee to be delivered to Konstantine's office. The older man clambered to his feet while Mikhail spoke with the housekeeper and wandered off to the bathroom attached to the office.

Konstantine reappeared, and with slow, ponderous steps, returned to his desk and sank into his chair. "Questions?" he asked, his features drawn but eyes bright with eagerness. Determination.

His father-in-law's face was gaunt. His skin bore a yellow tinge, while two bright red balls sat above his cheekbones. He sounded utterly spent, with a weariness that went straight to the marrow. Yet, his resolve kept him going, and he never complained.

"No, everything is straightforward. You keep impeccable records."

"When I took over from my father, the paperwork was messy. It took effort to organize everything. What you see here is the work of many years."

"Why isn't your son taking over? Or your daughter?"

Konstantine barked out a laugh. "My daughter? Huh! That one is brainless and incapable of running a business of this complexity. She has trouble choosing her nail polish color. And my son." He heaved a heavy sigh, audibly releasing his frustration. "The boy has been a disappointment since birth. He inherited his mother's cruel streak, and while I'm ruthless and act when necessary, my men accept I'm fair. My son is callous and lacks leadership qualities. The person taking power after I'm gone requires strength, determination, and an iron will. He must approach his decision-making with an even hand, harsh when needed, but never vacillating. I have watched you for years and admired your conduct. Your grandfather is one of my friends. You will be good for my daughter and produce grandsons worthy of the Smirnoff blood. With you in charge, I have no fear that everything I've built will burn to the ground."

Konstantine meant every word. This was important to him, yet Mikhail had this niggling feeling—no, not true. After his early dawn interactions with Konstantine's children, he wondered if he should walk away instead of stepping into the midst of a power struggle. Yet part of Mikhail understood the man's wish to leave a legacy.

Dragging his mind back to the present, he didn't comment on Konstantine's assertions, deciding to humor the man. "What else do you want me to see?"

"You're an experienced businessman who can turn your hand to any problem. I want to give you signing authority on my accounts." His gaze locked with Mikhail's, and a shrewdness crept into his eyes. "Don't use this right until I am no longer here. While I have breath, I prefer to authorize payments."

Mikhail dipped his head in silent agreement.

"I need your word," Konstantine insisted.

"You have it." Mikhail replayed Konstantine's assertion of Mikhail's business experience. It was true he understood Smirnoff's business-speak, yet he encountered brick walls when he pushed for memories. Those walls in his mind were far-reaching and scary. Impenetrable. Why couldn't he remember the past? Why? He bubbled with frustration but kept his expression composed.

In his memory, his life started here at the estate, but

when Konstantine spoke to him, he had no difficulty dredging up the correct responses, the right experiences to join the discussion. Konstantine had mentioned a grandfather, but Mikhail couldn't grasp a face to match the name.

The mystery woman floated in and out of his memories, fleeting and insubstantial, yet he sensed her importance. When she appeared, warmth suffused him. Happiness. Contentment. He felt whole when he thought of her, and he wasn't sure what this meant. Then there was the tiger...

Realizing he had drifted again, he found Konstantine had also gone silent. Something had upset the older man because a tear ran down his face.

Mikhail stood, and when Konstantine glanced at him, he said, "I'll sign whatever papers you want. Let me know when you're ready for me."

"My lawyer is visiting this afternoon," Konstantine said. "I will need you to sign documents at two-thirty."

"I'll be here." Mikhail offered a polite nod and left the office. No one loitered in the passage outside, and his steps slowed. Instead of returning to the main reception room where he was confident he'd find his wife or one of the many relatives who crowded the estate, he let himself out a side door leading into the garden.

A contented chuff reverberated through his mind, but his steps didn't slow, and he didn't analyze the weirdness of the strange sound echoing through his head. The pine scent tinged with flowers and grasses drew him deeper into the garden, away from prying eyes, and the two silent men who followed him whenever they spotted him leaving the main house.

Mikhail ignored their presence and kept walking until he reached the copse of trees surrounding one side of the estate. The green fragrance grew more potent, and he inhaled deeply, letting his breath and tension free. He freed his mind to drift and didn't try to force his way past the walls in his brain. A vision of the woman floated into prominence, and he clung to that, holding the image in his mind's eye.

Who was she?

His footsteps slowed, and a surprising feline purr rumbled from him. The woman wasn't a classic beauty, not like his wife. Her body appeared strong rather than feminine, and her large breasts drew his eye. She radiated strength and determination. A woman like this, standing at his side, would be invaluable, and he wished he knew her identity.

Longing crept through him—a hint of despair.

Another weird growl rattled his brain, and his two silent guards burst from the trees and raced up to him, weapons extended.

"Get down," one snapped.

Mikhail ignored the order.

"Where is the animal? Which way did it go?" the other demanded.

"It sounded like a big cat."

He discounted their orders and hiked farther into the coolness of the trees. A bird glided from a branch, attracting his attention. It was the same bird that had peered into his window. Instinct had him nodding at the bird, and he swore human intelligence glinted in those yellow eyes before it flew from sight.

Mikhail continued along the forest path and into the sunshine before returning to the main house. His steps slowed, his intuition warning him not to set foot in that house again, but he could hardly stay out here.

Sighing, he entered the front door.

A fist smashed into his face. Mikhail ducked, but not fast enough.

Pavel.

The blow crunched into Mikhail's nose and knocked him into the wall. A picture crashed to the ground, and the two guards burst through the doorway.

Like him, they hadn't thought anyone would attack him inside the house, not during daylight hours. The two men waded in and grabbed Konstantine's son, dragging him away.

"What is the meaning of this?" Konstantine asked, appearing at the end of the passage.

"He started it," the son snapped. "I want him out of here. He's not family. He's making you tired and insists on talking business when you should be resting. It should be me working with you in your office."

While Konstantine and his son indulged in a glowering contest, Mikhail gingerly prodded his nose. One guard reached out to grip his arm, but Mikhail shrugged him off and stood by himself.

"Do you require medical aid?" Konstantine asked, without taking his gaze off his son.

"No," Mikhail mumbled, although his nose might be

the worse for wear. Blood covered the hand he had clamped to his face. He headed straight for the curved stairs leading up to the house's next floor. Five minutes later, he stood in his bathroom to survey the damage. Not as bad as he'd thought. He cleaned off the blood and tested the depths of his pain. To his surprise, the throbbing was significantly less.

Strange.

Someone knocked on his door, which he'd locked against intruders. The knock repeated.

"Mikhail, are you all right?"

Bridget. None of the tension left Mikhail's shoulders.

"What do you want?" he called.

"I heard Pavel punched you. Do you need help?"

"What? A knife to the gut?"

There was a moment of silence, then a loud expulsion of breath. Mikhail imagined Bridget's expression and humor flashed through him.

"I'm sorry about that. Look, we can't talk through the door."

"Fine, but I'm searching for weapons before you get comfortable." Mikhail opened the door and stepped back, regarding Bridget warily. He was bigger than her, but he doubted he'd escape injury or death if she had a gun.

Some of his suspicion must've shown on his face because she huffed and held out both hands for his inspection. "I don't have any weapons. Check."

Not trusting her, Mikhail closed in and patted her down. Her startled intake of air told him she hadn't expected this. Once satisfied, he gestured her inside his bedroom. He closed the door and observed her as she scanned his bedroom.

"I like what you've done with the place," she said.

Huh. The lack of the room's personality had already jumped out at him. He'd wondered why he didn't have belongings. Even his toiletries had been new. His clothes and footwear, too. What man didn't have gadgets or a phone? When he'd asked, Konstantine had told him someone had stolen his briefcase during the unfortunate vehicle accident. He owned a phone now because Konstantine had presented him with one.

"What do you want?"

"Your nose isn't that bad. Papa told me Pavel broke it."

"No, it bled, but it's fine now," Mikhail said. "You avoid me unless your father is present. Why are you here? To stick a knife into my ribs?"

"We should talk."

"About whether I complained to your father?"

She winced. "I could be an asset to you. I'm well-versed in the workings of a business."

Mikhail folded his arms and leaned one hip against the wall. "How? Konstantine claims women can't handle finances and staff. He says they're more enamored with fashion and nail polish colors. How have you learned to run a business? In fact, how do I know you're not talking bullshit?"

"You don't, but those shopping trips I take aren't for gown procurement. I run a boutique and have done so since I was eighteen and bored with the social round."

"How do your father and the rest of your family not

know this? Why are you trusting me with your secret?"

She bit her lip before releasing it and lifting her chin. "I'm hoping you'll help me."

"How?" And more to the point, why should he?

"I get the impression you don't want to be here."

"You're my wife. Where else would I be?" Perhaps if he played dumb, she'd drop information. So far, everyone had acted cautiously when speaking around him. They treated him as if he had an infectious disease.

"We could work together. I want to learn the ins and outs of Papa's business. Despite what he says, I can handle the job. I might not have the right equipment between my legs, but my brain is excellent." Her hands fisted in her lap. "I can do this."

Mikhail stared at her impassioned expression and believed her. Most men would envy him. He had a beautiful wife and the ear of a man spoken of in fear and awe. This man was handing him the keys to his power and great wealth. While the business strategies fascinated him, Mikhail despised Konstantine's treatment of his employees, and the illegal sectors filled him with disgust. He'd witnessed the damage drugs inflicted on people and their families, society.

"You've told me you can do the job, but you haven't given me a reason to help you. At the risk of repeating myself, you and your brother sneaked into my bedroom and tried to kill me. Both of you. My question—why the hell should I trust you?"

"You're married to me," she said, slightly defensive.

"Ah, but you don't want me, and you'd be happy if I

told Konstantine I wanted a divorce. Not that it would make a difference. He wants our marriage."

"What about you? What do you want?"

The woman with green eyes stalked through his mind, and his heart squeezed tight. He reacted more to his mystery woman than his wife. "When did we wed?"

Her expression turned inscrutable, and his bullshit antenna pinged an alert.

"What would your father do if I told him I didn't want you?"

She cocked an eyebrow. "Ah, but I'm the perk you receive for agreeing to run his business after he dies. I'm part of the package."

"Do you love your father?"

"He's my father."

"That's not an answer. I know you don't respect him."

"Why should I? Respect needs to be earned."

He'd irked her, yet he felt no guilt. He didn't like her. Didn't trust her. "I'll think about it," he said.

She froze. "You will?"

"Yes, on the condition you don't try to kill me again."

She bounded to her feet, her pretty face ablaze with excitement. She headed toward him, intending to hug him. He sidestepped to avoid her embrace, every part of him seizing at the idea of physical contact with her.

She pulled up short, her brows rising. "Do I disgust you?"

"I don't trust you not to stick a knife in my ribs," he shot back.

She grinned. "Should be an interesting night when we

share a room again."

Not if he could help it.

22

Mikhail hadn't recognized her.

Edwina sighed hard because she didn't know what to do next. Short of knocking Mikhail out, it'd be challenging to free him from Konstantine's clutches.

"Stop worrying," Gregory said gruffly as they sat, sharing breakfast.

"It's hard not to stress. Mikhail seems content to remain at Konstantine's estate. He thought I intended to harm him." She bit her lip, exhausted, and squeezed her eyes shut to hold back tears.

Ivan briefly gripped her shoulder. "If Mikhail were in his right mind, knowing he'd hurt you would horrify him."

Edwina poured herself more tea. "The wound is closing, and the ragged edge is smoother. Whatever poison coated the blade was the problem. The healer assured me I'll recover."

Gregory growled, the snarl very feline. "It's gonna scar."

She set down the teapot. "Rather be alive with a scar than a dead leopard."

"True," Ivan agreed and reached for a piece of toast. He scraped butter over the surface. "You should stay here tonight. Let Roscoe and his team grab Mikhail."

"I can't sit here, doing nothing when Mikhail's life is at risk."

Ivan and Gregory made eye contact.

"What?" she demanded.

"Mikhail must've done something exceptional to win you," Ivan said. "You're loyal, determined, and brave. Exactly what he needs in a partner. Did you know he wanted to pacify his grandfather? He intended to keep his mistress and leave you at home."

Edwina picked up her teacup. "If he still thinks any of that will happen, he should reconsider before I make him." She paused, the urge to cry grabbing her again. "Fighting words, eh?"

"From the second he bedded you and you claimed him, he didn't give Clarice a second thought. Oh, he helped her because he's not a bastard, but when she came on to him, he told her he was no longer interested," Gregory said, pushing away his plate. All that remained was a strip of bacon rind and a smear of egg yolk.

"You fascinate him," Ivan agreed. "Your refusal to blend into the background grabbed his attention."

"What? It's been all of five minutes. He might change his mind. He might decide he'll marry Smirnoff's daughter, and once the old man dies, which won't be long, judging by his scent, he'll take over his business and change it to suit his preferences."

"That's stupid talk," Ivan snapped after dumping a spoonful of ruby-red jam on the middle of his toast. "If you think Mikhail will treat you like that, think again. You claimed him, so don't give up. We'll rescue Mikhail and fix whatever is wrong. We're his friends, and you're his wife."

Edwina sighed, her shoulders slumping because it had shocked her when Mikhail had attacked her with that knife. The ache in her ribs reminded her how close she'd come to a serious injury.

She shoved aside her fears, took a deep breath, and swallowed a mouthful of tea. "Did Roscoe say when he'd be in touch?"

"This afternoon," Ivan said. "He intends to surveil in his bird form before he contacts us. Mikhail wouldn't willingly stay at Smirnoff's estate. One, he wanted to spend time with you. And two, he loathes the way the man does business. You should know that."

"I do," Edwina said. "But this is hard. You didn't see his expression when he sprang at me with the knife. There wasn't a scrap of recognition. If I didn't know better, I'd say he was a cyborg."

The house phone rang in the distance for two rings before it stopped. Edwina tensed.

"If it were Mikhail, he'd ring our cell phones," Gregory said, correctly reading her mind.

The housekeeper appeared in the doorway, carrying the portable handpiece. "It is Mr. Mikhail's mother," she said. "She wishes to speak to her son."

Edwina winced; if she wasn't mistaken, Gregory and

Ivan reacted similarly.

"I'll take the call," Ivan said, holding out his right hand for the phone. "Sasha, how are you?"

"Don't Sasha me, young man," a woman's rich voice sounded down the line, loud and imperious enough for Edwina and Gregory to hear without straining. "Where is Mikhail? Is it true?"

"Is what true?" Ivan asked.

Edwina frowned. Had she learned about Mikhail's kidnapping?

"The notice in this morning's paper," Mikhail's mother said impatiently.

"What notice?" Ivan jerked his chin toward the pile of mail and the day's newspaper that Rita had left on the oak sideboard.

Gregory sprang from his chair to retrieve the paper.

"Mikhail's marriage notice," Sasha snapped. "I want to talk to my son."

Edwina made an inquiring face at Ivan, and he shook his head.

"He's not here right now," Ivan said.

"Where is he?"

Gregory unfolded the newspaper and laid it flat on the table. He and Edwina scanned each page and turned to the next. About halfway through the paper, they came to a social page.

"Fuck," Gregory whispered, his forefinger tapping an article on the top right side of the page.

The three gazed at the story and the accompanying photo of Mikhail and a blonde woman.

"When did Mikhail marry Bridget Smirnoff?" Sasha demanded. "Why didn't he tell me? Why didn't you tell me?"

A heavy weight settled on Edwina's shoulders, her mouth as dry as a desert. She picked up her teacup. Her hand trembled, and she gripped the cup harder to halt a liquid splash on the tablecloth.

"This isn't true," Ivan said, glancing at Edwina with concern.

"Mikhail isn't answering his phone," Sasha said. "You tell him to contact me today, or I'll descend on his house and not leave until I see him in the flesh." The call ended with a sharp click.

"Crap," Gregory said in an understatement.

"Do you think it's true?" Edwina asked, wondering if her marriage was legal. He was her mate, but—

"Your marriage was legal with witnesses," Ivan said firmly. "I don't know what crap Smirnoff and his daughter are pulling, but he can't be married to her because you're his wife."

Edwina nodded, but the tea in the pit of her stomach sloshed around dangerously, and the pain in her chest became distracting. She set down her cup and pressed on the spot with her fingers while trying to maintain control. If this weren't all kinds of warped, she'd laugh. She, who hadn't wanted a man, had mated with a tiger. Meantime, he married another woman with Bratva connections.

"What is going on?" she whispered once she had a better grip on her control.

Ivan's gaze held concern and kindness. "You know how

hard Mikhail worked to avoid entanglement in the mafia world. He wouldn't change his mind on a whim. He didn't walk into the Smirnoff family without coercion, dammit. Something else is happening here. Edwina, try to remember what Smirnoff said to Mikhail in the cafe. Every single word."

Edwina thought back, shook her head. "I've told you everything I heard. Smirnoff doesn't trust his son. He implied his son would run his business into the ground and destroy everything he'd built."

"That's what I don't understand. Why did he set his mind on Mikhail when he must've known Mikhail wanted to restrict himself to legal activities?" Gregory asked.

"Yeah," Edwina agreed. "Surely, he has known his son's weaknesses for some time. Why didn't he choose one of his men and train them? Why Mikhail?"

Ivan tapped his hand on the coffee table, his expression creased in thought. Finally, he sat back with an irritable scowl. "Only Mikhail can tell us. Getting him out of Smirnoff's clutches is a priority."

"How?" Edwina asked, voicing her frustration. "He's not leaving the estate and didn't recognize me. Who's to say he'll know either of you? He didn't acknowledge Roscoe, and they've worked together for years."

"We need to return tonight," Gregory said.

"Agreed," Edwina said. "About his mother. We should tell her the truth. Tell her that Smirnoff has kidnapped Mikhail, and we're trying to retrieve him. We want to keep her safe. She strikes me as courageous and likely to march up to Smirnoff's gates to demand an audience with her son."

"Edwina is right," Gregory said. "Sasha should remain at home. If Smirnoff grabs her, he might exploit her to control Mikhail."

"Who is gonna tell Sasha?"

"One of you should," Edwina said. "She thinks Mikhail married Smirnoff's daughter. It's best to keep me out of the messaging until we retrieve Mikhail. We can untangle the issue once Mikhail is safe."

"I'll call Sasha back," Ivan said. "Although she'll have questions I can't answer."

"Do your best," Edwina said. "She'll have faced problems when Mikhail's father changed the direction of the family business. I bet she's mentally strong. She's a shifter, right?"

"Yeah. She won't be happy about her father-in-law's interference. They don't play nice together," Gregory informed Edwina.

A trace of bitterness took Edwina unaware. Mikhail meant everything to her. He was her mate, the one her leopard craved. Edwina felt his absence like a nagging tooth, yet she couldn't shout to the world about their marriage. She shoved the emotion aside as a waste of brain power and focused.

"This is what we should do. Tell Mikhail's mother to stay out of this issue, or it might end up getting Mikhail killed. Inform her we have an excellent security team on the job, and the minute Mikhail is available, he will call her." She paused and forced herself to carry on. "Tell her he'll contact her in the morning."

"But what if we can't—" Ivan started.

"We will. The longer Mikhail is in Smirnoff's hands, the greater the possible damage. We don't know what the drugs will do to his feline, and we shouldn't wait to find out. Ivan, I'll contact Roscoe while you're speaking with Sasha."

"Edwina is right," Gregory said. "We can't let this continue. What if one of the Smirnoff family discovers his otherness?"

23

MIKHAIL DIDN'T TRUST BRIDGET but understood her resentment, her desire to brush him aside and claim leadership of her father's business affairs.

However, their marriage—that raised questions. If she disliked him, why had she married him? They had separate rooms. Why? Smirnoff wanted grandchildren and made no secret of this. The hard knot in his belly contracted, and Mikhail came to a decision.

Information.

He urgently required intelligence because everything about his position had his senses prickling.

Last night everything had become too much—he'd panicked and slashed the big cat with his knife. Heat collected in his cheeks when, in hindsight, the animal had seemed more curious than threatening.

Other things puzzled him. Why did he feel like a prisoner if he was part of the family? The guards were always loitering, even manning the office door, when Smirnoff had Mikhail closeted with him going through business matters. So many things didn't add up. Should he ask his father-in-law or his wife? Since she'd tried to kill him, he couldn't trust her. Oh, she'd told him she'd work with him, but what did he know? His brother-in-law was easier to read. He wanted Mikhail gone and didn't care how he achieved this feat.

Hell, all of this made his head hurt, but knowledge was the key. It was time to snoop, eavesdrop, and gather intelligence; failing that, he'd resort to nosy questions. Time to make nice with the aunts and uncles who treated him like an exotic pet. That had been weird, too.

But right now, he thought he'd start with his wife and ask why they weren't sharing a room like a typical married couple.

Decision made, he went in search of Bridget. He had an enticing carrot in mind to sway her to his way of thinking. Now it was time to see if she'd bite.

"WE MOVE TONIGHT," EDWINA said.

Roscoe frowned at her for a long time, lengthy enough to make her skin prickle and her feet want to shuffle. Edwina refrained from the last with difficulty and remained silent despite her urge to burble in defense of her statement.

"Why?" Roscoe asked.

"Because the longer Mikhail stays in that house, the

greater the danger. He didn't recognize either of us. That worries me."

"What if he refuses to leave?"

Edwina froze and realized her mouth had dropped open. "He won't."

"He attacked you last night and returned with the guards once you'd escaped," Roscoe said.

"If Mikhail were in his right mind, he wouldn't do that," Edwina protested. "I'm sure he'll acquiesce once he realizes the situation."

"And if he doesn't?"

Edwina's muscles tightened, and resentment filled her. But no. Roscoe was right. Just because she wanted Mikhail to leave didn't mean everything would go to plan. This was real life, not a fairy tale. "That's a fair point. What do you suggest?"

Roscoe grinned, the action so foreign, so unexpected that Edwina gawked.

"This isn't funny."

His smile faded. "No, it isn't, but I wanted to test you."

"Did I pass?"

"You did. I agree with you. Mikhail can't stay there any longer. If he were thinking clearly, he'd try to escape on his own. We know which room is his, so we return tonight. I take it you're coming with us?"

"Yes."

"How are your ribs?"

"They're healing slowly. I'll be fine."

Roscoe nodded. "We'll take extra care tonight."

"And if they're waiting for us?"

"We'll go with Plan B."

"Which is?"

"Take them out individually and get to Mikhail before the guards realize anything is amiss."

WHEN MIKHAIL SEARCHED FOR Bridget, he discovered she'd gone shopping.

"When is she expected to return?" he asked the housekeeper, whom he discovered in a cozy lounge. The middle-aged brunette shrugged, apparently uninterested in Bridget's whereabouts. Her black uniform rustled as she flicked a duster over a piece of Dresden china. "She goes out for the entire day. Will that be all?"

Frustrated, Mikhail stepped back, allowing the woman to continue her path around the sun-dappled room. "Thank you."

He strode from the lounge, his mind busily working. His headache wasn't as bad today, and he wasn't muddled. Unfortunately, that left him open to visions of the mystery woman. She stared at him with accusing eyes as if she expected him to go to her. But where? The more he wondered, the more confusion ailed him.

Pressing his fingers to his temples, he turned his mind back to Bridget, and inspiration struck. Since Bridget wasn't home, this was the perfect opportunity to search her room. But he had no idea where her room was located. Instinct had him inhaling deeply. Myriad scents assailed him, which was strange. Bridget's was among them, but if he was truly catching the residents' trails, they were too confusing for his mind to decipher. He retraced his steps.

"Excuse me. How do I get to Bridget's room?" He started to offer an excuse and stopped. The employees didn't appear to gossip or offer opinions. Instead, they crept around like terrified mice.

"Use the main staircase. The room is on the same level as yours but in the other wing. Second, no third door once you turn into the wing."

"Thank you."

Mikhail left the room, ignoring the visual holes the housekeeper drilled into his back. Long strides took him down the passage until he reached the sweeping staircase. He took the stairs two at a time and turned to the left. If anyone saw him, he'd say he was meeting Bridget.

Luckily, he met no one, but when he tried the door, he found it locked. Was she in there after all, or did she keep something inside her room she didn't want the rest of the family to see?

His room had a balcony, as did the empty guest room next door. He checked the door of the neighboring bedroom. Unlocked. Mikhail slipped inside and stilled because the clothes and footwear on the floor suggested someone occupied this room. Several computer monitors sat on a desk, their screens dark. He might've investigated them if he'd had time, but examining Bridget's room was more important.

When no one shouted an alarm, he closed the door behind him. He rapidly searched the drawers and en suite before deciding one of the younger cousins occupied this room. Next, he opened the terrace door and slipped outside. A window was open. Luck indeed. Mikhail exited the room and pulled the door closed after him.

It was a matter of minutes to gain entrance to Bridget's bedroom. This space was much neater. Mikhail took in the desk, chair, double bed, and feminine furnishings. A walk-in wardrobe contained racks of clothes and dozens of folded jerseys and sweatshirts. Another wall held myriad shoes, all stacked in shiny pairs, according to color. He quickly searched and learned nothing except his wife was neat and organized.

He searched the desk next and hit pay dirt—a folder containing photos of him. The photographer had taken the pictures at different times because he wore varied clothes and different people posed with him. Two men of a similar age, an older gentleman who carried a cane, and a woman in a red evening gown, clutched his arm and leaned close to whisper in his ear.

He swallowed hard and studied the angles of her face. The way she held her head hinted at strength and personality. Aware of the passing time, he flicked through the photos again.

Not a single name jumped out at him, but recognition flickered—at some images more than others. He replaced the photos, confident these people were important to him. Bridget or the photographer must've followed him to snap these images. He glanced at the band on his ring finger. It was shiny and caught the light. It seemed new. If Bridget was his wife, why wasn't she in his memory? Each figure in the photo was familiar, but not one of them was Bridget.

They weren't sharing a room. The ring appeared new. The Smirnoff family members treated him like an interesting specimen.

He sat on the bed to wait for Bridget's return. It was time for answers, and he hoped Bridget could help him.

THE SKY HAD DARKENED, the clouds on the horizon turning black with the promise of a storm before Bridget arrived home. Mikhail had combed Bridget's room and gone to his afternoon meeting with Smirnoff before returning to await his wife.

She'd told him she ran a business, so he doubted she'd spent the day shopping. Before he could build another head of steam, the bedroom door opened, and Bridget flicked on the light. She came to a dead halt on seeing him.

After a glance at the lock, she closed the door behind her.

"What do you mean by breaking into my room? My locked room." Her brown eyes flashed as she glowered at him. Her gaze zapped to the folder of photos sitting on the bed at his side. "You've been poking around in my belongings."

"Who are the people with me?"

Her chin lifted while defiance settled in her expression.

"Who is the woman? I know her but can't remember her name."

"I don't know." Honesty rang in her words. "Papa hasn't learned her identity yet."

"And the other people?"

"Gregory and Ivan—your school friends. The older gentleman is your grandfather, and the woman is your companion. Your mistress."

Mikhail weighed her words, matching the names she mentioned with the photos. Her response struck him as true, but the information didn't mean much to him. The knowledge didn't stir a single memory from his sludgy brain.

His gaze swept her and settled on the sparkly engagement ring and wedding band. "We're not truly married, are we?"

It was the only explanation that made sense.

The color fled her cheeks. "Yes, we are."

"What date did we marry?"

"I told you we married six months ago. You could've asked anyone here."

"The specific date," he demanded. "Where is our marriage certificate?" He had a vague idea he'd seen one and recalled placing it in his pocket. Had that been six months ago? "Where was the ceremony held? Who married us?"

"Papa has the certificate in his office."

"Why?" Mikhail fired back. "What date, Bridget?"

She stomped over to the bed and dropped the packages beside him.

"Bridget?" This time, he wanted answers. Definitive ones.

"I told Papa this wouldn't work."

"What wouldn't work?" Mikhail demanded.

"Papa is determined that you're the right person to take over from him. Pavel thinks it should be him. I wish Papa would consider me, but I'm a female, and my little brain can't run a complicated business." Bitterness coated her words, and a sense of hopelessness as if this were a sore subject. She sounded as if she'd given up on running the family business.

Mikhail pushed that aside. "What did you do to me?"

"I didn't do anything except follow Papa's orders. He's convinced he can mold you into the son he has always wanted."

"And that would be why Pavel keeps trying to kill me."

"Do you blame him?"

"I haven't done anything to warrant it."

"Ah, but you have Papa's approval, something neither of his children has," she said lightly.

"What did your father do to me?" Mikhail asked, his tone brooking no refusal.

"He has pet scientists, and they've developed a drug that steals people's memories yet leaves them highly functioning. It's useful for people who see something they shouldn't." She made a scoffing sound. "You're lucky they've perfected the drug. The earlier candidates didn't fare so well."

Mikhail stared in disbelief. He'd been right. Something *was* hinky in this house. "How is the drug administered?" He'd been careful with his food and the liquids he consumed. Nothing had tasted odd. He hadn't even understood why he'd become suspicious.

"They knocked you out in the cafe and gave you an

injection. You were unconscious for longer than they expected, and Papa thought they might've turned you into a vegetable, but when you came around, you seemed okay."

So much to unpack in those few words. Was that why he had headaches all the time? They'd told him one pain pill a day was enough, but his skull felt like it was splitting open. He'd take another tablet once he got back to his room.

"You seemed okay," she repeated.

Fury had him gripping his hands together when he wanted to wring her neck. "How long does the injection last?"

"Around a month. The scientists are working on refining the drug."

Mikhail's mouth twisted. "I see."

Her gaze met his then, her eyes wide. "Your memory is coming back."

"No," Mikhail said, his tone hard. "But I've suspected something is amiss, especially since your brother makes it no secret he wants to get rid of me."

"Pavel is an idiot. He cannot see the big picture."

"And you do? How long did your father think he could control me? What did he think might happen after he died? Who will oversee my drugging?"

"Papa expects me to carry out his wishes. If I don't, one of his friends will ensure I receive nothing from his will."

Mikhail bit back a snarl and continued his questioning. "Did the scientists do other tests on me while I was unconscious?"

"Papa was worried you might wake up and find them

poking and prodding you. He wanted you to think your injuries were minor." That was something, at least, if she was telling the truth.

"Bridget, it's time for honesty. I don't want to stay here. The security guards are constantly watching me. Your brother wants me gone, preferably to my grave. I can't trust you. Konstantine is teaching me about his business, gradually telling me insider details, yet I'm a prisoner here. Your father gives me tasks I can do here and gets other employees to do the legwork, which tells me he hasn't worked with me long enough to trust me. He's uncertain of me yet."

"Aren't you the clever one? At least he's giving you the chance to learn the business. I'm the pretty trophy wife, expected to hang off your arm."

"What happens if I demand you share my bed? Have you or your father considered that?"

Her expression turned wary, and she backed up a step.

"And if a child results?"

"I don't want children."

"They wouldn't be legitimate. So many discrepancies in your story once I start to poke and pry for answers." He still had so many questions. "What if the drug has long-term negative effects?"

"The scientists assured Papa the drug was quite safe."

"You'd be happy to take the drug each day?" When she winced, he said, "Yeah, that's what I thought."

"What do you want from me?"

"The truth. For a start, is my name really Mikhail?"

"No." She strode to the door and wrenched it open.

"Get out."

"What? You're kicking your husband from your bedroom? What about my rights?"

"Get out," she snarled.

"I'll tell your father we're having marital problems."

She whirled toward him, her eyes full of ire. She crossed the carpeted floor with giant steps and shoved him toward the door. "Get out!"

Mikhail didn't fight her fierce pushes and let her herd him to the door. On the threshold, he dug in his heels.

"We could help each other," he said. "Think about it."

24

IT RAINED, HEAVY AND unrelenting, the temperature plummeting. The surface water turned the track into a quagmire, and their vehicle skidded and slid, no matter how hard Gregory tried to steer it to the center.

"The rain will keep the guards inside," Ivan said, breaking the taut silence. "My bet is they'll make a cursory check of the grounds before hustling back to shelter. That will benefit us." He glanced at Edwina, who sat in the rear, her knuckles white from gripping the seat. "Are you positive you're up to this?"

"Yes. If this changes, I'll let you know and step back," she promised. No way in hell was she letting her mate stay in this place for one minute longer.

Ivan's phone beeped, and he studied the screen. "Roscoe and the others are in position."

"We're five minutes out," Gregory promised.

Ivan tapped his screen and pocketed his phone.

When Gregory pulled up alongside a black truck, the doors opened. Three men exited the vehicle, and Edwina saw they were disrobing, ready to shift. She followed suit. They'd already discussed their plan, and each understood their place in the rescue attempt.

Edwina shifted to her leopard form, her transformation more sluggish than usual. She centered her mind as her parents had told her during her first change and pushed away the pain. Finally, she stood in her leopard form. The others were waiting and scrutinizing her difficulties.

She released a grunt, and the others burst into action. Roscoe took to the wing, struggling against the wind before he entered the currents higher in the sky. He disappeared into the darkness, and Edwina transferred her attention to the tiger in front and their surroundings.

The hole in the fence was still present, and they squeezed through. Rain dripped off the trees and plants and plopped on her face. Thunder sounded in the distance, and a shiver ran through Edwina. Water splashed beneath her paws, and mud splattered her belly.

Ahead, one of Roscoe's shifters froze. A security guard hustled past, his body curled inward against the driving rain. A hood covered most of his face, restricting his vision, and it was clear he was desperate to escape the inclement weather.

The problem with the weather was that Mikhail wouldn't likely venture outdoors. Not in this deluge. They hadn't factored in heavy rain when they'd discussed their plan. The longer Mikhail stayed here, the worse the danger for all of them. Fear followed her footfalls as they slinked closer to the property.

Tonight, they crept nearer the house without spotting Mikhail. They paused at the garden's edge, and Edwina was positive each of them was wondering what they'd do now.

The main door opened, the quick flash of light bringing joy. Mikhail. He glanced both ways before stepping away from the house and slipping into the shadows. He didn't wear a coat, yet the rain didn't deter his determined steps.

The crunching of gravel had Mikhail pausing, then sliding farther into the darkness. Edwina detected what he'd heard—the approach of two security guards, and judging by their tension, they knew Mikhail had left the house. A hidden camera or another type of warning system?

The two men halted not far from where Edwina crouched in the undergrowth.

"Where is he?" one asked, frustration shimmering in his voice.

"No bloody idea. He hasn't tripped another of the warning systems, so he must still be close to the house."

"What are we meant to do when we catch him?" the first grumbled. "I don't see how Pavel expects to get rid of his brother-in-law. Miss Bridget and Mr. Konstantine will ask questions."

"Pavel intends to do it himself. He has a real hard-on for this guy."

"What's the husband like?"

"The indoor staff like him. Say he's a gentleman. Polite and undemanding. They say the boss is happier when he's around and holding his own against the cancer. I mean, he's not getting worse."

"Huh! I wouldn't put it past Pavel to be poisoning his father. Man's a callous bastard."

"Wait, something is moving in the trees over there. He must've lucked out and hit the blind spot."

"What are we going to tell him when we confront him? He's Konstantine's son-in-law."

"We won't recognize him at first, or at least that's what we'll pretend. Play dumb and make out we're doing our job."

The two men brushed past Edwina so closely she was positive they'd notice her glowing eyes. Concerned, she focused on the ground until both men were safely past.

Was it Mikhail they'd spotted or one of their team rustling through the bushes?

She lifted from her crouch and peered from her hiding spot. Hard to ascertain anything but shadows once away from the well-lit house.

A bird flew from the house to the trees. It landed in the branches with a loud rustle, and a curse escaped from one guard.

Edwina held back her snicker even as she understood Roscoe's message. Mikhail was loitering in the trees, and this might be their best chance to hustle him from the estate. Edwina slinked forward, listening intently for additional security. Two guards were easy to handle, but more would present a problem.

Their footsteps were loud enough for Edwina to keep track of their whereabouts without difficulty, but locating

Mikhail proved more difficult. Only when she glanced upward and spotted Roscoe did she get a clue, thanks to him pointing with one clawed talon.

She slunk cautiously along a narrow path through the trees and slowed when she spied Mikhail. He stared straight at her, his blue eyes focused on her.

"What are you doing here?" he asked in a rough voice. "You shouldn't be here. It's dangerous."

Edwina's top lip curled. It wasn't safe for him either.

Aware he might have a weapon, she padded toward him, closing the distance slowly to telegraph her intention. Mikhail stared before turning his back and retreating deeper into the forest.

Impossible man. Did he not understand this was a rescue?

A tiger approached Mikhail from his right and another from his left while Edwina trailed her husband. The others were a distraction for the guards while they focused on Mikhail. Overhead, Roscoe released a caw of alarm.

Mikhail's head jolted, his big body freezing against a large pine. He scanned, reminding Edwina of a predator. Worry seeped through her. What would they do if Mikhail refused to leave with them? When they'd discussed this, Ivan had laughed and told her not to be stupid. Now she wasn't so confident. He should've recognized her scent, at least.

He hadn't.

What the hell had they done to him?

Mikhail smelled the foreign tang seconds after the bird shrieked. The black leopard was following him, and this time it wasn't his mind conjuring false images. He instinctively inhaled, but the creature's smell wasn't familiar. A chuff from his right had his head jerking in that direction. Tiger. Another low chuff came from his left. A second tiger. He blinked hard, barely stopping himself from fleeing.

No point. They'd leap before he'd taken two steps.

Both beasts prowled closer, closing in on either side. Tigers like the one he kept imagining. Another throb speared his brain. Why was this happening to him? If he mentioned the anomaly to the doctors, they'd lock him up or ply him with a battery of tests.

The animals continued to stare with their unrelenting gazes. Magnificent beasts. One crept close enough to nudge him. Not his imagination. Not a psychotic break from reality. Sweat formed on his back, clammy yet chilling at the same time. His muscles tensed as he wondered if they'd attack. He had no weapon this time.

The beasts stood so close he could smell them, reach out and run his fingers down their stripes. A grunt sounded behind him, and he stumbled. The black leopard. Was it the same one from the previous night? It looked the same, but what did he know?

The tigers sidled closer still. Mikhail's nose wrinkled as he drew a breath of air over his tongue and through his nose. While he hesitated, working to tamp down his alarm, the pair padded straight to him without hesitation. One gave him a hard nudge, sending him two steps along the track. Subtly, they herded him toward the property's perimeter.

He walked stiffly, his knees knocking. On the bright side, they weren't trying to eat him. Yet.

Surely Konstantine would've mentioned pet tigers. The security team would've warned him about walking alone without a weapon. His vision wavered in and out, dizziness taking him by surprise. The leopard barked out a warning, and a tiger edged closer. Mikhail grabbed hold, stopping himself from face-planting.

A flashlight flickered in the distance. The tigers slipped off the path, dragging him with them to hide from the approaching guard. Well, that answered one question. The tigers shouldn't be here.

Disorientation grabbed him by the throat, throwing his thoughts into a weird place where tigers exchanged shapes, flickering from beast to human and back. His heartbeat increased to a jerky speed, and the pain inside his head increased tenfold. One tiger released a growl.

Mikhail backed up rapidly, every instinct telling him to run. Return to the house and think about this. Hell, every corner he turned in this place held danger.

One tiger stepped closer, his bulky, muscular body blocking Mikhail's path. Mikhail was vaguely aware of a bird calling, twice this time.

The tiger's growl emerged with a touch of menace, the intensity increasing when Mikhail tried to detour. Mikhail halted, his breath coming quicker. In the distance, that bird cried again. Weird.

"Enough mucking around," a feminine voice said.

Pain struck his temple, and he hit the ground, his vision darkening to empty blackness.

Ivan shifted and hauled Mikhail over his shoulder, heading for the gap in the fence even as he muttered at Edwina. "Why did you hit him?"

"He doesn't recognize us. We can't leave him here, and he wouldn't leave without a fight."

"What if you've injured him?"

Guilt slid through Edwina. She hadn't thought. She'd merely acted.

Roscoe released another of those high-pitched warnings, and they detoured, slinking into the thick bushes and hiding until the guards passed. Roscoe cried out again, letting them know the path was clear, and they hustled, joining up with Roscoe's men.

"We'll discuss this later," Edwina said before shifting back to her leopard form. Hell, Ivan was right. They'd known Mikhail wasn't functioning correctly. What if she had made things worse? Her chin dipped briefly to her chest, the guilt terrible enough that she wanted to slink away and hide.

If she'd made a grievous error, she'd live with it. Bottom line, they couldn't leave Mikhail in Smirnoff's charge. While Mikhail appeared healthy, it wasn't normal for a person to forget their past. The previous evening, he'd acted shocked. His behavior hadn't differed much tonight when confronted with Ivan and Gregory in their tiger forms. Somehow, Smirnoff had stolen Mikhail's memories. Perhaps the healer would better understand what was happening once she'd examined him.

Roscoe called out yet another warning, and they slipped into the shadows.

"Why is that bird hanging around?" the guard asked his partner. "It has been making a racket all night."

"Don't know. Perhaps it's a mating thing."

Edwina heard the man's shrug in his voice. Beside her, one of Roscoe's team silently shook. She'd bet that gem would make its way back to the boss.

Finally, they returned to the fence gap and exited Smirnoff's property. Still in human form, Ivan crawled through and dragged the unconscious Mikhail after him while Roscoe hovered above, keeping watch.

The entire time Edwina expected the security guards to notice the intruders, and this fear accompanied her back to where they'd left their vehicles. Edwina shifted and grabbed her clothes from the rear of the truck. She dressed rapidly before turning back to Ivan.

"How is he?"

"Still unconscious," Ivan said.

"He didn't want to come with us," Gregory said. "He kept trying to return to the house. Edwina did the only thing possible."

"We could've gagged him," Ivan protested.

"With what?" Gregory demanded.

"We could've ripped up Mikhail's jacket and used that."

"There were too many guards coming and going. More than last night," Gregory countered. "Edwina did what neither you nor I wanted to do."

Roscoe appeared behind them. He scanned their tense

expressions. "We need to hustle. How's Mikhail?"

"He needs the healer," Edwina said before Ivan or Gregory could reply. "He didn't recognize us, and his behavior is odd. Not like Mikhail at all."

Roscoe nodded. "I'll meet you at the healer's, and we'll talk."

Ivan placed Mikhail into the rear of the truck. Five minutes later, they were on their way.

"Fuck," Gregory said. "There's a vehicle coming."

Edwina and Ivan ducked out of sight, and Edwina kept her hand on Mikhail, but he didn't stir.

"What's happening?" Ivan asked.

"They're slowing. Damn, they're waving at me to stop. What do I do?"

Roscoe slowed behind them and got out while Gregory wavered. Roscoe spoke to the man, and Edwina heard through the window Gregory cracked open.

"What are you doing out here?" a man with a gruff voice asked. Suspicion coated his words.

"We were doing a spot of night hunting," Roscoe said easily. "In the forest over there."

"This is private land," the man said.

"No, we hunted in the public forest," Roscoe said, keeping his tone light and non-confrontational. "I checked the boundaries before we came out."

"What were you hunting for?"

"Birds," Roscoe said. "A collector hired us to capture ten local owls."

"Owls!" The man had relaxed at Roscoe's words. "I didn't hear any guns, but I figure you wouldn't need guns to collect owls."

"Nope. Killing the birds defeats the purpose."

"Did you get any?"

"Not tonight, but we've found a nesting site. I'll check with the collector and ask if he wants eggs."

The man's eyes narrowed, but he finally nodded. "You should take care driving on these roads. Don't get too close to Smirnoff's estate. Accidents happen."

Roscoe gave an easy laugh, but tension slipped into the vehicle. "The collector constantly changes his mind about his needs. We might not have this job in an hour after we speak with him."

"Drive safe," the man said, and they inched past.

"We're lucky we got Mikhail out tonight. I doubt we'd have been as lucky on a third visit," Ivan murmured. "They seem to have upped the security."

"Our problems aren't over. Mikhail doesn't recognize us," Edwina said. "What do we do next?"

25

"WHERE'S MY WIFE?" MIKHAIL huddled in the bed, with not the slightest recognition in his expression.

"He's becoming agitated," Edwina murmured, her heart aching. Her mate had forgotten he'd married her. Her throat hurt, and all the adrenaline from Mikhail's extraction had drained from her, as had the high emotions at finding him safe. Unfortunately, he hadn't escaped Smirnoff's hands unscathed. "The healer told me we should back off and give him space."

When Ivan and Gregory hesitated, she grasped their arms and hauled them from the room. They found Roscoe waiting for them.

"Has he improved?"

"No." Tears stung Edwina's eyes. "He's confused. Disorientated."

"His eyes don't look right," Ivan said.

Gregory shook his head, his worry for his friend written

into his expression.

"What did the healer say?" Roscoe asked.

"She thinks it's the drugs they used to suppress his memories and hopes he'll improve once they leave his system. He keeps requesting his wife and told me his father-in-law would retrieve him because he's important to the business. Whatever drug they've used is interesting. He can operate without a problem but has no recollection of the past." Edwina's breath caught, the knot in her throat forcing her to stop speaking. "Physically, he's okay. A few bumps and bruises, but no one has abused him."

"He's determined to get to his wife," Ivan said. "We've had to watch him closely to ensure he doesn't leave the house."

"I thought he'd be more comfortable in his own home," Roscoe said, his tone thoughtful, his golden eyes bright with intelligence. "But it occurred to me Smirnoff might send his men to search for Mikhail. We should take him someplace where Smirnoff won't think of searching."

"Somewhere with high security until the drug wears off," Ivan said.

The door to the room where they'd put Mikhail wrenched open. "Where is my wife? I want Bridget."

The surge of hope on hearing his words shrank. This was her mate, and he didn't want her or recall their hasty marriage in Scotland.

She straightened her shoulders. "Bridget isn't here. Can I help you with something?"

"Who are you?" He raised one hand to prod his temple, his face paler than usual.

"My name is Edwina," she said. "We're friends, although you don't remember me after your accident. This is Ivan and Gregory. You went to school with them; they're your closest friends." She gestured at Roscoe. "Roscoe is also a friend, although a more recent one. Is your head aching?"

"I need my special headache tablets. Bridget says I should take one each day. The doctors told her this was important for my recovery." He winced. "My head is throbbing so bad. I can scarcely think."

Roscoe exchanged a glance with Edwina. "I'll call the healer and get her to meet us at my place. Pack a bag."

"Gregory and I will stay here," Ivan said. "We'll behave normally and keep our eyes peeled for Smirnoff or his thugs."

"I have spare rooms, one of which is secure and will work for Mikhail. We don't want him blundering around the countryside in his state," Roscoe said.

A few minutes later, they departed.

"Are you taking me home?" Mikhail asked, shading his eyes against the sun.

Edwina pulled a pair of sunglasses from her handbag and handed them to him. "Yes," she said. "Put these on and rest your eyes. It might help your headache." She'd noticed him pressing his temples with his fingers. A sudden suspicion occurred. "Do you have headache tablets at home?"

"Yes," Mikhail said.

"How often do you take them?"

"The doctor told me the pills were strong and not to take more than one a day."

265

"How many have you been taking?"

"My head hurts," Mikhail said.

Possibly more tablets than was safe. "When did you take the last tablets?"

"Head hurts," he muttered.

"All right, you rest. We'll have you home in no time."

"I'll call the healer once we arrive," Roscoe said.

Mikhail didn't react, instead sat hunched with his fingers pressed to his temples.

The drive to the isolated property didn't take long. Mikhail staggered when she helped him from the vehicle's rear, and Roscoe hurried to her aid. Edwina frowned when Mikhail showed no awareness of his surroundings.

"My guess is they've been giving him the tablets to keep his memories at bay, but the pills have side effects. Either that or they have an addictive quality, and we're seeing the withdrawal symptoms," Edwina said, almost grinding her teeth together to prevent her furious growl.

"Yeah," Roscoe said. "I wish we could give the healer more information. It sounds as if Mikhail's head has caused him problems, and he has taken more tablets than necessary."

"That would explain his confusion. The first night we saw him, he seemed more with it. This time he's confused, and his head pain is bothering him."

"At least they haven't had their hands on him for long. We'll have to hope the side effects will pass."

"I wonder if there's a way of getting a pill sample."

"We could ask Mikhail for a description of the bottle, but it might prove difficult to access the estate again,"

Roscoe said. "We might source the pills directly from the manufacturer. My men have noted the recent estate visitors. We'll track those vehicles and go from there."

"Plan," Edwina said, appreciating Roscoe's help.

They took Mikhail to a guest room, and he seemed relieved to lie on the bed with his eyes closed.

"I'll watch him," Edwina said.

"I'll summon the healer and start researching the medical side." He departed, leaving Edwina to her ruffled thoughts. What was she going to do if Mikhail didn't improve?

Almost as if he'd read her fears, Mikhael cried out, his big body thrashing. "Bridget!"

Edwina's skin turned icy cold. Had he shared a bed with the other woman? A growl rolled up her throat, fierce and mean. This was her mate they'd messed with, and if she got her hands on Smirnoff, she wouldn't be responsible for her actions.

A woman arrived with a pot of tea and a plate of sandwiches and left them with Edwina. Half an hour later, the healer came.

"Take a walk around the garden," she ordered Edwina. "The fresh air will help you. Don't worry about your man. I'll take care of him."

"But—"

"Don't worry," the healer broke in with her gentle voice. "Roscoe has told me everything. I'll do tests. The drugs in his system are causing the problems. If he's no longer taking them, his shifter half should help him heal."

Edwina hoped the healer was right because if Mikhail

didn't recover, she would take down Smirnoff and his complicitous family. She'd unleash fiery hell on them.

MIKHAIL WOKE SLOWLY, HIS head fuzzy and his body stiff and sore. Dappled light came through the curtains, and he blinked against the light, his eyes ultra-sensitive. Had he drunk too much? He cast his mind back, unable to grasp specific thoughts or an idea of what had happened. His mouth was dry, his throat parched.

"Mikhail?"

The feminine voice wasn't familiar, but it held concern and caring, and he turned his head in that direction. It took him ages to focus. A brown-haired woman with bright green eyes sat on a chair near the bed. Those green eyes drew him with their familiar intensity.

"Who…" He licked his lips to ease the dryness. "Who are you?"

Emotions flickered over her face too fast for him to decipher, but uppermost was disappointment.

"I'm Edwina," she said, her accent strange to his ear. "Are you thirsty?"

"Yes." When he nodded, searing pain shot through his temples.

"And you have a headache," she added, apparently reading him better than he could her. "I'll get you a glass of water and headache tablets. No, don't move. You haven't been well and will feel weaker than usual."

Mikhail was glad to obey because his muscles twanged a

protest each time he moved. She was back in an instant and helped him to sit. White-hot pain roared through his skull, and a groan escaped him. He trembled, hot sweat coating his skin. Some of the water in the glass she held to his lips splattered over the side and onto her cream blouse. He half expected her to snap sharply because other people had when he'd vomited on them. *Wait.* The memory slipped from his grasp before he could squeeze it for truth or fiction.

"Easy," she said. "Drink slowly. There's plenty more water if you want it."

The cool liquid soothed his parched mouth and throat.

"Okay," she said when he ceased drinking. "I have something to help your headache. Let me get you another glass of water."

He sat, half-reclined and shaking, waiting for the woman's return. Weak as a cub. He gave a half laugh, half sob because he'd muddled his thoughts. The saying was helpless as a... Ah, heck. He didn't know. Not that it mattered, but he hated feeling stupid.

"Here you go." She steadied him while he accepted the white tablets from her. They differed from the others. They'd been a pale green and larger. Not that they'd helped much.

"Are these stronger than the green ones?"

"No, a different brand. We thought they might help more than the previous ones."

He would've nodded, but his head throbbed too much, and he hated to make the discomfort worse. He shoved the two pills into his mouth and, with a shaky hand, drank water to swallow them down.

"Light," he croaked.

"Is it too bright?"

"Yeah."

The woman stood and tugged across a curtain. It cut the light filtering into the bedroom, and he ceased squinting.

"Why don't you try to sleep?"

"What's wrong with me?" he asked. His mind was fuzzy and full of rippling, aching pain.

"We're not sure, but you've been having headaches. The healer suggests you sleep as much as possible."

"Yes. Tired." Was it his imagination, or was he slurring his words?

"You sleep, and I'll check on you later. Do you need the bathroom?"

"No."

"I'll fill the glass for you in case you're thirsty later. The en suite is right through that door."

"Thanks." Mikhail closed his eyes and sank into the oblivion that dragged at him.

Edwina left the bedroom, quietly locking the door after her. The last thing they needed was for Mikhail to wander off while they were making plans. She headed toward Roscoe's study and tapped on the door.

"Enter."

She pushed through the doorway and stopped on spotting several of his men with him. "Sorry, I didn't mean to interrupt."

"Take a seat," Roscoe said. "We're planning what to do

next."

Edwina slipped into a seat. "Were you able to identify the doctor visiting Mikhail?"

"Yes," Roscoe said. "He's not an actual doctor. He's a scientist on Smirnoff's payroll. I have two men in position to grab him when he leaves work."

"What's next?"

"Once we speak with the scientist, we'll decide our next move. Hopefully, Mikhail will improve soon and give us more information. We were right to bring him here. Smirnoff has his men combing the countryside, searching for Mikhail. He went to Mikhail's estate, but it was a civil visit. They bowled up to the front gate and asked to speak with Mikhail. They took Mikhail's grandfather with them, so Ivan let them inside. He told them Mikhail wasn't present, and Ivan thought they believed him. He told the grandfather he was worried because it's not like Mikhail to disappear this way."

"Did Mikhail's grandfather say anything about Bridget and Mikhail's marriage?"

"No," Roscoe said.

"Thank you for your help," Edwina said.

Roscoe grinned, making Edwina stare because it was an unusual sight. "I still expect you to work for me. You're smart and think on your feet. Most people would've frozen when someone knifed them. You kept your head and got yourself back to the meeting point, despite your pain."

"Thank you," Edwina said, the scar itching beneath her clothes. "The future is murky right now. Who knows what will happen?"

A knock came on Roscoe's office door.

"Come in."

The door opened. It was one of Roscoe's men. He wore a forbidding expression as he handed over a newspaper. "Front page."

Roscoe opened the paper on his desktop. "Bloody hell. Edwina, look at this."

26

Mikhail woke from a deep sleep with a damp pillow and a dry mouth and throat. He swallowed several times, but his mouth remained uncomfortable. With a groan, he pushed to a sitting position and spied a glass of water on the bedside cabinet. He reached for it, every muscle in his body aching. His fingers trembled when he picked up the glass, and several water droplets escaped the rim.

The liquid was blessedly cold as it slid down his throat, assuaging the dryness. His thoughts turned to the woman with the green eyes. She'd been kind to him. No threats. No visible weapons. He'd pulled a knife on her, though, hadn't he? The vague recollection of her shock slipped into his mind to haunt him, standing out among the other thoughts that knocked together and tangled him into confusion.

He drank all the water and returned the glass to the bedside cabinet. His head still ached, although not as much as it had before he'd slept. Mikhail prodded at his memories. He had a wife. Bridget.

Except, something about their marriage wasn't right. He'd learned something important...

A whoosh of air exited him, and belatedly, he winced because the huff of frustration had set off drums inside his skull. Damn, he couldn't remember. If he left the teasing thoughts alone, the answers would pop into his head when he wasn't focusing so hard. Or maybe the mystery woman could help. She didn't send tension through his muscles while Bridget...

He hadn't felt comfortable in that big house unless he was in the office with Konstantine. His father-in-law had wanted him to learn the business and take over from him.

"What did you do before?" a small voice at the back of his head asked.

Mikhail focused on that tiny voice and tried to supply an answer. The longer he tried, the worse his head hurt. His breath caught as he stood and struggled to internalize the aching throb.

The room where he'd slept wasn't familiar. He drew back the curtain and immediately let it drop, gasping at the bright eye-searing light. Mikhail stumbled around the room's confines, not recalling the furniture or the shelf of popular novels. This room, like the one in Konstantine's mansion, bore no private mementos. Despite his pounding head, the small voice told him to leave.

It was time to seek answers.

EDWINA STARED AT THE front-page newspaper story, open-mouthed and shaking her head in denial. "What do we do now?"

"First, we obtain a copy of the marriage certificate. We know Mikhail didn't marry Bridget, but if Smirnoff has bribed officials, he'll have a marriage certificate in the system. We'll check the dates against Mikhail's diary of engagements and might get lucky. My bet is the forgery is excellent." Roscoe glanced at the man who stood in the open doorway. "We need a copy of Edwina and Mikhail's marriage certificate as well."

"I'll start on that," the man said. "I'll contact Ivan or Gregory to ask if Mikhail had the certificate."

"Thanks," Roscoe said. "Report back if you learn anything new."

The dark-haired man lifted a hand in farewell and left the office.

"I presume Mikhail has a copy since the minister gave him paperwork." Edwina sighed. "Mikhail's mother is going to be a problem."

"Remain here with me," Roscoe said. "That will keep you out of Sasha's way."

"But what about Mikhail? They're saying he's been abducted and offering a reward for his return."

Roscoe checked his watch, leaned over, and flicked on a radio.

The news. Not that she could understand a word. Frustrated, she tapped her right foot while she waited for

Roscoe to interpret.

After five minutes, Roscoe switched off the radio. "The Smirnoff family says intruders entered their property and kidnapped Mikhail. They're offering a reward for information leading to his safe return. Anyone who has information should contact the police."

"None of that is true."

"We extracted Mikhail clandestinely," Roscoe said.

"Mikhail isn't married to Bridget. He's married to *me*. Smirnoff wants to regain control of Mikhail, and we can't let that happen."

Movement from behind Edwina had her whirling in her seat. Mikhail staggered through the open door, and she hurriedly jumped to her feet. She crossed the distance between them and wrapped her arm around his waist, steadying him. "What are you doing out of bed?" And how had he unlocked the bedroom door?

Mikhail tried to take a step and almost took them to the floor. Roscoe stood and used his muscle to help her guide Mikhail to a chair.

"Heard you talking," Mikhail muttered. "Needed to know."

"Know what?" Edwina asked, using her hand to feel his forehead. His skin was clammy, his cheeks red. He'd pulled on clothes but had misbuttoned his shirt, and his feet were bare.

"Head sore," he said.

"How long since he had painkillers?" Roscoe asked.

Edwina checked her phone. "Barely two hours. It's too soon for more."

"What you talking about?" Mikhail's voice slurred, his words slow, as if he was having trouble forming thoughts.

"We've been discussing your marriage to Bridget Smirnoff," Roscoe said.

"Hinky," Mikhail muttered.

He had that right.

"When did you get married to Bridget?" Edwina asked, and every word was a knife to her heart. They weren't married. They couldn't be. She knew this, yet apprehension slid through her.

Mikhail's brow furrowed, but neither she nor Roscoe pushed him to hurry his answer. Mikhail was obviously in pain and having trouble stitching his thoughts together.

Edwina made a mental note to ask the healer about a sleeping draft—something natural that hopefully wouldn't react with the drugs Smirnoff had pumped into him.

"Bridget? Dunno." Mikhail slumped in his chair, his face almost colliding with the wooden desktop.

"You need to rest," Edwina said, standing in her concern.

"No. No! Answers," Mikhail said.

"You want answers about what?" Roscoe asked.

Mikhail grimaced and ran an unsteady hand over his head. The tugging of his fingers disordered his hair, and he no longer resembled her well-groomed husband. He appeared vulnerable, and her heart twisted at his obvious pain.

"Uh." Mikhail lifted his right hand, flashing an unhelpful gesture. "Not right," he said finally.

"Let's get you back to bed. Roscoe and I will find answers for you. Right now, your job is to sleep and heal."

"Heal?" His focus was absolute, as if this was the only information he could trust.

"Yes, sleep is an excellent healer," Edwina said. "You must sleep at least for an hour. I'll come to check on you and bring you something to eat. How does that sound?"

Mikhail's frown didn't reduce, and frustration rose off him in palpable waves.

In the end, Roscoe had to help her get Mikhail back to his room.

"I'll get you more water," she said, noting the empty glass. Liquids might help to flush the drug from his system. "Here, drink this."

After he drank the water, she refilled the glass again.

"Need answers," Mikhail insisted. "Girl with green eyes, help."

Edwina stilled, her hope rising. Had he remembered what they were to each other? "I promise Roscoe and I will help you learn the truth. Your job is to rest and sleep." She hoped Mikhail understood because he seemed confused. She'd expected the longer he went without the drug, the better his memory would become, but that wasn't happening.

"If you need one of us, we'll be around. All you need to do is shout, and someone will come," Roscoe said.

"I'll check in on you in an hour." Edwina infused cheerfulness into her voice when the emotion had packed up and gone on holiday. The situation bore an irony that wasn't lost on her. She hadn't wanted marriage, and

Mikhail had wished to wed her merely as a smokescreen. Now she was fighting for their relationship, and Mikhail had no clue.

The phone summoned Roscoe, and he headed to his office while Edwina hovered until Mikhail dropped off to sleep. She finally crept from the room and searched for a cup of tea. She'd barely taken her first sip when Ivan called.

"Sasha has left. I had to fill her in on part of the story. I informed her Mikhail's grandfather had enticed Mikhail to meet with Smirnoff. Then, I told her we were still piecing together the rest but didn't believe Mikhail had married Bridget." Ivan paused long enough for Edwina to slip in a question.

"Do you think she believed you? And what about Mikhail's grandmother? She helped to engineer my meeting with Mikhail."

"I don't think Sasha knew. You do *not* want to see Mikhail's mother in a temper."

"How did you get her to leave?"

"I told her Smirnoff wants Mikhail to run his business, so her son was safe for now."

"The Smirnoff family is offering a reward for information leading to Mikhail's return."

"Crap. I hadn't heard that. Neither has Sasha." Ivan paused, and Edwina could almost hear him thinking. "I'll call Sasha and get in front of this recent development. Be upfront and tell her we're working with Roscoe. Believe nothing she reads in the paper."

"What if Smirnoff contacts her?" Edwina asked.

"Sasha hates Smirnoff. He's more likely to get Mikhail's

grandfather to call her."

"We should prepare her for that possibility. We can't tell her we have Mikhail. Not until he's more lucid. He has no idea who we are and probably won't recognize Sasha." Edwina didn't mention her disappointment at being unable to introduce herself as Mikhail's wife.

She slapped down her pique and concentrated on the immediate future. "Hopefully, once the drugs wear off, he'll contact Sasha himself."

"Yeah." Doubt rippled down the line. "I hate to say this, but it'd be better if Smirnoff died and the Smirnoffs fought a leadership battle."

"We can't lead Smirnoff here. You and Gregory can't come here. If we must meet, we'll arrange another place."

"Excellent point. The last thing we need is a gunfight with Smirnoff's people. Talk to you later. I'd better run interference with Sasha before she jumps into this mess."

"Good luck," Edwina said and disconnected.

Roscoe had finished his call, his expression grim. "Smirnoff knows we have Mikhail and wants to make a deal."

27

Edwina gasped, her heart hammering her rib cage. "Does he know, or is he guessing?"

"He called me," Roscoe said.

"What's our next move?"

"I've called in my aerial team, and they'll keep watch to give us an early warning," Roscoe said. "Short of taking out Smirnoff, I'm unsure what to do."

"Can we pay someone to take him out?" Edwina asked.

Roscoe grimaced. "It doesn't seem sporting to kill a man with limited time left."

"That might be our sole option. Leave a power vacuum and let them battle it out within the family."

"I'll speak with my team. Maybe one of them will have a bright idea to solve our problem."

"You heard that Mikhail's mother is...concerned about her son and demanding answers."

"I've heard she's a force to be reckoned with."

"I'm not sure Ivan can hold her off for much longer. Mikhail is still sleeping, but his headaches worry me. Could I contact the healer for something stronger than our painkillers?"

"I'll call her because I'm worried. I thought if we removed him from Smirnoff's clutches, Mikhail's feline would do the rest."

"I thought the same."

A raucous bird call sounded overhead.

"Crap," Roscoe said. "They're here."

"Smirnoff?"

"Someone from that house. Can you shoot?"

"Weapons aren't a thing in New Zealand. I can use a knife and fight hand-to-hand. That will have to do. Let me check Mikhail first."

Edwina hustled to Mikhail's bedroom and found him asleep. Good. That made things easier. She closed the door and hoped like hell this situation didn't turn to custard.

Edwina found Roscoe in consultation with two of his men—feline shifters like her. She listened carefully even as her pulse raced. They had to keep Mikhail safe.

A car pulled up outside, and Edwina glanced out the window. A woman climbed from the vehicle. Tall with blonde hair swept up in a casual knot, she wore black trousers and a tailored white blazer. The sun caught on her hand and bounced off her rings. Edwina's stomach bucked with foreboding.

"Is that Bridget Smirnoff?" Edwina asked. The woman walked with confidence and arrogance as if the world owed her. Edwina grimaced at the plain cotton trousers she wore with a black T-shirt. Ah, well. She couldn't do anything about it now.

The woman rapped on the door, and the knock sounded authoritative.

Huh! How could a summons to enter have authority? She was overthinking this, but one thing was certain. She didn't intend to hand over her mate to keep the peace.

"Is she alone?" Roscoe asked.

"Cass hasn't called a warning to say otherwise," one feline said.

"She drove the vehicle," the second shifter said. "If you're letting her inside, we can do a thorough search and let you know."

"Do that," Roscoe said. "Don't let her see you."

Edwina and Roscoe waited for the men to leave via the rear door. The knock came again.

"How are we going to play this?" Edwina asked.

"We'll let her in and see what she wants," Roscoe said, holding his head a fraction to the side. To a human, the way he did this would be a quirk, but it was a birdlike gesture and denoted watchfulness. Nothing got past this man. "We'll treat her like a guest until we learn otherwise but take care. She's a Smirnoff."

"Why don't you let me answer the door? I don't know if she's expecting a woman."

Roscoe gestured for her to go ahead, and Edwina strode to the door when a third, much louder knock rattled the door.

"Hold your horses," Edwina said. "I'm coming." She opened the door and went on the offensive. "What is your hurry?"

Bridget looked down her nose at Edwina and pushed past her. Edwina let her, but her temper pulsed with dislike. This woman had taken one look and decided she was the hired help.

"Miss, I don't know who you are, but please, what do you want? I have a lot to do, and I don't need rude visitors interrupting me when I'm trying to work."

"Where is the owner of this house?" Bridget demanded.

"Harold Oldham?" Edwina asked, needling Bridget.

"I wish to speak to Roscoe."

"Why?" Edwina asked.

"No business of yours," Bridget snapped. "I demand you get Roscoe for me. *Now*."

"Why?" Edwina persisted. "It's my job to keep undesirables away."

"He has something that belongs to me."

"I see," Edwina said, her temper burning. She did *not* like this woman. "Why don't I show you to the lounge while I see if Mr. Roscoe is available?"

"Tell him it's urgent," Bridget snapped.

"This way." Edwina maintained an impassive expression as she opened the door to a formal lounge and stood aside for Bridget to enter. The other woman brushed past her, elbowing Edwina on the way.

Edwina closed the door with a loud snick and sought patience with a deep breath. People like Bridget Smirnoff thought that having money meant they didn't require manners. She sucked in another breath and unclenched her hands before returning to Roscoe's office.

"You have something that belongs to her," Edwina said.

"Huh," Roscoe said with a faint grin.

"I seem to amuse you," Edwina said. "I've noticed your lips curving three times when you hardly ever crack a smile."

"Why don't you check on Mikhail, then come and join us? I'll keep the important conversation for your arrival."

"Fine." Edwina strode along the passage and noiselessly opened the door to Mikhail's room. He was still asleep, breathing deeply and evenly, and she took heart from that. She closed the door and retraced her steps. Murmured voices came from the lounge, and she stepped inside.

"No, we don't want refreshments," Bridget snapped. "Go away and let me speak to Roscoe."

"I'm not your slave." Edwina walked farther into the room and took a seat opposite Roscoe.

"You let the hired help listen in on your private conversations?" Bridget's glare was hot enough to singe Edwina's hair, but Edwina didn't cower. She had dealt with her grandmother, and it would take more than Bridget sniping at her to make her turn tail.

"How can we help you?" Roscoe asked.

Bridget cast her a scornful look before focusing on Roscoe. She stretched her lips into a smile, but it was patently insincere.

Neither Edwina nor Roscoe spoke. Instead, they waited for Bridget to get to the point.

"My husband is missing," Bridget said finally.

Anger rushed through Edwina so fast and forcefully she felt dizzy. Mikhail was her mate. *Hers.* And this

285

woman was not going to get her grubby hands on him. She'd protect him with everything she had while he was vulnerable.

"Did you want to hire us to find him?" Roscoe asked.

Bridget made a rude sound. "I'm not stupid. You're a close friend. I think Mikhail disappeared because of you. You're hiding him from me. *His wife*." She thudded her hand against her chest, her gaze fierce.

"He's not your husband," Edwina said, unable to hold her tongue any longer.

"Who are you?" Bridget demanded.

Edwina ignored the question. "You're not married to Mikhail. You're telling everyone you're married, but it's a lie."

Bridget angled her chin, her gaze full of ire. "We exchanged vows six months ago."

The woman didn't enjoy being challenged. Maybe if she poked and prodded, Bridget would become angry enough to blurt out helpful information.

"Where did you marry?" Edwina shot back. "Who designed your wedding dress? Why wasn't your marriage reported on the social pages?"

"I don't have to answer your questions," Bridget spat.

Edwina noticed the bright color appearing on the other woman's cheeks. Excellent. Her plan was working, and when she glanced at Roscoe, she received a slight chin lift. His lips twitched, and a sense of comradeship filled her. She belonged here. Bridget did not.

"Perhaps he decided he'd made a mistake," Edwina said.

Bridget bared her teeth. "We love each other."

A snort escaped Edwina before she could halt it because this was a big fat fabrication. Mikhail loathed everything the Smirnoff family stood for. Crime paid for Bridget's designer clothes and expensive jewelry.

"Mikhail isn't at his estate. My father's men have checked and spoken to Mikhail's mother. She doesn't know his location, and I believe her. She was upset. You're Mikhail's friend, and you know where he is. If you don't take me to him, I'll inform my father, who will take matters into his own hands. He won't display my patience."

"Is that a threat?" Edwina asked.

"A promise," Bridget said sweetly.

The door opened behind Edwina without warning, and her heart sank when Mikhail ambled inside. He appeared more alert than earlier, despite his crumpled clothes.

"Mikhail!" Bridget was on the move and throwing herself at him before Edwina could react. She curved her arms around his neck and pressed close.

Edwina's leopard growled, low and mean.

"Steady," Roscoe said in a low voice.

"Mikhail, I was so worried. You disappeared without warning, and no one knew what had happened to you." She kissed his cheek.

Mikhail met Roscoe's gaze, and Edwina saw the second Roscoe's shoulders relaxed. Then Mikhail angled in her direction, and his eyes widened. "Edwina, you're here. I thought I'd imagined you." He shook off Bridget, and every bit of tension seeped from Edwina. He remembered her.

"Who is this woman?" Bridget demanded.

"I'm his wife," Edwina said, her tone sweet. "His actual wife."

Bridget took half a step back, then halted her retreat. "Mikhail, I'm your wife. Tell her."

Mikhail scowled at Bridget. "What the hell are you talking about? We've never met in person. Edwina and I are married. She's my wife."

Edwina's relief was so great that she swayed for a moment. He'd remembered. The drug had left his system, or at least most of it had. Currently, his brows squeezed together in confusion.

"You're Bridget Smirnoff. Why are you here?"

"Because you're my best chance at freedom and gaining everything I want," she snapped, and in one smooth move, she pulled a gun from her handbag.

Mikhail stepped in front of Edwina. "What the devil do you think you're doing? Why would I help you? Your father is a pain in my backside."

"Those drugs worked," Bridget muttered, but she hadn't counted on acute shifter hearing.

"What drugs?" Mikhail demanded, his brows drawing together.

"Do you remember meeting Smirnoff at the cafe?" Edwina asked. She wasn't positive about how much he recalled.

"I think so. Yesterday?"

"No, it was almost a week ago," Roscoe said, his attention fixed firmly on the gun. "Edwina and I, plus some of my team, have been searching for you ever since. Smirnoff drugged you in the cafe and took you to his estate. He told you that you'd married Bridget, and as his son-in-law, he wanted you to take over his business."

"What the hell?"

"We are married," Bridget butted in with a trace of almost panic.

"Smirnoff is teaching you the intricacies of his business and expects you to run the business when he passes," Roscoe said.

"That's true," Bridget said. "You promised you'd teach me the complexities of my father's business."

Mikhail lifted his hand to his head, his fingers pressing into his temples. Edwina watched with concern. He hadn't recalled everything. But at least he remembered they'd married. That was something.

"And this is all about you," Edwina said, not trying to hold back her sneer. Mikhail owed the Smirnoff family nothing. "You would've killed him with the drugs you gave him to conceal his memories and wouldn't have cared. All you want is to get your way."

"Do you want my brother to take over the family business?" Bridget asked. "I'd be much better and do an excellent job. You must help me."

"You've already done enough damage," Edwina said. "Put the gun down before someone gets hurt."

In answer, Bridget squeezed the trigger.

28

EDWINA CRUMPLED TO THE floor after two rapid flashes and loud reports from the weapon. Another shot, and Roscoe dropped.

"Stop! Give me the gun," Mikhail demanded, cold sweat forming on his back. *Edwina had to be all right. She was his mate. His other half.* Anger took over and the urge to wring Bridget's scrawny neck. "Look at what you've done."

Bridget's face paled, and the hand clutching the gun shook violently. While her father and brother were involved in crime and violence, she was not. Her inexperience showed, but her jaw had set with her determination. She blinked rapidly, her mouth working. No words emerged.

Mikhail spiraled between anger and soul-sucking fear. He sucked in a panicked breath, and the coppery scent of blood tainted it. His legs trembled, and snarls of fury filled his head, butting against the painful and tender spots in his brain. He staggered, almost face-planting as he stumbled toward Roscoe. Mikhail crouched beside his friend.

"Return to the estate. You must help me," Bridget cried.

"Why?" Mikhail spared her a scathing glance before he pressed his fingers to Roscoe's neck. His pulse thumped beneath Mikhail's fingers. He huffed out a deep breath. Roscoe would recover. But Edwina... He crawled across the floor, unsure his legs would support his weight.

"Stay away from her," Bridget ordered. "She is unimportant."

Hell, no! Mikhail ignored Bridget, his pulse thrumming louder than his panicked feline. The *bang, bang, bang* in his ears overpowered everything. A sick sensation swirled through his belly on seeing the pool of blood around Edwina's head. He couldn't lose her, not now.

Fearing the worst, he turned her over. Blood trickled from a wound in her shoulder while a small dart protruded from Edwina's arm. He yanked it out and whirled on Bridget. "What have you done?"

"She was in my way," Bridget said.

"She is my wife," Mikhail thundered.

"She means nothing. My need is more important. Please, I'll give you anything. Help me."

Rapid footsteps sounded in the hall. A man cautiously poked his head around the corner. One of Roscoe's men.

"Call a healer," he ordered.

The man retreated. Bridget relaxed a fraction, lowering the weapon. A mistake on her part because Mikhail sprang with a furious feline yowl. Two men darted through the doorway.

"No!" Bridget shrieked, but the three men overpowered her, despite her thrashing and litany of curses.

"Watch that weapon. It spat darts and bullets." Mikhail scrambled to Edwina, not hiding his urgency and desperation now. His breath stuttered as he felt for a pulse. *There!* A faint, thready beat.

"What did the gun fire at her? What drug is it?" he demanded.

Bridget shrugged. "Don't know. Don't care. She was in the way. I hope she dies."

The healer and her assistant rushed into the office.

"Edwina first. Roscoe has a stronger pulse. Bullet wound in her shoulder and darted with an unknown drug," Mikhail said.

"Your memory has returned." Satisfaction filled the healer's words, although she focused on Edwina. Her assistant busied herself with Roscoe.

Mikhail stood, pausing to stabilize his balance. "What drug does the dart contain?" he asked Bridget. Those vicious growls ripped through his head again, and he ached to hold his skull and beg for mercy. *Show no weakness.* The rumble subsided, and the pain lessened. Mikhail breathed again.

"Mikhail, it isn't too late to return to Papa's estate. Untold riches and power await if we work together. Please, Pavel mustn't learn of this. We must leave now. Now that she's gone, we can work together. We'll make excellent partners." She wrenched free of her captors and sidled closer to press her breasts against his arm. "In all ways."

Mikhail let his disgust show. "Lock her up where she

can't escape. Smirnoff's organization can implode from the inside. I want nothing to do with it." He turned his back on Bridget. Edwina remained unconscious, although it looked as if the healer had halted the bleeding.

"I'll do tests to ascertain the drug then dig the bullet from her shoulder. Young man, your wife won't be happy when she awakens. She bears a scar from your knife, and now a bullet wound."

"Mikhail! Stop. You must help me. Please. I beg of you."

Mikhail whirled on Bridget, fury scraping him with sharp talons. "*I owe you nothing.* My memories are fuzzy, but you are *not* my wife. Take her away."

Roscoe issued a throaty groan.

"He's coming round," the assistant healer said.

Tension eased from Mikhail when Roscoe sat up without aid. His vision was blurry because he rubbed his eyes and blinked.

"Bridget shot you," Mikhail said. "It was an experimental weapon and fired darts and bullets."

"My focus is shonky. Shadowy." He rubbed the back of his neck. "Hell. Brain, too. What happened?"

"Bridget arrived. Don't know why. Do you know?"

Roscoe started to speak and came to a befuddled halt. "No."

"Maybe one of your men will know," Mikhail suggested because he had nothing, and they needed information. "I'll speak with them. Will you take care of Edwina? Bridget darted her and shot her."

"Go," Roscoe said. "I'll watch things here."

"Weapon?" Mikhail asked.

Roscoe pushed upright with a groan. He lumbered to his desk and pulled out a key. He removed a picture from the wall, opened a safe, and handed Mikhail a gun.

"You remember my men? Don't shoot them by mistake." He lowered his voice. "They're shifters and will heal, but bullet holes will shorten their tempers. If you fire, make certain of your target."

"I will," Mikhail promised and checked the safety.

"It's loaded." Roscoe gingerly prodded his scalp. "Someone is banging inside my head with hammers."

"Know the feeling." Mikhail didn't linger. He strode through the house, instinct giving him directions. The various scents aided him, and he accepted the knowledge without question.

Several men loitered in front of the cottage. They glanced at him and stood straighter, but not one of them pulled a weapon. *Roscoe's men.*

"Roscoe can't recall what happened and why Bridget Smirnoff came. Did he tell any of you?"

"Edwina and Roscoe met with her. Bridget demanded your return to the Smirnoff estate. She expected you to teach her the business and continue to work with her father. That's all I heard before the gunfire." His brow crinkled. "The discharge wasn't loud."

An experimental weapon in Smirnoff hands. Not ideal for their opposition. Had they used it on him? His memories were damn fuzzy, and Roscoe demonstrated similar symptoms. He concentrated and only fragments of the last week made sense. The harder he pushed to fill the gaps, the fiercer his headache.

"Thanks," he said. "Roscoe is awake, and the healer is attending him. His memory is spotty, but he'll survive. What happened to Bridget?"

"We've locked her in a secure room," a shifter replied.

"Excellent. I have ideas, but I'll run them past Roscoe first." Mikhail returned to the house and sought Roscoe. His housekeeper had made Roscoe and the healers hot drinks. "How is Edwina?" he asked. She'd bled way more than a shifter... His thoughts trailed off when he recalled the tiger who'd haunted his mind. *He was a shifter.* A roar almost deafened him. He winced before realizing the sound had been internal. Mikhail pictured an animal, and claws burst from beneath his fingernails.

"Stop!" Roscoe barked.

The tiger image burst, and the claws receded. Mikhael's breath came in hot pants, panic at the control slip bursting over him.

Mikhail glanced at the healers, who were whispering together. The older one set down her tea and hurried from the room with the younger one on her heels.

"Edwina?" Mikhail murmured, staring after them.

"Wait until their return. They assured me she'll recover. She has regained consciousness, but Margot told me she displayed confusion. My memories are still hazy."

"I am a tiger shifter," Mikhail said, gazing at Roscoe. "Until now, I'd forgotten."

Roscoe's brow puckered. "But your shifter half?"

"Was present, but I didn't understand. Thought I was crazy."

The younger healer entered the room. "She is asking for

you."

Mikhail sped down the hall, his long strides propelling him toward Edwina.

Edwina sat, propped up by pillows. Her face was pale, but her smile lit the room. It lit him. Mikhail was at her side in seconds.

He grasped her hands. "How are you?"

She stared, tears shimmering in her beautiful green eyes. "You remember me?"

"You're Edwina, my beloved wife."

"I'm not your marked mate," she snapped back.

"Ah! There's my feisty lady." Mikhail laughed, his joy ringing out. "Because I'm a foolish male," he said. "The minute this is over, I will remedy the situation. How are you? Is your feline healing the wound?"

"The hole is knitting together but will leave a scar. Mikhail, what should we do? We can't leave Smirnoff's business to implode because our people might suffer in the explosion."

Mikhail frowned. "What do you propose?"

"Ever since my mind started working better, I've tried to fashion a way to turn this situation to our advantage." She bit her lip. "One solution came to mind. Return to Smirnoff's estate and wait until the old man succumbs to his illness. You must learn the business inside out and teach Bridget. Show her how your companies function, and if she goes outside the law, that's not on you. From this morning and things I'm remembering, she's desperate to run the business. I suppose her father won't consider her because she is a woman?"

"Correct," Mikhail said.

"Make a deal. Tell her you'll teach her if she leaves us, your businesses, and employees out of her schemes. This is the nonnegotiable condition for teaching her. If she backtracks later, we'll destroy her."

Mikhail froze, his brows rising. Shock flared through him like a shooting star as he gaped at his wife. "But Bridget and her father have told everyone she and I are married. What about you? What about us? What if Konstantine lingers?"

"That might present a problem," Edwina agreed. "When I saw Smirnoff last, he was haggard and smelled of illness. You could tell Bridget you'll give her a maximum of three months and no longer."

"What about her brother? Pavel is a hotheaded loose cannon. This situation is a bomb waiting to detonate. It might kill us all."

"I know," Edwina said. "But if we make this sacrifice our future will be safer, our lives stable. Our children and their children will have decent lives without Smirnoff family pressure. If an unknown takes over Smirnoff's organization, the problems might intensify. At least Bridget is a known quantity."

"Edwina is right," Roscoe said. "Her idea, while radical, will have lasting benefits for everyone. I volunteer to act as your security guard. My contribution to this plan."

"But what if they kill me? Or Bridget takes you out in a jealous rage?" Mikhail voiced his greatest fear.

Edwina's chest heaved, and she closed her eyes. When she reopened them, he could tell she'd come to a decision.

"I'll return to Middlemarch. Once Konstantine dies or the three months end, contact me."

"But we're newlyweds," Mikhail protested, overwhelming dread seizing his mind. "I want to mark you, claim you as mine. Spend time with you. Love you."

"This is for your family, your employees, and those who count on you to keep them safe. This is bigger than us." She reached for his hand and laced their fingers together. "Besides, it might be fun to play my grandmother. She deserves everything she gets."

"But what about your music?" Mikhail asked, desperate for a different proposal. "I promised you could hire teachers and take courses."

Warmth filled her smile as she studied him. "I'll find an online course or a short one I can finish while you're helping Bridget. I'll continue with my music writing."

"This is a crazy idea. Are you certain?"

"Yes," Edwina said. "If I'm safe and your mother stays away from the Smirnoff family, you'll focus on completing your mission."

"It's a sound plan," Roscoe said, placing a hand on Mikhail's shoulder. "Once you're finished with the Smirnoffs, collect Edwina from her home and bring her back so she can work for me."

Mikhail grumbled, taking heart from Edwina's grin.

"Stay alive, Mikhail," she said. "If you die, I'll end up alone and write songs of lost love that will depress everyone."

"Once this is over, we'll honeymoon," he promised. "We'll go somewhere quiet to enjoy each other's company."

"Promise?" Edwina said.

"I promise." Mikhail pulled her into a loose embrace. His lips met hers, and he kissed her. He heard a faint grumble from Roscoe, but he didn't release his wife. Her touch soothed him and cleared his confusion. The door opened and closed—presumably Roscoe leaving, but he didn't stop kissing his wife, holding her.

Edwina was his beloved wife. His soulmate, and he wanted to remember this moment to sustain him until they could be together again.

29

EDWINA SAT ON THE deck of the holiday cottage she'd rented for her visit to Middlemarch, a guitar in hand and a notebook sitting on the wooden table to her right. The winter sun held welcome heat, and a hint of spring danced in the air. She picked up her drink bottle and sipped her water. Although she hadn't heard from Mikhail, Roscoe had fed her snippets. Not that they reassured her. Every day Mikhail stayed in that vipers' nest, the more she stressed and worried. According to Roscoe, Pavel had attacked Mikhail twice before Bridget had ordered a hit on her brother. She hadn't heard more, and every email or message from home sent her stomach swirling and tension stalking her mind.

Edwina yawned and grimaced. Sleep did not come easy these days, and the bed felt empty without her mate. "Mikhail, please stay safe," she whispered.

A car pulled up at the security gates, and Edwina

groaned. Her grandmother. *Again*. Periodically, her grandmother visited Edwina to order her to return home and cease her childish behavior. *At her age, she should have a husband. How could she afford to stay at this place? It was expensive.*

Edwina rose and hit the button on her remote to open the gate. From the moment Valerie McClintock climbed from behind the driver's side, her glasses lenses glinting in the sun, Edwina vibrated with tension. She respected her grandmother, she did, but sometimes she hated her.

"I've arranged an outing," her grandmother said, her chin jutting with determination. A wave of familiar lavender perfume drifted to Edwina. "Todd Fisher will pick you up at six for dinner."

Edwina silently counted to five. "He can try to collect me, but I won't be here at six."

"Why not?" her grandmother demanded. "Never mind. Make tea and tell me in a civilized fashion."

Civilized. Wow! Her grandmother had a cheek. She was the one who'd barged in without an invitation.

"I've run out of milk," Edwina said with petty glee. Oh, she was bad. "It will have to be black tea."

Her grandmother winced. "I suppose lemon will do."

"Sorry, no lemon either," Edwina said, not even bothering to suggest she run to the office and ask for milk.

"You're older now," her grandmother said in a strident voice. "And should prepare for all civilities. You require a job and a husband."

Same old. Same old. "Grandmother, please call Todd and tell him I'm not available. Not tonight, and not any night. I have other plans, which I would've told you about if you'd bothered to ask."

"You're wasting your life. Since you arrived home from the gathering, you've stayed here. How can you afford it? All you do is play your stupid guitar."

Edwina sucked in a breath. "That is not all I do. I've started an online music degree. Coursework and assignments take time. Sometimes, I help Emily at the café and babysit for Isabella."

"You should have your own children," her grandmother fretted.

Edwina preferred to wait, spend quality time with Mikhail, complete her music degree, and enjoy life first. Not that she'd discuss this with her grandmother. Children were a topic for her and Mikhail. Her grandmother's input was unnecessary. She reminded herself to visit Gavin in his clinic for another contraception shot.

"You haven't visited your parents," her grandmother said.

Because Edwina was still angry at them for acceding to her grandmother's wishes. She pressed her lips together and gripped her temper.

Her grandmother frowned. "You said you didn't meet anyone at the gathering. Suzie met a billionaire."

She'd met someone too but couldn't tell her grandmother he was working on a hazardous project, and she'd come home to spare Mikhail worry over her safety.

"I know," Edwina said. "Suzie and I speak with each other most days."

"He's a bear," her grandmother said.

"I'm looking forward to meeting Suzie's husband in person. We've spoken via video calls."

Her grandmother pinched her lips together, and Edwina almost smiled at the telltale thud of her forefingers against her plaid skirt. Suzie had a billionaire husband—a successful businessman—while Edwina was hiding in this cabin and babysitting other people's children.

As always, she sent silent prayers skyward for Mikhail's safety. He was doing this to keep his employees safe and people like Clarice and her son.

"Edwina! Are you listening to me?"

Edwina started and blinked. *Mikhail had to survive.* "Sorry, I was wondering about my assignment."

"Music of all things. It's not even useful. You can't sail through life with your head in the clouds."

"Yes, Grandmother," Edwina said, tired of the verbal game. She wanted to complete her assignment and check the lyrics Suzie had emailed.

"I'll expect you at the family dinner on Sunday," her grandmother said in her no-nonsense voice.

"Yes, Grandmother."

"Wear something nice," her grandmother added.

Edwina cursed under her breath. When would she escape the matchmaking? She'd contemplated telling everyone about Mikhail but didn't want nosy questions. Had they fought? Did his family disapprove of her modern ways?

She'd known this separation would be difficult, but a fulfilling marriage without trust and safety was impossible.

If that meant waiting while Mikhail did this vital job, then so be it.

Since her grandmother seemed to want reassurance, she dipped her head. "Yes, Grandmother." But she visualized wearing tight jeans, a top that exposed the curves of her breasts and a leather jacket along with spiky heels. That delightful vision and her grandmother's probable reaction kept her smiling cheerfully until the elderly woman departed.

SATURDAY AFTERNOON, MIDDLEMARCH

Edwina returned from training with Isabella, her entire body coated with sweat. They'd gone for a run first. Even though her legs had quivered from the exertion, she'd completed an entire Isabella workout afterward without complaint.

She recalled Isabella's faint praise with satisfaction. "You've improved."

Roscoe's offer intrigued her, and although she'd discuss it with Mikhail, she thought she'd accept a part-time job. It would give her a break from her songwriting and music course and might even offer inspiration.

Edwina stripped off her clothes and dumped them in the laundry basket. She'd turned on the shower when she heard a knock at the door. The temptation to ignore the summons was strong, but it was probably her mother or grandmother, and they'd spot her rental car. Sighing, she grabbed her robe and left the bathroom, belting the garment as she hustled to the door. A peek out the window had her frowning. She didn't recognize the vehicle. The red sedan looked like a rental. Perhaps one of the new guests had taken a wrong turn?

The knock came again, more insistent.

"Great timing," she muttered, stomping to the door. A familiar pine scent hit her seconds before she flung open the door. She let out a girlish shriek, clapped her hand across her mouth in consternation, then she was in his arms and burrowing against his bulky warmth.

"You're here." She touched his face, reassuring herself he was solid. "Is it done? We won't have trouble from the Smirnoff family?"

"It's done," Mikhail said, his expression soft and full of tenderness.

She tugged him inside and closed the door. "I've been with Isabella, doing a training session. I was about to get in the shower."

"I've come straight from Dunedin Airport," Mikhail said. "I'd be happy to share a shower."

"Do you have clothes?"

"I'll get my bag in a minute. First, I want to kiss you." His big hands slid down her back as if he couldn't stop himself from touching her.

She clutched his broad shoulders. "I can't believe you're here."

"Ivan gave me your letters. I read them on the plane," he said. "I was hoping we could manage a honeymoon in Tahiti before we fly home."

"Yes," she said, standing on tiptoes to kiss him. She'd

make it work.

Mikhail took over the kiss. It was romantic, and everything she'd ever dreamed of. She fell into the magic and happiness, almost giddy knowing that this test of their relationship was over and they could start a life together for real.

Mikhail pulled back, his eyes glowing with his feline. "Why don't you start your shower, and I'll grab my bag and join you. Do you have plans for this afternoon?"

"I promised Isabella I'd babysit for her and her husband. They're dropping their son Kian off, and he's staying overnight."

"No problem. We'll have time for a snooze first?"

Anticipation spread in Edwina. "We will. I intended to take Kian for a run once it gets darker."

"I'd enjoy that," Mikhail said. After another toe-curling kiss, he slipped outside to get his luggage.

Edwina grinned after him, her fingers pressed to her swollen lips. She dashed to the shower and stepped under the warm water, washing away the perspiration lingering from her workout.

Mikhail appeared in the bathroom, clad only in his boxer briefs. "I left my bag in your bedroom. Is that okay?"

"Yes! I've missed you." Edwina nudged open the shower door and gestured for him to enter.

"We'll have time to catch up," Mikhail said, shucking his underwear. "Lots of time."

Edwina grimaced. "I have a family lunch tomorrow."

"Excellent. I look forward to meeting your grandmother."

"She doesn't know about you," Edwina said.

"Yet," Mikhail said with a grin.

Edwina grabbed her facecloth and squirted a blob of citrus body gel onto it. She rubbed it over Mikhail's chest, admiring his muscles, despite his dropped weight. "Were you able to avoid more doses of the drug?"

"Yeah, the drugs were in the headache tablets they gave me. Bridget and I decided it was best to pretend I was taking them, which is what I did. I was careful about what I ate and drank. It helped that Bridget understood I'd walk if anything went wrong. She wanted control so badly she ensured my safety. It was easier once Pavel wasn't part of the equation."

Edwina gestured for him to turn and cleansed his back. "She arranged her brother's death. That's cold."

"In the end, she shot him herself," Mikhail said. "Although he didn't say much, I think Bridget went up in Konstantine's estimation. He still doubted her ability to run the business, and I taught her in private."

"Will she stick to her end of the deal?" Edwina asked. "I'm not her fan."

"I might disagree with her decisions, but she's honorable in her own way. Bridget won't interfere with my business or allow her people to upset you. She admired the way you stepped back and allowed me to help her. She wouldn't have done the same."

He smiled down at her. "I've looked forward to this day. I don't know what it is about you, Edwina. You crept into my heart and disarmed me with your mental strength and bravery. I missed you, more so once the drug wore off properly, and I remembered everything."

Edwina kissed him lightly on the lips and exited the shower. Mikhail turned off the water, and she handed him a towel.

"I love you, Edwina."

Heat and gladness fused in her body. "Yeah?"

"Yeah. I can't believe my blind luck in finding you. When I think what might've happened—if I'd allowed Clarice to sway me. I would've lost the greatest treasure I possess."

"We're together now."

"We are." It sounded like a solemn pledge.

"Are you hungry?"

"I'd prefer to make love to my wife and claim you, so no one will make the mistake of believing they can steal you away."

"That wouldn't happen."

"I refuse to give any man a chance." Mikhail rubbed the towel over his chest and back, his gaze not leaving hers. Then he dropped the towel and stalked closer. He swung her into his arms and headed toward the bedroom.

30

EDWINA CUDDLED CLOSER TO Mikhail, her feline as deliriously happy as her. She loved him and had tumbled into this state early in their relationship. She'd worried about becoming a mere wife with no power, and while change would occur, Mikhail would compromise. Of this, she was confident. They'd discuss their path together.

Their naked bodies rubbed in delicious friction, and Mikhail cupped her buttocks and drew her nearer until she pressed against his hot, hard arousal. Edwina's pulse thundered as she nipped his bottom lip and savored his scent, his closeness.

His growl made her laugh. This was how sex should be—full of fun and satisfaction. A shudder worked through her body as he explored her mouth. Their tongues danced together, and they climbed a path to deeper arousal and pleasure. His fingers traced her jaw before drifting lower to rub the fleshy part where her neck and shoulder met. Another shudder, laden with joy and anticipation, stole through her.

"Edwina," he whispered.

"Mikhail."

His rumbly laugh brought a smile to her lips. She rolled, pushing him into the mattress and letting him take her full weight. She laughed, which held triumph until he lifted her and took one nipple into his mouth. The first draw sent pressure rampaging through her, and she gasped, aware of the emptiness between her thighs. He held her in place with effortless strength, teasing her until she moaned.

"Ah, Edwina. I need to taste you." Before she could reply, he had her on her back and her legs splayed. Seconds later, his mouth was on her sex, licking and sucking and making her tremble with awareness. It wouldn't take much for her to topple into climax.

"Need you inside me," she whispered. "I've been waiting for over three months. I crave your hard cock pushing inside me, filling me."

Mikhail let her hips touch the mattress again. "Do I need to use a condom?"

"No, I visited the clinic yesterday." She stilled. "Do you mind?"

"We have plenty of time."

Their lips met in a tender kiss. He notched his cock to her and pushed inside. Their unified groan had her grin widening.

"Does that feel better, sweetheart?"

"Deeper," she ordered. "Yes, that is perfect."

Mikhail withdrew, then surged back into her until he could go no deeper. She felt the pulse of his cock. He rocked gently against her while his hands glided down her back, and fingertips explored her curves. Every inch of her skin he stroked tingled.

The delight intensified when the shivers collided with the sensations inside her. Edwina gasped, her mind turning a weird corner.

"I thought heroines in romantic novels who shout or gasp in ecstasy were silly and a figment of the author's fertile imagination."

Mikhail halted, buried deep within her, his eyes wide and startled. She wriggled against him, kissed his tanned throat, the intensity of her pleasure growing when her stirring massaged a tender spot deep inside her.

"Please move."

He shook his head, a grin flirting with his lips. "We will discuss romantic heroines as soon as we finish."

"Mikhail."

Thankfully, he responded by moving faster, thrusting harder into her as they strove for a shared climax.

A shared climax. Edwina choked back a laugh that tried to emerge as a scream because she was certain most women didn't screech in pleasure either. Noise might wake the kids or neighbors, but each stroke had her inching closer to satisfaction. Ripples of intense bliss coursed through her body, bright color streaming behind her closed eyes. Mikhail held her tight, his release echoing hers as they reached their peak.

When their heartbeats quieted, they cuddled, their

breath mingling as they lazily kissed. His powerful arms enveloped her, and she felt warm, safe, and loved in his embrace. She ran her fingers through his hair and neck before deepening the kiss. He pulled away, only to rest his forehead against hers with a contented sigh. Edwina felt connected more than ever, but one tiny thing bothered her. He hadn't marked her yet. She gave the thought a violent nudge until it dislodged and floated away. Mikhail cared for her. He'd traveled from Russia to collect her when she was certain he had important business. A man didn't sacrifice for a woman he didn't care for.

She hid her insecurities and rushed into speech. "I missed you and worried Bridget would go against her word. That she'd knife you in the back or her father would linger for months. Selfish, I know, but I hated the idea of losing you before our marriage started. And just so you know, Bridget wouldn't have survived if she'd hurt you." Edwina meant every word because Isabella would've helped her.

Mikhail brushed the hair from her face. "From the moment you marked me, I looked at you as mine rather than a means to an end. Once we learned how far Smirnoff would go, I waited to tie our lives together because of the danger. To you and to me. You remained unmarked for that reason, not because I didn't care."

"I'm not in danger now."

"No, we're all safer with Konstantine and Pavel gone," he agreed. "Bridget will do her best to avoid us and will cease demanding protection money from our people."

"Then why am I still waiting for you to mark me?" Her

voice was plaintive, and hearing her tone, she bit her lip. She was no longer a child, and this was juvenile behavior.

"We hardly know each other." Mikhail stroked his hand over her head, and her feline released a contented purr. She felt rather than saw him smile. "I want you one hundred percent confident in our relationship. We should spend time together. No," he said when she opened her mouth to protest. "I want to go on our honeymoon and learn everything about you—the good and the bad—and for you to do the same. I missed you desperately. It was bloody hard not contacting you. Brief communication via Ivan wasn't enough. You're so much younger than me. I—I—"

Edwina lifted her head. "What?"

"I worry the age difference will cause problems."

Edwina couldn't help it. She snorted. "You're a tiger shifter, and shifters typically age slowly. You're fit and in your prime. It should be me worrying about holding your interest."

His frown softened to tenderness, and her heart beat faster.

His blue eyes glowed as his gaze crawled over her, the sensual gleam deepening to heat. "Oh, you interest me and keep me on my toes, never standing for any BS. But really, you're reinforcing my point. We need time to become used to each other, to understand how the other thinks. Grow together as a couple."

Edwina nodded, understanding what he was trying to say. Neither of them had wanted a marriage, but she was clear about her future. Still her music, but she also wanted a life with Mikhail and everything that encompassed.

"How long were you thinking?"

"Depends. We need time for our honeymoon and to settle into a life together. You want to work for Roscoe." He stated this last, rather than asking the question.

"I've been training with Isabella. Isabella told me security work is waiting around with not much happening and that most companies have dozens of procedures to mitigate the danger."

"Roscoe assures me this is true," Mikhail said. "I can't say I won't worry, but I won't stand in your way. My work with Bridget was more dangerous than anything you're likely to face."

"Thank you. I want to finish my studies, so I'll ask Roscoe if I can work part-time." She glanced at her watch. "Isabella and Leo will arrive soon with Kian. Sometimes, I go to the lodge and sit on the deck with a gin and tonic. My grandmother thinks I'm turning into a lush. Would you like to go with me? The view is spectacular, and I told Isabella that's where I'll be. They have kid's cocktails, and I promised Kian one the next time I looked after him."

"That sounds civilized. I can't think of anything I'd rather do." He kissed her and parted their bodies. "I could do with another shower."

"Me too," Edwina said and waggled her eyebrows. "We have time for multi-tasking."

Mikhail rolled to his feet. "Lead the way."

THE NEXT MORNING, AFTER a leisurely breakfast and

a walk, Edwina said, "Are you ready to face my family? I'm expected for lunch and haven't mentioned you to Grandmother. I'm still annoyed at her for maneuvering me and taking your money. You'll come as a surprise since she assumes I'm single. It's driving her crazy that I'm staying here rather than with my parents because she can't work out how I'm paying for the cabin."

"I hope she has sleepless nights," Mikhail said. "What are you going to tell her?"

"The bare minimum. She'll recognize your name but doesn't need details."

"I haven't spoken to my grandmother much, but I told her she wasn't to discuss my business or you with her friend. I'm sure she did as I asked because I didn't hold back on my temper."

"My grandmother doesn't know a thing," Edwina said. "Perhaps I'm an ungrateful wretch, but she treated me like a possession—hers to do with as she willed. I have feelings, dammit."

"I didn't treat you much better, carting you from the Scottish castle against your will."

She bared her teeth. "Ah, but you've learned from your error and understand I will geld you if you misbehave. My grandmother believes she has the right to make my decisions, and my stubbornness astonishes her. Thanks to you, I can afford to stay here. If I had to live with my parents, she'd be much worse. As it is, she keeps organizing dates for me. She wants someone useful to the family."

Even after she'd returned home, her grandmother ordered her around and expected Edwina's compliance.

She fingered the wedding band she'd slipped on five minutes earlier. After not wearing the jewelry, the shiny ring kept snagging her attention.

"I bet you're much like your grandmother," Mikhail said. "You're stubborn and have decided views."

"Ah, but I've been on the receiving end of her bossiness since I was young. I know what it feels like and won't make the same mistake with my children or grandchildren. Please, if I lean in that direction, tell me to pull in my head and stop acting like a general."

Mikhail picked up her left hand and kissed her fingers. His eyes danced with humor. "I'm sure Ivan and Gregory would enjoy deflating an enlarged ego."

Edwina stood on her tiptoes and quickly kissed his lips, loving his scent. He smelled of fresh air and pine trees, a faint hint of tiger, and a healthy dose of her. Their combined scents pleased her greatly and put a spring in her step. "We should hustle. Do you want me to drive?"

"You know where you're going, but I expect a conducted tour during the drive."

Edwina pointed out places of interest and made a slight detour to take Mikhail through the heart of Middlemarch. She showed him the school hall where they held meetings about town-related stuff, Caroline's clothing store, the police station, the vet and doctor for feline residents, the Storm in a Teacup cafe, and other buildings.

They pulled up outside her grandmother's house ten minutes late. She slid a sidelong glance toward her husband. "Are you ready for this?"

"Your grandmother might consider our marriage a

victory," Mikhail said.

"But she'll be all sorts of pissed because I didn't tell her I'd married," Edwina said cheerfully. "She'll want to know why I came home without you."

"Her curiosity will go unquenched."

"Exactly, and that will irk her something fierce." Edwina climbed from the car just as one of her younger sisters ran out to greet her.

"Grandmother is cranky because you're late." Her sister's eyes widened on spotting Mikhail. Her nostrils flared as she dragged in his scent. "You..." She clapped her hand over her mouth, her green eyes bugging out.

"Gina, this is Mikhail, my husband."

"*Ooh*," Gina said.

Edwina held out her hand to Mikhail, trembling a little. It was always tricky confronting her grandmother, and this time, her nervousness peaked higher than usual. "We'd better go inside before Grandmother gets even more grumpy."

Mikhail resisted her tug and, instead, pulled her to him. He bent his head and kissed her with tenderness and passion until her uneasiness disappeared. "I love you," he said and winked at her.

"You have lipstick on your mouth," Gina blurted.

Mikhail pulled a handkerchief out of his pocket. "We can't have that." He wiped away the crimson lipstick and tagged after Edwina and her sister.

Edwina heard voices in the dining room and led Mikhail in that direction. She paused in the doorway, her gaze landing on a man she didn't recognize.

SHELLEY MUNRO

"Grandmother, did you forget to tell me something?" she asked in an icy voice.

"You're late," her grandmother said. "This is Logan White. I invited him to dinner because I wanted you to socialize with people your age. It's not natural for you to stay in that cabin alone."

"It's a hotel property," Edwina said. "Not a rustic cabin in the heart of the forest."

"Say hello to Logan," her grandmother said.

Her grandfather held a frown, but he directed it at his wife rather than Edwina. Gina darted past and slid into her usual seat.

"Is there another chair?" Edwina asked, moving farther into the dining room with Mikhail on her heels.

"Who are you?" her grandmother demanded.

Edwina ignored her grandmother and tugged Mikhail toward her parents. "Mum. Dad. This is my husband, Mikhail Lermontov. We met at the gathering. Mikhail, my parents Janet and Malcolm McClintock."

"Married!" her grandmother shrieked, her narrow nose quivering with indignation.

"Grandfather, my husband, Mikhail. Mikhail, this is Logan McClintock." She turned to her grandmother, facing her fully for the first time. "Grandmother, meet my husband."

Her grandmother darted forward and shifted the collar of Edwina's blouse. "You're lying. Where is your mark?"

"Mother," her father protested. "That was rude."

"Valerie," her grandfather said a beat later. "What are you doing?"

"They're not married. Edwina is playing a prank on us," her grandmother said, agitation in every line of her body.

Mikhail snapped to attention at Edwina's side. "I didn't think we'd need to produce our marriage certificate to prove our marital status, but we are husband and wife."

"But you're not mates," her grandmother snapped back.

"Don't be silly, Valerie," her grandfather said, drawing his lanky body up and rising to his full height. "Use your feline senses."

"That means they've shared a bed," her grandmother announced.

"You're right," Mikhail said. "Your grandmother is rude and cantankerous when she doesn't get her way."

The room went silent, and Edwina had to work hard to keep her mouth from quirking upward.

"Grandmother, Mikhail and I are mates, no matter what you try to tell yourself. I love him with all my heart, and in a few days, we're flying to Tahiti for two weeks for the honeymoon we've put off since the gathering. Then we'll fly home to Russia."

"Wait. Lermontov," her grandmother said. "You're Katie's grandson."

"I am," Mikhail said. "But don't congratulate yourself on maneuvering Edwina into your snare. We married after a mature discussion, where she agreed to be my wife. Our marriage has nothing to do with you. In the future, I suggest you leave any negotiations to Edwina's parents. Don't maneuver Edwina's brothers and sisters."

"What Mikhail said," Edwina agreed. "I love you, Grandmother. I don't know why sometimes because you're constantly interfering in our lives, but you're family. You need to find new interests or focus on fundraising for the community instead of wasting your energy on us. We know you're available for advice if needed, but my parents have done an excellent job. You must stop organizing us because you'll lose our respect if you don't."

"Edwina," her father said, and pride shone in his green eyes for the first time in her memory. "You're quite right. Mother, you interfere all the time. We'd appreciate it if you ceased."

"I'd like to add something before we change the subject. Grandmother, that loan you gave to Mum and Dad and are charging them interest and expecting the principal repayment. I suggest you forgive them the loan and call it a gift."

"No," her grandmother snapped.

"If you don't," Edwina said. "I'll drop more truth bombs. Ones you won't appreciate."

"That's blackmail," her grandmother said, her eyes narrowing behind her rimless lenses.

"Yes," Edwina said. "It doesn't feel nice, does it? Right, what do I need to do to help with lunch?"

Her mother stood and hugged her while her father shook hands with Mikhail.

The rest of the afternoon was smooth sailing, although Edwina caught her grandmother's glare several times. Edwina scowled right back, and her grandmother looked away first.

Later that night, Edwina lay in bed with Mikhail's arms

wrapped around her.

"Thank you for your support, Mikhail."

"Always," he said, tugging on a strand of her hair. "I love you."

"You are my heart mate. We're lucky everything turned out all right," Edwina murmured.

"Not luck. Fate."

Edwina chuckled. "That too." She reached up to kiss her mate, and their kiss and the resulting lovemaking lasted for a long, very satisfying time.

EPILOGUE

A BRIGHT ORANGE AND white fish streaked past, so close to her nose that Edwina gasped. Excitement and wonder filled her, and she rolled her body in the water, searching for Mikhail. He swam easily behind her, his gaze almost as blue as the Bora Bora Sea, even through the snorkel mask.

A flash of movement to her right snared her attention, and Mikhail halted beside her, pointing to the coral reef. Two leopard rays swam over the top of the reef, their rippling progress like a ballet, so graceful were the spotted pair.

After a week of swimming, snorkeling, and lazing around their over-water bungalow, she should be used to the stunning beauty of the island, but seeing the fish in their natural habitat and watching the glorious sunsets above the mountains never failed to stun her.

Mikhael tapped her on the shoulder, and she surfaced, treading water, and letting the small waves nudge her toward the shore.

"Are you hungry?" Mikhail asked.

"Famished," she said with a grin. "Did you see the angelfish? And the clownfish that almost collided with my nose. I don't know which of us was more surprised. And the starfish. They're such pretty colors. I'm a little sad about leaving tomorrow, although I'm looking forward to our stopover in New York."

Mikhail's mouth twitched. "You've mentioned this a time or two."

"Thank you for this awesome holiday."

Mikhail drew Edwina close for a kiss, and his lips lingered, tasting of salt and the ocean. "Spending time with you—my darling wife—is reward enough. It was you that kept me going through the Bridget situation when I wanted to wring her neck."

"Charming."

"That is not a word I'd ever associate with Bridget Smirnoff," Mikhail said drily. "Now if you'd mentioned barracuda..."

Edwina grinned. "Do you want to go ashore for a meal at the restaurant, or have something delivered to our bungalow?"

"I've made plans for our last dinner." He tapped her nose before lifting her onto the stairs that led from the water to their thatched bungalow. "Secret plans. This afternoon I'd like to relax and watch the water. The guy who delivered our breakfast told me he'd seen a pod of dolphins close to the lagoon."

Edwina released a happy sigh. "I love the sea. Don't get

me wrong. I love the forests and mountains too, because it means we can shift and run in privacy, but it's fun seeing the fish and birds, falling asleep to the wave's music, and waking to that incredible view. And that bathtub. It is amazing."

"We could order a tub for two at home."

Edwina laughed. "We'd never get our work done. Your shower is enough of a distraction."

"Our shower."

Edwina reached for Mikhail's hand and threaded their fingers together. "*Our* shower is the best. I'm craving a French baguette with ham, cheese, and tomato. How does that sound?"

"Perfect with a cold beer."

"Done." Edwina picked up the phone and ordered their lunch, adding a fruit platter at the last minute. She wouldn't get much delicious tropical fruit at home.

When their food and drinks arrived via canoe, Mikhail and Edwina lazed on their private sun terrace and cooled off in their plunge pool. As always, their conversation ranged over myriad topics and was easy and fun. Mikhail challenged her in the best way. Heck, even her grandmother had thawed enough to smile at him when they'd dropped around to say goodbye. Her father had privately thanked her for forcing her grandmother to forgive their loan, and she'd told him the truth of what his mother had done.

"I sort of wish I could hear the confrontation between my father and grandmother. My dad is easygoing and avoids arguments, but he was furious after I told him what had happened."

Mikhail propped himself up on one elbow and leaned closer to steal a kiss. "But it worked for us in the end."

"It did, although my grandmother—if she knows what is good for her—should never take credit."

Mikhail's rich chuckle made her smile, and she adjusted her bikini top and sat up. "How would you feel about an afternoon nap?" She waggled her eyebrows at her husband. "I want to be well-rested for wherever we're going tonight."

Mikhail stood, and before she could rise, he scooped her off the lounger and into his arms. He carried her into the cool bedroom with its carved wood panels on either side of the king-size bed. A plain white quilt covered the bed, but the central turquoise stripe added color and contrast while the multitude of pillows invited a weary traveler to rest awhile.

"I might take a quick shower," Edwina said. "Care to join me?"

"Yes."

"That was easy," Edwina said.

"With you I am easy."

She laughed, enjoying the effortless intimacy that had sprung up between them. She turned on the rain shower and rapidly stripped off her red bikini. Mikhail disrobed and stepped behind her, his warmth and protectiveness enveloping her like a cozy blanket. He cupped her breasts and teased her nipples until her breath caught, and she shivered with anticipation.

Mikhail grabbed a fluffy loofah and squirted a dollop of

shower gel onto it. Then, he swirled it over her body, front and back, and ended this with a swat on the backside. "I think you're clean now."

Edwina turned to argue, but the sensual gleam in his blue eyes and the faint trace of gold that shone in them gave her a clue. Even if she had missed his erection, the hint of cat told her everything. She grabbed a fluffy white towel and rapidly dried herself before stepping into the adjoining bedroom.

Mikhail must've drawn the wooden shades before he'd come to the bathroom, and now the screened windows let in subdued lighting. Excitement prickled in her. They'd made love often since he'd come to collect her, and they knew each other's bodies well.

Mikhail appeared in the doorway, splendidly naked and with that determined light in his eyes even more evident.

She cocked a hip. "See something you like?"

"I see someone I love," he returned, and everything in her softened. She held out her arms to him, and he came to her before toppling them both on the bed. Sometimes, their loving was slow and dreamy, and at other times, fast and furious. It seemed like this time might be of the latter variety. Their mouths collided, tested for fit, and heads tilted as they pressed close to one another. Every kiss, every caress lured her in—seduced her. Mikhail kissed down her neck and across the top of her breasts. He corralled her with his bigger body, enticing and cajoling her with each touch.

When he finally entered her, she was trembling and drowning in his sensual assault. He filled the empty spaces in her. He was her everything.

"I don't know what I did to deserve you, and I keep thanking fate for throwing us together," she whispered.

"It was fate. I almost chickened out at the last moment, but then I saw this bold and sassy woman in a slinky red dress who dared to challenge me. That was the second when our fates joined."

Edwina snickered. "Chickened out? You? That word isn't in your vocab."

"Ask Ivan and Gregory. They had to talk sense into me." He kissed her and did a lazy thrust of his hips that filled her to the hilt.

She seized his shoulders and held tight as he quickened his strokes and moaned when he hit the perfect spot. His lips went to her throat, and his rough tongue flitted over the base of her neck. Her pulse jumped when he repeated the action. He rocked his hips, pushing his cock deep, and then she felt the scrape of his teeth. Edwina's heart skipped a beat when he repeated the action, and she swallowed hard, pleasure fizzing through her body in all directions.

Mikhail teased her with the flicker of his tongue, followed by the scrape of his teeth again. Then, before she could say anything, he bit down, drawing blood. Pain spurted along her nerve endings, but the rock of his hips and the drag of his cock over her clit distracted her. The pain surged again, this time combining with pleasure. Feelings and emotions swelled inside her, sparking through her with each drag of Mikhail's tongue.

The lazy strokes pushed pleasure higher, as did the massage of his tongue over the wound he'd inflicted.

Without warning, she exploded, her gasp and the rapid spasms of her sex dragging her into intense bliss while a connection clicked into place, a moment of quiet joy. Mikhail lifted his head, and his eyes were golden. He increased the pace of his thrusts while maintaining her gaze. His eyes closed momentarily, his muscular body shuddering in her arms. She held tight to her man, savoring his closeness and the intimacy that arced between them.

When Mikhail opened his eyes again, they were a normal, sexy blue. He smiled and studied the mark he'd made at the juncture of her shoulder and neck. "I love you, Edwina. My mate." His voice rang with a satisfaction that echoed in her, and when he stroked the raised welt, she felt it everywhere. She returned the favor, caressing the mating mark she'd left on him months earlier.

"That drives me crazy," he murmured, his voice deep.

"I know," Edwina said in a soft voice. "Thank you for claiming me."

"I wanted to give you time, but there was never a doubt in my mind. We're a team. Mates."

"Fated mates," Edwina said before she kissed him again and surrendered to his love.

I HOPE YOU ENJOYED Edwina and Mikhail's adventures in love. Edwina was a bratty teenager when we first met her. Her growth through the various Middlemarch romances was a joy to write, and I really like the strong woman she has become.

The next Middlemarch Gathering romance belongs to Suzie. We already know that she hooks herself a billionaire, but there is resistance because, like Edwina, Suzie wants to study music. Let's see how this romance shakes down...

Read about My Highland Billionaire at Shelley's website. (www.://shelleymunro.com)

ABOUT AUTHOR

USA Today bestselling author Shelley Munro lives in Auckland, the City of Sails, with her husband and a cheeky Jack Russell/mystery breed dog.

Typical New Zealanders, Shelley and her husband left home for their big OE soon after they married (translation of New Zealand speak - big overseas experience). A twelve-month-long adventure lengthened to six years of roaming the world. Enduring memories include being almost sat on by a mountain gorilla in Rwanda, lazing on white sandy beaches in India, whale watching in Alaska, searching for leprechauns in Ireland, and dealing with ghosts in an English pub.

While travel is still a big attraction, these days Shelley is most likely found in front of her computer following another love - that of writing stories of contemporary and paranormal romance and adventure. Other interests include watching rugby (strictly for research purposes), cycling, playing croquet and the ukelele, and curling up with an enjoyable book.

Visit Shelley at her Website
www.shelleymunro.com

Join Shelley's Newsletter
www.shelleymunro.com/newsletter

ALSO BY SHELLEY

Paranormal

Middlemarch Shifters

My Scarlet Woman

My Younger Lover

My Peeping Tom

My Assassin

My Estranged Lover

My Feline Protector

My Determined Suitor

My Cat Burglar

My Stray Cat

My Second Chance

My Plan B

My Cat Nap

My Romantic Tangle

My Blue Lady

My Twin Trouble

My Precious Gift

Middlemarch Gathering

My Highland Mate

My Highland Fling

My Elusive Mate

My Valiant Princess

My Highland Wedding

My Highland Billionaire

Middlemarch Capture

Snared by Saber

Favored by Felix

Lost with Leo

Spellbound with Sly

Journey with Joe

Star-Crossed with Scarlett